A CHRISTMAS KISS

"What are you doing?" asked Mack.

"Waiting."

"For what?"

"We're under the mistletoe, Mack. What do you think I'm waiting for?"

"You want me to kiss you?"

Her lower lip came out in a sexy semi-pout. "It is traditional. I'm very big on holiday traditions. Aren't you?"

"I don't want to kiss you," lied Mack.

Cecily slowly licked her pouty lower lip. "You don't? Don't you like me, Mack?"

Mack groaned. "I like you. I don't want to kiss you, that's all. There's something you need to know about me, Cecily. I won't be good for you."

"You don't have to be good, Mack. Bad works for me. Now, you're not going to make me order you to kiss me, are you?"

Lowering his head, Mack could have tried for a quick brush of lips and a quicker escape. But once his mouth was on hers, his brain—the little he had left—ceased to function.

Primitive and powerful, instinct took over. Mack's arms went around Cecily, and he jerked her against him. A noise somewhere between a moan and a purr sounded deep in her throat. Mack swallowed that, too, and all the other small gasps and sighs coming from her delicious mouth. . . .

Books by Dixie Kane

DREAMING OF YOU

CHASING LILY

MAKING MERRY

Published by Zebra Books

MAKING MERRY

Dixie Kane

ZEBRA BOOKS
KENSINGTON PUBLISHING CORP.
http://www.kensingtonbooks.com

ZEBRA BOOKS are published by

Kensington Publishing Corp.
850 Third Avenue
New York, NY 10022

All Kensington titles, imprints and distributed lines are available at special quantity discounts for bulk purchases for sales
promotion, premiums, fund-raising, educational or institutional
use.

Special book excerpts or customized printings can also be
created to fit specific needs. For details, write or phone the
office of the Kensington Special Sales Manager: Kensington
Publishing Corp., 850 Third Avenue, New York, NY 10022.
Attn. Special Sales Department. Phone: 1-800-221-2647.

Zebra and the Z logo Reg. U.S. Pat. & TM Off.

First Printing: October 2003
10 9 8 7 6 5 4 3 2 1

Printed in the United States of America

This book is dedicated to my cousins: Bill, Marilu, Nancy, Jeanie, Ken, Jan, Jay, Teresa, Kenda, Stanley Roy, Martin, Christy, Sidney, and Freddie.
Merry Christmas, primos and primas!

PROLOGUE

Christmas Day

Cecily Barton née Culpepper stood between her father and her brand-new husband, greeting guests at her wedding reception. Each time Cecily caught a glimpse of the diamond band on her left hand, she felt her heart flutter.

She was a married lady.

The thought made her stomach knot. Cecily smiled weakly at the next guest. "Hello, Mrs. Whistler. So happy you could come." She *was* happy. Knot or no knot, of course she was happy. It was her wedding day, the day the society editor at the *Houston Chronicle* had named— effusively, in Cecily's opinion—the wedding of the decade, possibly of the century. Nerves. That's what had her tummy in a twist. She was nervous.

Why? She couldn't be having wedding night jitters. She and Neville had made love. Neville was a wonderful lover. The wedding? No, that had gone beautifully. She hadn't been nervous before or during the ceremony, so why now? She hadn't inherited Cyrus's avowed ability to predict disaster—which only extended to the financial markets in any event—so it couldn't be that.

"Cecily, what are you frowning about?" asked the next guest in line, an old friend of her father's.

"Was I frowning, Mr. Seaton? I can't imagine why."

"Impatient to dance with your husband, no doubt." Mr. Seaton gave her a dry kiss on the cheek. "Best wishes, my dear. Hello, Neville. Congratulations." He moved on.

Maybe she was nervous about their travel plans. Tomorrow morning she and Neville would leave for their honeymoon in Rio de Janeiro. Brazil had been Neville's idea—she had suggested Paris. But, as Neville had pointed out, they had both been to Paris. London, Rome, and Athens were also scratched off the list for the same reason. Cecily sighed. And a very romantic reason it was.

Neville wanted them to honeymoon in a place neither of them had been before. That way, he said, their shared memories of the honeymoon would not be tainted by memories of other visits with other people. Rio would be special because it would be theirs alone.

A break in the line of guests gave Cecily time to look at Neville. She was so lucky to have found a man like him: handsome, intelligent, honorable, and rich enough that her father hadn't chased him off. Cyrus Culpepper had approved of Neville Barton from the first, or at least from the day he received the report on Neville's financial status. Her daddy, mindful of his own net worth, had always done his best to protect Cecily from fortune hunters.

Neville caught her glance and leaned over to whisper in her ear. "How many more people must we greet? I want to dance with my wife."

"I think we can stop soon. Wasn't it clever of me to limit the guest list to two hundred of our closest friends?

If I had left it up to you and Cyrus, everyone either of you had ever thought about doing business with would have been invited."

"Very clever. Cyrus and I were wrong to look upon this as an opportunity for a little business schmoozing."

"You certainly were." The knot in Cecily's stomach began to unwind. She gave Neville a saucy grin. "It's very nice to have a husband who can admit when he's wrong."

"As well as one who doesn't come burdened with family. That cut down the list of invitees. Not to mention saving you from having to deal with a mother-in-law."

"True. But you have a family now, Neville. Cyrus and me, for starters. More to follow." Cecily blinked. Thinking about the baby Bartons to come had made her eyes go misty.

Neville gave her hand a squeeze. "Did you really like your wedding present?"

He'd given her an oil painting by an obscure, and likely to remain so, artist. "I love it." She didn't, but she didn't absolutely hate it, either. After all, it was the thought that counted. Neville had obviously thought that since she had a degree in fine arts and had worked at Objet d'Art, a trendy gallery, a painting from that gallery would be the perfect gift. It wasn't his fault that her former boss had foisted one of Diego Alejandro's gloomy paintings off on him.

"See here. I don't recognize you, sir. Were you invited?" Cyrus spoke loudly.

Cecily turned to see if a gate-crasher had managed to get by the security Cyrus had arranged. A man in a business suit, followed by two men in police uniforms, stood in front of her father.

"No, I was not invited, Mr. Culpepper. However, I have

a right to be here." Walking past her, the man stopped in front of Neville and pulled a badge from his pocket. "Detective Adkins of the Houston Police Department. Neville Barton, you're under arrest. You have the right to remain silent. . . ."

One

Three years later

"I am not an orphan!" Hannah Barton yelled.

Nancy Phillips, a licensed social worker for the Texas Department of Protective Services, got out of the beige sedan. She unlocked the trunk and took out a suitcase, then walked to the passenger door of the car and opened it. "Come on, Hannah. You have to get out of the car now. This is where you'll be staying for a while." She waved her free hand in the direction of the Gothic stone building situated in parklike surroundings.

"You can't fool me! I know what that place is. It's an orphans' home. I am not an orphan!" Hannah Barton repeated, louder this time. "I have a father. His name is Neville Barton."

A frown creased Mrs. Phillips's brow. "Yes, Hannah. We know that. But your father is nowhere to be found."

Hannah refused to look at her. "I don't care. I'm not going to an orphans' home."

Mrs. Phillips reached into the car and unhooked Hannah's seat belt. "Now, now, Hannah. Calm down.

We'll make every effort to find your father, and any
other relatives you might have. The department has a
special group of people whose job it is to find a relative
to take care of you. Until we do, we've arranged for you to
stay with the nice people at Little Lambs Children's
Home, right here in Katy."

Hannah had lived in Katy, Texas, for as long as she
could remember. Katy was where her father would
come looking for her. Reluctantly she got out of the car.
"I don't want to go there. And I don't need to be
adopted. My dad doesn't have to adopt me. Does he?"

Mrs. Phillips took her by the hand. "No. The agency
will attempt to find your father first. But from what Mrs.
Beasley said, you haven't seen your father in a very long
time. Do you remember him?"

"No-o-o, not exactly." Hannah jutted out her round
chin. She hadn't ever seen her father. She hadn't seen a
picture of him until three years ago—the picture had
been in the *Houston Scoop*. "But he remembers me. I
want to wait for him at Gran's house."

Catching Hannah's chin in her hand, Nancy gently
tilted her head so that their gazes met. "You can't stay
all by yourself, Hannah. I'm sorry, but your grandmother isn't coming home. She's with the angels now."

Hannah scowled at the woman. She was not a baby.
She was eleven years old, and she knew what people
meant when they said someone had gone to live with
the angels. "I know what that means," she told Mrs.
Phillips. "My mother died when I was five. My grandmother is *dead*. My ma told me to stay at Gran's until my
dad came to get me. I have to stay there, or he won't
know where to find me."

"We left a forwarding address at the post office. That
way, if anyone writes to you at your old home, the post-
man will take the letter to the Little Lambs home."

"He will?" Hannah asked, narrowing her eyes. Miss Phillips *seemed* nice. But grown-ups lied. "Are you sure?"

"Yes. And you can write to your father, too, if you want. Do you have his address?"

Reluctantly Hannah shook her head. "No."

"Come on, Hannah." Mrs. Phillips led her up a flight of granite stairs to a large wooden door. "This isn't going to be so bad. There are nice children here, some your age. Just think. In a couple of weeks you'll have lots of new friends to share Thanksgiving dinner with."

Hannah didn't want new friends. And she didn't care about turkey and dressing. She couldn't think of one thing she had to be thankful for. Well, maybe one. She wasn't like those other kids. She wasn't an orphan. Almost an orphan, maybe, but only until her father came for her.

"I know this is scary," said Mrs. Phillips, opening the door. She gave Hannah a little push across the threshold, then steered her to a door marked *OFFICE*. "But everything's going to be all right, Hannah. You'll see."

"I've got a stepmother," Hannah blurted. Even a wicked stepmother would be better than an orphans' home. Probably. Hannah was smart enough to know that not all stepmothers were evil—and the woman her father had married hadn't looked mean. Hannah had seen her picture in the newspaper more than once.

"Yes, Hannah. We know about her, too. She'll be contacted. Your grandmother never mentioned any other relatives?"

"No. She never said much about my dad, either." More often than not, when she had said anything about Hannah's father, Gran had been saying words Hannah was not supposed to say. She didn't think Mrs. Phillips needed to know that Gran cussed.

"Sit down, Hannah." Mrs. Phillips pointed to a wooden

bench. "You wait here while I have a word with Miss Perkins. "How did you know about your stepmother?"

"I read stories in the *Houston Scoop,*" said Hannah. "That was Gran's favorite newspaper." She had started reading the paper the same year there were stories about her father's engagement. Gran had cussed a blue streak when that news had come out. Cecily was the name of the woman who had married her daddy. Cecily Culpepper Barton—that was her full name. She was Hannah's stepmother.

And a madcap heiress.

Hannah had looked up those words in the dictionary. *Madcap* was another word for lunatic, and *heiress* meant she was rich. Her dad had married a crazy rich woman. The *Scoop* stories had said her daddy was a successful . . . Hannah couldn't remember the word, but it meant *businessman*. She hadn't understood why he'd had to marry a lunatic, and she hadn't wanted to ask Gran about it.

She wished her mom had been around to ask. Of course, if her mom had been around, her dad wouldn't have married some other woman. Her mother had told her he had left to make his fortune, and that when he had done that, he would come back and get them.

Hannah was sure he would have come, right after he got married. She was pretty sure a businessman would have to have lots of money to be called a success. Probably her dad had wanted enough money *and* a second mother for her before he came to get her. But something bad had happened to her dad at the wedding. He had been arrested for stealing money, and the police had put him in jail. Gran had said that behind bars was where he belonged. But he didn't stay in jail. He got out and ran away.

She would run away, too. If she knew where he was, she'd run straight to him. She didn't care if he had stolen money. He had only done it so he could make his fortune and come to get her. Hannah swallowed the lump in her throat and watched as Mrs. Phillips knocked on a door. "Do I have to stay here?" she asked, her voice small.

"Yes, Hannah. Don't worry. This won't take long. I'll be back in just a few minutes."

Hannah's shoulders slumped. Miss Phillips was not going to let her go home and wait for her father all by herself. No one had let her stay by herself after Gran had gone to the hospital. She had been staying with Mrs. Beasley, the next-door neighbor, ever since the ambulance had come to take her grandmother away. That had been two weeks ago. Mrs. Beasley had taken Hannah to the school bus stop at the end of their street every morning, insisting that she go to school. She had taken Hannah to the hospital once.

That had been scary. Gran had looked very small in the hospital bed, like she'd shrunk or something. And there had been tubes in her nose, and machines beeping in the background. The sign on the door had said *ICU*. Hannah knew what that meant. She watched *ER*.

Hannah had held Gran's hand, and Gran had squeezed her hand. Mrs. Beasley had told her to tell Gran goodbye. She had been crying. That had made Hannah cry, too.

Hannah felt like crying now, too. She didn't want to to stay at some dumb orphans' home. But she was too scared to run away. She didn't know where to run.

Mrs. Phillips returned. "Miss Perkins will be with you in just a few more minutes. I'll stay with you until then."

"What's going to happen to Gran's house?" asked Hannah. And her things?"

"I'm not sure. The house may belong to you now. We haven't found anyone related to your grandmother besides you. Someone will figure that out, and if you are her only heir, they'll appoint a guardian to look after your property."

"If it turns out to be my house, can I go back and live there?"

"Sure. The day you turn eighteen. Until then, you need an adult to look after you."

"I can look after myself." Hannah muttered the words to herself. She could, too. But she wished her dad would come soon. It would be nice to have someone to help her take care of herself.

Back at her office at the Department of Protective Services, on Friday, Nancy Phillips reported to her supervisor, Paul Beeson.

"The girl is right, you know," said Mr. Beeson. "She isn't an orphan. She has a father."

"Yes, Neville Barton, the crook," said Nancy. "Do you realize that Hannah has never even seen her father?"

"That's not so surprising. No one knows where he is."

"No. I mean she's *never* seen him. He left his wife when she was pregnant. From what the neighbor told me, Hannah's mother had some romantic notion that he would return someday. That's the story she told Hannah, too."

"She doesn't believe that, does she?" asked Mr. Beeson.

"I'm pretty sure her grandmother told her the truth about her father—she let Hannah read the stories about him in the newspapers. But I think Hannah wants to believe what her mother told her. Especially now that she's alone in the world. Except for her stepmother. The trouble is, Hannah has never met her, either."

"Barton's wife? You think that Cecily Culpepper is still married to him? I thought she had divorced him years ago."

"I don't think so. We'll have to check, of course. But

if she and Barton are still man and wife . . ." Nancy
trailed off.

"Then the statute on missing parents will apply to
Hannah's case."

Nancy nodded. "Right. If a parent can't be located,
the department tries to locate a relative of the missing
parent—I told Hannah that much."

"Well, I hope you're right about the marriage still
being in effect. Hannah's stepmother will be offered
the opportunity to take custody of Hannah as the kid's
managing conservator. If we're lucky, she'll agree."

"I hope so. But what on earth would a woman like
Cecily Culpepper want with an eleven-year-old child?"
asked Nancy, not really expecting an answer.

"What would she want with a husband she hasn't
seen since the wedding? If she's still married to Neville
Barton after three years, she must intend to stay married. As to whether she wants her husband's child, we
won't know until we ask her, will we?"

"I don't think we should tell Hannah about this. I
wouldn't want her to be disappointed. Not until we
know for sure that her stepmother will want her."

"Does Hannah know about her father's crimes?"

"She must, if she read the *Houston Scoop*."

Mr. Beeson shook his head. "Some father. Deserts his
wife when she's pregnant, never even says boo to the
kid. And from what I read in the papers, the woman he
married is a flake. She's the one who is always in the
headlines, isn't she?"

"That's her—Cecily Culpepper. They write a story
about her every year around Christmas—because every
year she manages to do something outlandish." Nancy
sighed. "Poor Hannah."

"Poor is one thing she won't be—not if the Culpeppers
take her in. Cyrus Culpepper is one of the richest men
in Houston." Mr. Beeson handed Hannah's file back to

Nancy. "Her case should be settled fairly quickly, assuming that Cecily Culpepper is still Cecily Culpepper Barton. We don't have to do a home study on stepparents, so the process should move right along. All we have to do is verify that she's still married to Hannah's father."

"I haven't seen anything in the news about her getting a divorce," Nancy said. "But that's only the first hurdle. If she is still married to Barton, she may not want a stepdaughter. I don't think she has any idea that her husband was married before, much less that he had a daughter—that was never mentioned in any of the stories I read about him or her."

"Then she's in for quite a surprise, isn't she?"

Nancy nodded in agreement. "I only hope we can settle this matter before Christmas—I wouldn't want Hannah to be this year's installment of Cecily's Christmas curse."

Two

Cecily Culpepper, staggering under the weight of four overstuffed shopping bags, stopped at a shop window on the second level of the Galleria. "Have we been in here?"

Cecily's oldest and best friend, Olivia Penn of the department store Penns, equally burdened, looked in the window. "Yes. That's where you got the ceramic owl for Margo, remember? But you never told me why that is the perfect gift for your father's secretary."

"Margo collects owls. She has owls on her desk and on her credenza." Cecily looked in the store window again. "This *is* where we found the owl, isn't it? Good grief. Whose idea was it to go shopping the day after Thanksgiving?"

"Yours. And retailers everywhere thank you," Olivia said fervently. "But I think we've done enough for today, especially since we never made it to Penn's. Lunch?"

"All right. If I can't remember where we've been, it's time for a break. Let's see if we can get into La Madeleine."

Once the two women had placed their orders at the

counter and were seated at a table, Olivia asked, "What
are you doing for Christmas this year? Any plans?"

"No plans. Just wishes. I wish . . . I wish . . ."

"You wish you were married, with children," said Olivia.

"How did you know?"

"Cecily. We played dolls and mommies together when
we were six. You told me then. And you mentioned it
every week or so after that, up until three years ago. As I
recall, the exact number of children was the only vari-
able in your wish."

"I *am* married." Cecily made a moue of disgust. "Sort
of. But no way am I going to be the mother of that
man's children. I should have been more careful about
what I wished for when I was six."

"What were you going to wish for today?" asked Olivia.

"I don't know. That's the problem. I don't know what
I want. I just want . . . something I don't have. And since
I have everything anyone could possibly want . . ." Cecily
shrugged.

"You don't have a man. Start **with** that. Why don't
you have yourself a merry little holiday fling?" Olivia
wiggled her eyebrows suggestively.

"Because. I'm married."

"Barely. When are you going to do something about
that?"

"Like what?"

"D-I-V-O-R-C-E," Olivia spelled. "Face it, Cecily, it's
time to move on."

"Move on from madcap heiress to gay divorcée? And
that would be an improvement . . . how?"

"You would be free to find another man," Olivia answered promptly. "Since you apparently feel it's necessary for you to remain faithful to that . . . husband of
yours as long as you wear his ring."

Cecily held up her left hand. "I am not wearing his
ring."

"I was speaking figuratively," said Olivia.

"I did promise to forsake all others," Cecily reminded her.

"Neville forsook first. I'm pretty sure that's a loophole."

"To be perfectly honest, being married isn't what's keeping me from making merry. I'm just not interested in men. Men are no darn good."

Olivia sucked in a breath. "Bite your tongue. Men have their uses."

"Name six."

"Sex. Taking out the garbage. Fixing flat tires. Paying bills. Sex. Opening jars. Oh, and did I mention sex?"

"I get the picture. All right. It's not that men are no good. It's that I'm no good at choosing a good one. I'm scared of making another mistake. More than scared. I'm terrified." Cecily gave Olivia a rueful look. "Now you know. I'm a coward. A *dumb* coward. You can't argue with that—look who I picked to marry."

"You can't possibly make another mistake that bad." At Cecily's raised eyebrow, Olivia said, "I meant that there can't be another man as bad as Neville in your future. Plus, you've learned from your mistake. Think of how much wiser you are now than you were then."

"I don't *feel* wiser. Not where men are concerned. Trust me, Olivia. I'm not ready for a date, much less a holiday fling. I may never be ready."

"Cecily, sweetie, I know you think love and marriage should somehow enter into the picture. Trust *me*. Not necessary. Find a man to enjoy. Get a divorce and have an affair. Or vice versa."

Cecily felt her lower lip attempting to move into pout position. She bit it. "There's no one I want to have an affair with. And I can't get a divorce. I don't know where Neville is."

"You don't have to know. The lawyers will take care

of it, no matter where he is. Besides, Cyrus is bound to know where Neville has gone to ground."

"If he does, he hasn't shared the news with me. He probably thinks I would run off to join him. Cyrus doesn't trust me."

"He does, too," said Olivia. "Your father dotes on you."

"Doting. Trusting. Two different things. Cyrus may dote, but he stopped trusting me when I made a fool of myself over Neville Barton."

"Have you tried to talk to Cyrus about Neville?" Olivia asked around a mouthful of chicken salad sandwich.

"Of course not. The mere mention of Neville's name makes his blood pressure skyrocket. As long as I'm facing up to my shortcomings, I have to face the fact that I haven't done anything to restore Cyrus's trust in my good sense. To the contrary, I've become the darling of the tabloids, Houston's own madcap heiress." Cecily slapped her forehead with the heel of her hand. "Duh. I know why I'm feeling restless—it's that time of year."

Olivia gave her a blank look. "The day after Thanksgiving?"

"It all starts with Thanksgiving. Whispers, sly looks, those tacky front-page headlines in the *Houston Snoop*— I mean *Scoop*. Everyone's waiting to see what wild thing Cecily Culpepper will do this year."

"Well . . ." Olivia patted her mouth with a paper napkin. "What will you do?"

"Not. One. Thing. This Christmas is going to be different. I'm tired of frittering my life away doing silly, impulsive things for the amusement of the masses."

"You're resigning your position as Houston's madcap heiress?"

"I am. I never wanted the job in the first place."

"I've always thought getting stuck with that moniker was plain bad luck. One little slip when you were seven-teen—jumping into that fountain on a dare. Just bad luck that a photographer from the *Snoop* was there to snap your picture. 'Dripping-wet girl with a rich daddy' equals 'madcap heiress' to the tabloids. I don't know why."

"Neither do I. But I'm giving up living up to that silly sobriquet. No more madcap heiress antics for me. From this moment on, I vow to be decorous and demure."

"Demure? Decorous? You?" Olivia shot her a dubious look. "Impulsive and outlandish is more you. But you could stop acting like an idiot. That would be good." Olivia took another bite of her sandwich and chewed vigorously.

"You thought I was acting like an idiot? You might have said something."

"Why? You knew. Until last year, you weren't hurting anyone but yourself."

Cecily lowered her eyes. "I know," she whispered. "Last year I was *really* dumb." She looked up. "This year will be different. I swear."

Olivia frowned, something she rarely did. She was determined to avoid Botox injections for as long as pos-sible. "Now, Cecily, don't go too far the other way. You don't need to enter a convent to atone for your sins. As sins go, they were pretty puny."

Cecily opened her mouth, ready to argue about the relative puniness of her sins. She thought better of it. Instead, she repeated, "I am going to be demure and decorous. And useful."

"You are useful. You volunteer at the Humane Society's animal shelter."

"Community service—part of the sentence for my crimes."

Olivia snorted. "Losing your license was punishment enough. And that's not the only useful thing you do. You take care of Cyrus."

"With a lot of help from Iris. I wish Daddy would marry her—you would think after twenty years he would have noticed that she's in love with him."

"Cyrus is not a people person. He's a money person. You could do what I do—work for the family firm. Nepotism has its place." Olivia was a buyer for the Penn department stores.

"Oh, Cyrus would give me a job, all right, but it wouldn't be a *useful* job. He'd just make up something useless for me to do. He knows I don't have a head for business. I missed out on Daddy's ruthless-entrepreneur gene and got my mother's shopping gene instead." Cecily flashed a smile at Olivia.

"Luckily, you got Marjorie's classic beauty gene, too—blond hair, blue eyes, and cheekbones. I covet your cheekbones."

Cecily snorted. "You've got cheekbones. And gorgeous red hair and green eyes."

"I got those from my daddy's gene pool. Aren't you glad you take after your mother? Imagine looking like Cyrus—especially now that he's decided to capitalize on his resemblance to old Saint Nick." Olivia sipped her iced tea. "If you don't want to work for Santa, why don't you go back to work at Objet d'Art?"

"Because. Working at the gallery was a frivolous job. Frivolous and boring. You know, in retrospect majoring in art wasn't very practical—especially since I have no real artistic talent." Cecily took the last bite of her turkey sandwich and chewed. "I wish I knew how to type."

"Do you want dessert?" asked Olivia, eyeing the display case where French pastries were temptingly arranged. "I'm giving up sweets for the holiday season. Maybe that way I won't put on five pounds like I usually do."

"I don't want dessert, either. Just coffee. I'll get it."
When she returned with the coffee, Cecily said, "I've
been thinking—I've had plenty of time to think while
doing my community service at the animal shelter.
After you get the hang of it, cleaning up dog poop is
pretty much a mindless activity."

"Is that why you're still doing it? Because it gives you
time to think?"

Cecily shook her head. "No. But what I think is, even
if I can't decide what it is I *want* to do, it's pretty clear
what I *need* to do. I need to do something useful. My
sole contribution to mankind up to this point is to
make a fool of myself every holiday season. Pretty sad,
considering I'm almost thirty."

Olivia choked on a sip of coffee. "Don't say that. I'm
six months older than you, and I'm years away from
thirty."

"Two years. Why did I ever think it was a good idea to
behave like a fool?"

"Oh, Cecily. You were hurting. Don't beat yourself
up for trying to hide your pain."

"My stupidity, you mean. And while we're on the subject of my intelligence or lack thereof, what did I ever
see in Neville Barton?"

"Charm. Intelligence. Wealth. A man who wasn't after
your daddy's money. You fell in love with Neville because
you thought he was honest, truthful, and courageous.
Not to mention rich as Croesus. It's not your fault that
he turned out to be a liar, a cheat, and a coward."

"And a thief. Don't forget that. Still, falling in love
with Neville doesn't say much for my ability to judge
men."

"Women make mistakes about men all the time."
Olivia leaned across the table. "Listen, Cecily. The problem with men is, they lie. Like any other skill, some do it
better than others. Neville was a master of the craft."

"I suppose that's true."

"It is true. Your judgement isn't any worse than any other woman's. Probably better than most. After all, you've had to deal with sycophants and fortune hunters ever since you were old enough to write a check. Neville was the only one who fooled you."

"One was enough."

"You can't think it was your fault that Neville was arrested at the wedding reception."

"Well, no. Except I did choose the wedding date—you know I always dreamed of a Christmas wedding. And I am responsible for every Christmas fiasco since."

"All right. For the sake of argument, I will concede that you contributed to your first bad Christmas by choosing December twenty-fifth as your wedding date. How can you blame yourself for Roddy's boat sinking?"

"That's easy—I was at the wheel. But the boat didn't sink. Not completely. It listed rather badly to port after I ran her onto that sandbar. Made getting around difficult. But it didn't sink."

"You didn't run it aground on purpose," Olivia pointed out.

"True. But I agreed to go on the Christmas cruise with Roddy and his silly friends. It seemed like a good idea at the time—being on the high seas and out of camera range when Jade and her paparazzi cohorts came snooping around. I knew they would want a follow-up story to the debacle of my Christmas wedding. They got their story, anyway. The *Snoop*'s chartered boat got to us almost before the Coast Guard did." Cecily stared into the depths of her coffee cup. "Maybe I am cursed."

"You are not cursed," said Olivia. *"Cecily Culpepper's Christmas Curse* makes an interesting headline, that's all. I think the alliteration has something to do with it."

"Last year's installment in the continuing saga of disasters was *all* my fault. From start to finish. Which we never did, because the police stopped us before we reached the finish line. The drag race was my idea, don't forget."

"I'll never forget that. Racing on a highway, even if it was in the middle of the night, was dangerous, Cecily."

"Dangerous and *stupid.*"

"I won't argue with that. You lived up to your daredevil image with a vengeance that time. But I still think the judge's sentence was too harsh. Suspending your driver's license for eighteen months? Plus three hundred hours of community service. Not to mention the fine. What was he thinking? It's not as if you were drinking and driving. No one got hurt. That stretch of highway was deserted."

"Except for that one state patrolman. And the sentence may be harsh, but it fits the crime." Cecily sighed. "I can't complain. It's not as if I have to walk or take the bus, for heaven's sake. Daddy hired my very own chauffeur for me."

"Of course he did. I said it before, and I'll say it again. Cyrus dotes on you."

"But he's not proud of me. How could he be? All I do is shop."

Olivia eyed the shopping bags piled around their table. "Speaking of shopping—I can't believe how much stuff I bought here. I was only going to check out the competition. If my father sees these bags, he'll have a fit."

"Are you going to switch bags?" asked Cecily. She knew that Olivia kept a supply of Penn's bags in the trunk of her car.

"Of course. You have to promise me we'll continue this shopping spree next week, at Penn's. Penn's is having a week-long pre-Christmas sale, starting Monday."

Cecily smiled. "I know. I got the flyer. I do love to shop." Her smile faded. "Oh, good grief. Olivia. Tabloid headlines. Shopping. I'm turning into my mother, an exhibitionist shopaholic. No wonder Cyrus is disappointed in me."

"You are not a teensy bit like your mother. How could you be? You don't even know her."

"I read about her—in the European tabloids. The contesa makes the papers in Italy, France, and England on a regular basis. Not only that, she attends every couture show in Paris and Rome. She shops. Just like me."

"Not at all like you. You don't buy couture from French and Italian designers."

"Because Cyrus insists on buying American."

"The only time you make the news is at Christmas, and then you're pretty much confined to the *Snoop*."

"Oh, well, I guess I'm only a pale imitation of my mother, then."

"You're not an imitation of anyone, Cecily Jeanne Culpepper. You're an original. And if Cyrus isn't proud of you, just the way you are, he should be. You're smart and pretty and fun. What more could a father want?"

"A little dignity?" Cecily set her empty cup in its saucer and moved the paper napkin from her lap to the table. "Maybe I *should* get a divorce. Cyrus would approve of that."

"Stop thinking about Cyrus. Think about yourself for a change. Your wish is never going to come true if you stay married to Neville Barton. You need to get rid of him so you can find a man and have the family you've always wanted."

"That's not what I want. Not anymore. And I'm not going to have an affair, either. Not until I've gotten a handle on this 'demure and decorous' business. Then, maybe, I'll think about it." Cecily paused. "For future reference, how do you go about finding a lover?"

"Why are you asking me? Oh. Because I've had a couple of—"

Cecily snorted. "A couple?"

". . . affairs this year. Not-so-significant others are all around you, Cecily. The pool of potential lovers is much larger than the pool of prospective husbands. Whenever you're ready for an affair, you won't have a problem. Not with all the second-husband wannabes hanging around."

Cecily shuddered. "Please. I may not know exactly what it is I do want, but I am absolutely positive I don't want a second husband. My lovers, whoever they may be, will have to be satisfied with sex. Are we done here?"

"Yes. I hope I remember where I parked my car," said Olivia, gathering up her shopping bags.

Cecily used her cell phone to call her chauffeur. "Jenkins? We're finished with lunch. I'll be at the front entrance in a couple of minutes."

"Will you miss Jenkins when you get your license back?"

"I don't think so. I like driving myself. But it is nice not having to look for a parking space. Especially at this time of year."

"My favorite time of the year—the sound of all those cash registers ringing warms my little retailer's heart. It used to be your favorite time, too, remember?"

"Yes," Cecily sighed. "I used to love Christmas." She squared her shoulders. "And I am going to love it again. The past few years, I've let Iris take care of decorating the house for the holidays—I just couldn't face holly and mistletoe. This year, I'm going to do it all—the tree, the wreaths, the garland, the poinsettias."

"Don't forget the mistletoe. It's past time you started kissing frogs again."

By Sunday night, the Culpepper residence was decked with more than boughs of holly. Cecily had decorated three trees—a large one for show in the center hall, a medium-sized tree in the family room, and a small one in her third-floor hideaway. She and Iris had wound ribbons of garland through the staircase banister and draped more over the archways and fireplaces. Cecily had balked at the mistletoe, even though the hackberry tree in the backyard was loaded with the parasite.

Iris had hung one sprig from the chandelier in the foyer, and she had refused to take it down. That small setback hadn't dimmed Cecily's holiday spirit. She went to bed feeling happier and more hopeful than she had in years. Even her subconscious was happy, supplying her with a delightful Christmas dream. Cecily dreamed she was wandering through a huge department store where everything was marked down 70 percent.

A ringing telephone woke her up.

Slitting one eye open, Cecily squinted at the clock on her bedside table. It was twelve minutes after two o'clock. Opening both eyes, she sat up and stared dumbly at the telephone. Fuzzy-brained from sleep, she instinctively knew that a phone call in the middle of the night could not be good. No one was calling to tell her she had won a prize, been elected to office, or been named woman of the year. That kind of news came in the light of day.

Besides, Cecily hadn't entered a contest, put her name on a ballot, or done anything to deserve an award.

That meant the call was bad news.

A cold lump congealed in the pit of Cecily's stomach. She did not want to hear bad news—not when she was alone in the dark. Maybe if she didn't answer, whoever was calling would give up. Maybe it was a wrong number.

The phone kept ringing. Insistently. Endlessly.

Cecily couldn't block out the sound, even with two pillows over her head. She had to answer it, but she did not have to do it in the dark. She turned on the lamp next to the telephone and picked up the receiver. "Hello?"

"Darling. Did I wake you?

Cecily moaned softly. That voice. That deep, soothing, compelling, *sexy* voice. *His* voice. "Neville."

"Yes." There was a pause.

A pregnant pause. Cecily had never understood that phrase before. Now she did. The silence was heavy with impending . . . something. Doom, most likely. "What?" she asked, a bit snappish.

"I did wake you." Neville's tone was contrite. Neville was good at contriteness. She could see him. His brows would be slightly drawn together, his witchy green eyes full of concern. Neville would be pushing his hair—that endearing black strand that conveniently fell onto his forehead whenever he needed to look boyish and innocent—away from his face.

"Yes, Neville. You did wake me. It *is* two o'clock in the morning."

"Is that the time in Houston? Sorry, darling. Time zones are so confusing."

"Which zone are you calling from?"

"That isn't important. Hearing your voice is what matters." Neville's voice cracked.

She wasn't falling for that. "Did you have a reason for calling?" Now she sounded positively waspish. Well, she had the right. But she didn't particularly want Neville to know that he could make her forget her manners.

"Yes. I know it's been a long time—"

"You could say that. Three years *is* a long time between calls." Neville's last call had been from a jail cell. He had phoned a plea for her to bail him out. She had. And her husband of sixteen hours had left Houston that same night for Rio de Janeiro.

Neville had not bothered to tell her good-bye.

". . . but you have been in my thoughts every minute of every day fate has kept us apart."

"Fate?" Cecily snorted an unladylike snort. "You conned immense sums of money out of half of Houston, you got caught, and you decamped with your loot. I wouldn't call that fate."

"I'm innocent, Cecily. You of all people should have a little faith in me. After all, I am your husband." Neville sounded hurt. Deeply and sincerely hurt.

Cecily kept quiet. She could pause pregnantly, too.

"I am still your husband, aren't I? You haven't gotten a divorce."

"No." He sounded nervous. Cecily held the phone away from her and stared at the receiver. Neville was never nervous. She must have been mistaken. Replacing the receiver to her ear, she said, "We're still married. Unless you've gotten a divorce. Have you?" Her heart began to beat faster at the thought of being a divorced woman.

A shuddering sigh came over the telephone line. Neville did shuddering sighs almost as well as he did contriteness and sincerity. "Of course not. I love you, Cecily. And you must care for me."

Cecily bit her tongue to keep from swearing at him. Using what her daddy called her "snooty princess" voice, she said, "To be perfectly honest, Neville, I don't feel anything for you." Her eyes widened in surprise. Hallelujah! That was true.

She didn't feel anything at all for Neville. Not love. Not hate. Nothing at all except a mild annoyance at being awakened from a really good dream. She would have felt that no matter who the caller was. Cecily stood on her bed and did a little dance. Too bad Neville couldn't see her hopping up and down on the mattress—she would have liked for him to know she was telling the truth.

"You're hurt. I should have called before now. But I

was thinking of you, darling. I wanted to spare you the embarrassment of being connected to an accused thief."

Cecily stopped dancing. She wasn't hurt. But if Neville wanted to think so, she was under no obligation to correct him. It wasn't as if he were going to suffer guilt pangs over the way he had abandoned her.

Neville continued, "But when I learned that you were still my wife—"

"Who told you?" asked Cecily, suddenly alert. Which of her so-called friends had been in contact with Neville?

". . . I had to take the chance. I saw your name— Cecily Culpepper Barton—in a Houston newspaper. The paper was several months old. But it gave me hope. Hope is something I've had very little of lately, darling."

"Neville . . ." Cecily faked a yawn. She was not sleepy. The shot of adrenaline she'd experienced on hearing her fugitive husband's voice had her wide awake. "You're beginning to bore me. Get to the point. Why did you call? What do you want?"

"Darling Cecily. I wanted to hear your voice. I wanted to tell you that I love you." Another one of those portentous pauses.

"And?"

"Where is the wedding present I gave you?"

"What? Why would you ask about that?"

"As a test of your feelings for me. You must have kept it, if we're still married. You haven't given it away, or burned it?"

Cecily had thought of doing both. "Not executed, sire, but banished. What does that have to do with—"

"Banished? What does that mean? You didn't donate it to some charity, did you?"

"No, Neville. Your wedding gift is still on the premises." The painting was hanging in the bedroom of the vacant apartment over the garage. Her chauffeur refused to

live there, preferring—admirably, in Cecily's opinion—
to go home to his wife.

Neville sighed. This sigh sounded genuine. Cecily
shook her head. It must be the connection. Her husband was incapable of any genuine emotion. "Good—
that proves you still care for me. Cecily. Darling. I want
you to meet me."

Cecily's mouth dropped open. Neville had managed
to surprise her. "Meet you? Where?"

"Anywhere you say. Except the United States, of
course. Please."

"I'll think about it." Cecily hung up the telephone,
then immediately regretted breaking the connection.
She didn't need to think about it. She ought to have
told Neville to go to hell.

Hell was exactly where Neville Barton belonged.

In his bedroom on the second floor of the Culpepper
manse, Cyrus Culpepper waited. He heard Neville mut-
ter something that sounded like "shit." Then the connection was broken. At the sound of the dial tone,
Cyrus carefully replaced the receiver in its cradle. Cecily
did not know he had arranged to have an extension to
her private telephone line installed in his bedroom.
Nor did she know that he had hired an international security firm staffed with former Interpol agents to keep
an eye on his no-good son-in-law.

Cyrus did not feel even a smidgen of guilt about spying on his daughter and the scoundrel she had married.
He intended to protect Cecily from Neville Barton. He
had failed Cecily the last time Neville had come sniffing
around. This time would be different. He would save
Cecily from Neville. From herself, if necessary. That
thieving con artist was not going to hurt his little girl
ever again.

Cyrus picked up his telephone and punched the number for the security firm watching the son of a bitch. He told them about Neville's call, then hung up. The other calls he had in mind would have to wait until morning.

This time, Cyrus vowed, he would see his son-in-law behind bars. Once Neville was where he belonged, Cecily would come to her senses, get a divorce, and get on with her life.

And about time, too. Cyrus looked at the calendar. Wouldn't you know it? Neville had crawled out from under his South American rock at the beginning of the holiday season. Cecily hadn't had a good Christmas in years, thanks to Neville Barton.

"Damn him," said Cyrus, tugging on his white mustache. "Showing up like the ghost of Christmas past. Well, he's not going to ruin another holiday for Cecily. This Christmas will be different."

Three

When the winter sun peeked through her bedroom window Monday morning, Cecily gave up trying to sleep and got out of bed. She dressed in beige wool slacks and a cranberry cashmere sweater and, ignoring the stairs, headed for the elevator. Cecily usually took the stairs from her third-floor retreat, but this morning she felt lazy.

After her wedding day fiasco, Cecily had given serious thought to moving to a different city. A different state. Somewhere no one would know who she was. Cowardly, no doubt, but learning her husband of two hours was a criminal had not left her feeling particularly brave. Or smart.

But Cyrus had suffered a heart attack—she blamed Neville for that, too—and she had stayed at home to oversee his recovery. Once the doctors had pronounced him good as new and given him detailed instructions on what he had to do to remain that way, Cecily had thought about moving out again.

Cyrus hadn't objected, exactly, but he had looked so

pitiful every time she brought up the subject of moving that she had given up the idea of her own house. Olivia cynically suspected that Cyrus had turned half of the third floor—formerly all attic—into a self-contained suite for Cecily for the sole purpose of keeping her at home and under his thumb.

Cecily preferred to think of the remodeled attic as a compromise. She had her very own place, including a bedroom, a sitting area, and a tiny kitchen. There was an extra room, currently unfurnished, which she could turn into a guest room or an office if the need ever arose.

Which it probably wouldn't. There were three seldom-used bedrooms on the second floor, along with Cyrus's suite. And what would she need an office for? What little work she did—volunteer work for a couple of charities, and keeping track of Cyrus's social appointments—required no more than a corner of her father's desk.

Her third-floor suite meant Cyrus had her close at hand. And not to cater to his whims, either. She knew Cyrus wanted her close so *he* could take care of *her.* Cecily stretched and yawned. She had to admit her daddy could be a little overprotective at times. She might have to have a talk with him about that someday soon.

But not before Christmas.

Yawning, Cecily exited the elevator into the central hallway on the first floor and walked down the hall to the large, sunny kitchen. She headed for the coffeemaker on the marble counter and poured herself a cup. "Morning, Iris." Iris Wilson had been the Culpeppers' cook and housekeeper since Cecily turned eight.

"Did I hear the elevator?" Cyrus asked from behind the business section of the *Houston Chronicle.* Only the top of his head was visible. Cyrus had snow-white hair—

it had turned white after his heart attack. He'd grown a beard while recuperating, and he had kept the short, neat beard topped with a fluffy white mustache once he realized it made him look like Santa Claus. He used his benign appearance to his advantage in his business dealings. No one expected Santa Claus to be ruthless.

"Yes. I'm feeling lazy this morning." Sipping her coffee, Cecily wandered over to the round oak table in the windowed alcove and sat down opposite her father. "Morning, Daddy."

From behind the newspaper, Cyrus grunted a greeting.

Iris set a glass of orange juice in front of her. She leaned closer and peered at Cecily. "You've got bags under your eyes. Didn't you sleep well?"

Cecily shrugged. "Not very. Something woke me up, and I couldn't get back to sleep." She had spent hours replaying the conversation with Neville over and over in her mind.

Lowering the newspaper, Cyrus studied her. "Go back to bed if you're tired. You don't have anything important to do today, do you?"

Cecily stopped herself from admitting that she didn't have anything important to do any day. Cyrus knew that. "I thought I might do some more Christmas shopping. Olivia said Penn's is having a special holiday sale, starting today. Is there anything in particular you want this year?"

"Another bull market would be nice. Why do you women get so excited about a sale? I can get you anything you want for cost."

"No challenge in that, Daddy. Besides, I'd have to know in advance what I wanted to buy for that to work. The fun of shopping is finding things you just have to have that you didn't know you needed."

Iris topped off Cyrus's coffee cup. "Sales make a woman feel virtuous. Like she's saving money."

"You could save more if you would just make a list and let me take care of it," Cyrus huffed. "Come to think of it, you would save a lot more money if you didn't shop at all."

"He doesn't get it," Cecily said, rolling her eyes.

"Nope. Can't say that he does," said Iris, winking at Cecily. "What do you want for breakfast?"

"Just coffee." She ought to tell someone about Neville's call. Not Cyrus, though. The mention of Neville's name was enough to make him apoplectic. "Anything interesting in the paper?"

Cyrus shoved the *Living* section across the table. "You're not mentioned. That's good."

Ducking her head to hide her wince, Cecily said, "The *Chronicle* isn't the *Scoop*, Daddy." The *Houston Scoop* would be interested in her middle-of-the-night conversation with her fugitive husband, but she wasn't about to give them the story.

"Cecily Jeanne Culpepper," said Iris, "breakfast is the most important meal of the day. Oatmeal or scrambled eggs?"

"Why can she have eggs when I have to eat this slop?" Cyrus pointed to his half-eaten bowl of oatmeal.

"Because her cholesterol is not through the roof, that's why. I'll fix you an egg-white omelet if you want."

"I want eggs with yolks, *and* bacon *and* sausage. Biscuits with real butter." Cyrus sighed pathetically. "But I'm not going to get it. Not with you two playing food police."

"You got that right," said Iris.

"I'll have oatmeal, too," said Cecily quickly. It was difficult enough keeping Cyrus on his diet without making him watch her eat egg yolks.

"You don't have to deprive yourself on my account. If I can't eat a real egg, I could at least see one. Have some bacon, too, why don't you? I could have a sniff."

"I want oatmeal," Cecily insisted. "I *like* oatmeal."

"Humph." Cyrus retreated behind the newspaper.

Cecily sipped her coffee and resumed worrying about Neville's call. She had a niggling feeling that she should tell the police she had heard from Neville, but the Houston Police Department was far from her favorite law enforcement agency—they were responsible for her married-but-not-very status, after all. They could have arrested Neville *before* she'd said, "I do."

Assuming the police were still interested in Neville— and she had no reason to think they were—what could they do with one telephone call? Tap her telephone? Cecily grimaced. She did not want strangers listening to her private conversations. Mentally she scratched the police off her list of people to tell about Neville's call.

She turned her attention to Iris. She could tell Iris almost anything, and Iris would keep her confidence. But even a hint that Neville was sniffing around again, and Iris would run to tell Cyrus. Iris shared Cyrus's opinion about Cecily's husband and what ought to be done to him. And Iris, like Cyrus, thought she couldn't or wouldn't see Neville brought to justice. Neither of them could understand why she was still married.

It was her own fault, of course. She hadn't been able to tell them that she was scared to death of being single again. Cyrus and Iris knew she was useless, and they loved her anyway. But if they found out she was weak as well as useless, they couldn't possibly do anything but pity her.

Pity was something she could not tolerate.

Even so, she should have filed for divorce from Neville the day after he left Houston. She would have, if she hadn't been so terrified of making another horrible mistake. But because she had decided to stay married until her self-esteem was restored—something that hadn't quite happened yet—and because she had been embarrassed to tell her father and Iris that she was a sniveling coward, they had concluded she still cared for Neville.

"You know what?" Cecily asked. "We ought to talk more. About important things."

"We talk," said Cyrus from behind the paper.

"Every day," said Iris. She put a bowl of oatmeal on the table in front of Cecily. "Where are you going today? The Galleria?"

"I was there Friday with Olivia. I may go back, but I'll start downtown at Penn's. The sale, remember?" Cecily ate a spoonful of oatmeal. At Penn's, she could drop by Olivia's office and tell her about the middle-of-the-night phone call. Olivia knew how to keep a secret, and she would have an opinion on what Cecily should do about the call. Olivia always had an opinion.

With a start Cecily noticed that Cyrus was frowning at her. "What's wrong, Daddy?"

"How are you going to get downtown? Is Olivia picking you up?"

"No. I'll call Jenkins as soon as I finish breakfast. He'll drive me."

Cyrus busied himself folding the newspaper. "Can't. I fired him."

"What? You fired Jenkins? When? Why?" Cecily sputtered.

"First thing this morning. If you're going to have a driver, I want one who is qualified."

"Jenkins knows how to drive. Why on earth did you fire him?" asked Cecily, dumbfounded.

"Been meaning to for several weeks. Jenkins didn't have a chauffeur's license. And he refused to live in the chauffeur's apartment. What good is a driver who lives halfway across town? We need someone close at hand."

"Jenkins's lack of credentials hasn't bothered you for twelve months," Cecily pointed out. "How could you fire the man with no notice?"

Cyrus twirled his mustache. "Easy as pie. I told him we no longer needed his services."

"Right before Christmas? Cyrus Jebidiah Culpepper! You should be ashamed of yourself." Iris glared at Cyrus.

"Today is not right before Christmas, Iris." Cyrus glared back. "Christmas Eve is right before Christmas."

"Right after Thanksgiving, then," said Iris. "How could you?"

"Jenkins has a generous pension from Culpepper Enterprises. I brought him out of retirement to drive for Cecily, remember? On top of that, when I fired him this morning, I gave him severance pay—two months' wages. Jenkins is not destitute, not by a long shot. He'll have plenty of money this Christmas, plus time to enjoy his grandchildren now that he won't be carting C. J. around."

"Why?" Iris asked, hands on hips. "You still haven't told us why you had this sudden urge to fire somebody. Some Santa you are. More like Scrooge, if you ask me."

"I never claimed to be Santa. Any slight resemblance I might have to the old gent is only in the eyes of the beholder. As to why I dismissed Jenkins, it's this way. I got to thinking. What if we needed a driver in the middle of the night? If one of us got sick, or something? Then what would we do?"

"Call nine-one-one?" asked Iris, refilling Cecily's coffee cup.

"Or a taxi?" asked Cecily. Something was wrong with the picture Cyrus was painting. Very wrong. While adding two spoons of sugar and a generous dollop of half-and-half to her coffee, Cecily tried to figure out what was going on in her father's clever and sometimes devious—but never criminal—brain.

"Are you thinking we might all come down with something life-threatening at the same time?" asked Iris. " 'Cause otherwise, I could drive you or Cecily, and you could drive Cecily or me to the emergency room. If the nine-one-one line was busy, that is." Iris took Cyrus's empty bowl from the table, rinsed it out, and put it in the dishwasher.

"You know, Daddy, I don't really need a driver. I could take taxis, or get my friends to take me around. I'll have my license back in another six months."

Cyrus's lower lip protruded from beneath his mustache. "I want a professional chauffeur. On the premises. Now. Who knows? If the new driver works out, I may keep him on after you get your license back."

"You will not. You hate having someone else drive you," said Cecily, beginning to be alarmed. "Are you feeling all right? Ohmigod. You had chest pains again, didn't you?"

"No, I did not. I'm fit as a fiddle. But if I had a driver, I'd get work done on the way to and from the office. That commute is getting longer every day."

Cecily calmed down. She was pretty sure Cyrus wouldn't lie about his health. Except for a lot of grumbling and an occasional attempt to sneak something by her or Iris, Cyrus did not fool around with his health. "You're supposed to be working less, not more."

"C. J. I want you to have a real chauffeur. A live-in chauffeur. And I want you to have him as soon as possible." Cyrus drew his thick, white brows together. His cheeks got rosier, a sure sign that his temper and his blood pressure were rising.

"Oh, all right. I'll call the agency and—"

"Not necessary. I'll take care of it." Cyrus got up and,

planting a kiss on the top of Cecily's head, said, "I'm going to the office. Do you want a ride downtown? Penn's is on my way."

"Yes, thank you. Are you sure you're feeling all right? I could call Dr. Miller and make you an appointment."

"I have an appointment—a regularly scheduled appointment with my cardiologist. Next week. I'm fine, honey. I'm going to make a couple of phone calls before I leave. Take your time with your breakfast." Cyrus left the kitchen.

Cecily watched him go, then turned to Iris. "Well. What was that about? He fired Jenkins. For no reason." Cyrus always had a reason for his actions. She sucked in a breath.

"What?" Iris narrowed her eyes. "You got an idea why he did it?"

"Maybe—no, that couldn't be it." For one brief moment, she had thought that Neville might have called Cyrus, too. But Neville knew how Cyrus felt about him— she'd had to talk long and hard to convince her father to put up Neville's bond money. Cyrus had wanted Neville to stay behind bars. Rightly, as it had turned out, since Neville had fled, forfeiting the bail that Cyrus had grudgingly supplied. Neville would not have called Cyrus. "Do you have a clue?" she asked Iris.

"Not a one. He'll fire me next. You mark my words. He doesn't like my cooking anymore."

"Cyrus likes your cooking. He just doesn't like a heart-healthy diet. And if he fires you, I'll hire you back." Cyrus would never fire Iris, not unless their long-standing affair ended. And that would happen only if Iris got tired of waiting for Cyrus to propose.

"That won't work. Cyrus will hire a French chef the minute I'm out the door. Too many cooks . . ."

"Iris. No one is going to fire you. You're part of the

family, dysfunctional though it may be." Cecily got up from the table and gave Iris a hug. "I'd better get my jacket. Daddy's probably ready to leave."

On the way to Penn's, Cecily tried—without notable success—to get Cyrus to tell her his reasons for firing Jenkins. Cyrus simply ignored the questions he couldn't evade. She could put two and two together, however. By the time she got out of the car, Cecily had a pretty good idea why Cyrus wanted a new chauffeur.

She could run her theory by Olivia—Olivia would tell her if she was on the right track. Cecily headed for the elevators that went to the executive office floors of the Penn Building. When she reached Olivia's office, she was told that Olivia was in a marketing meeting that would probably last until the afternoon. Cecily left a message telling Olivia to call her on her cell phone as soon as she was available, and resigned herself to a day of shopping.

After dropping Cecily off at the department store, Cyrus continued down Franklin to San Jacinto. He parked in the lot opposite the Criminal Justice Center. A few minutes later, Cyrus was sitting across from George Deeds, the Harris County district attorney. Facing a man on his home turf was not Cyrus's usual modus operandi. He'd made the concession this time because he wanted something from Deeds. Something big.

As was his habit, Cyrus got right to the point. "My daughter received a telephone call late last night. I happened to pick up the extension, and I overheard their conversation." Cyrus saw no need to tell the district attorney that the extension was one he'd had the telephone company install on Cecily's private line. "The call was from that bastard she married. He wanted her to meet him at some yet-to-be-decided spot outside the

United States. You can bet Barton has in mind a spot without an extradition treaty. If I had to guess, I'd say his next stop will be the Cayman Islands. My last report from International Operatives said Neville had left Brazil and was heading north. They think he's on his way to the Cayman Islands."

"Why is he on the move?"

"He's out of money."

George's eyebrows shot up to his receding hairline. "So soon? Barton left Texas with millions."

"He made some bad investments. And he spent a lot, too. A good portion of it on other women," Cyrus said, his tone expressing his disgust.

"Will your daughter meet him?"

"I don't know. She didn't say yes, but she didn't say no, either. I'd like to think she has better sense than to hook up with that scoundrel again. But I just don't know. It's been three years, and she's still married to him. Refuses to talk about divorce. Refuses to talk to me about Neville Barton at all, for that matter."

"Exactly what did she tell him last night?"

"That she'd think about it. Mark my words, Deeds. He will call again. Neville needs money, and he thinks he can get money from Cecily. He married her because she's my daughter. Blame myself. Should have seen through his bull. But he made Cecily happy, so I stayed out of it—except for the most minimal check of his financial status. Don't think I haven't kicked myself for not asking for a detailed report on his finances—but crying over spilt milk won't get it back in the can. You can bet that I won't be so lax when Neville Barton comes sniffing around my little girl again. This time, I'll see him behind bars."

"I'm not sure what you want me to do about this. The Caymans aren't within our jurisdiction any more than Brazil."

"I know that. Hear me out. You were district attorney when the police let Neville get away three years ago. Not your fault, but I expect you want to do your part to correct that mistake."

"What do you suggest?"

"As sure as God made little green apples, Neville will call again. Sooner rather than later is my guess. Tap my phones. Trace his call. Find out exactly where he is, and what his plans are for Cecily. If she continues to put him off, I think—no—I *know* that Neville may try to convince her in person."

"You think your son-in-law will return to the United States to claim his bride? After three years?"

"To claim her bank account. Or mine. I wouldn't put kidnapping past Neville Barton."

"You believe your daughter is in danger?"

"I do. I believe that a fugitive from justice is going to show up on my doorstep within the next few weeks. I want a police officer close at hand to slap him in irons. As a concerned citizen, I'm asking you to make an effort to capture a criminal. That is your job, isn't it?"

"Catching fugitives is a police job. Why didn't you go to them?"

"Because, George," Cyrus said, tugging on his mustache, "I did not contribute a substantial sum of money to elect the chief of police. As you well know, that is not an elected position. I came to you because I expect you to do your job. You're up for reelection soon, aren't you?"

Beads of sweat appeared on Deeds's brow. He took a handkerchief from his pocket and swiped it across his forehead. "Calm down, Cyrus. Of course I'll do everything in my power to help bring that SOB to justice. I just wondered why you came to me first, that's all."

"And now you know." Cyrus stood. "When you talk to the police, tell them I need a chauffeur. Oh, and make sure he comes with the proper credentials and a convincing résumé. You can fake that kind of thing, can't you?"

Deeds nodded. "I think that can be done. When the situation calls for it."

"I'm calling for it—I told my daughter I fired her chauffeur because he did not have the proper credentials. If I am to retain my credibility with her, her new driver must come equipped with a chauffeur's license."

"I understand," said Deeds.

"Good. Call me as soon as you and the police decide on how to proceed." To make sure Deeds understood the urgency of the situation, Cyrus added, "I'll expect that call today."

"As soon as possible." Deeds took out his handkerchief and blotted sweat from his forehead again. "Today might not be—"

"Today," Cyrus repeated. "One more thing. Try to get this over and done with before Christmas, will you? The tabloids have stuck Cecily with that silly 'Christmas curse' business. I'd prefer not to have the arrest take place on Christmas day this time. Cecily's been having a little trouble with the holiday season ever since her wedding day."

"Now, Cyrus, Chief Bronson explained that at the time. They had a hard time finding a judge to sign the arrest warrant—it was Christmas day, after all. And they had to arrest him before he left on his honeymoon—he was going to Brazil."

"Where he went anyway, thanks to a fake passport. The police should have planned ahead. If the police had done things right, Cecily wouldn't be married to that son of a bitch."

Deeds held up his hands, palms out. "You're right, of course. We'll do the job right this time."

"Do it quickly, too. It's past time Barton was out of my little girl's life."

Reaching for his telephone, Deeds nodded. "I'll call Chief Bronson right away."

Cyrus stroked his beard. "Thanks. I appreciate your help. Happy holidays."

Four

Detective Mack Armstrong of the Houston Police Department grumbled to himself as he steered his ancient Ford pickup away from Culpepper Enterprises and toward River Oaks and his new assignment.

Some frigging assignment—riding herd on a spoiled socialite.

While listening to his captain outlining his duties, Mack had managed to keep most of his gripes to himself. But he had let one smart remark slip out—he had questioned the necessity of helping George Deeds add to his reelection campaign fund.

Captain Morris had pointed out that arresting Neville Barton was a legitimate police activity. The man had been indicted on 347 counts of theft and had made fools of the department by jumping bail. Barton had jumped all the way to Brazil, and he'd taken his money with him. Morris had pointed out that having a man like Barton at large made it difficult to convince Houston's impressionable youth that crime did not pay.

Catching crooks was police work—Mack had no problem agreeing with that. But baby-sitting a spoiled,

richer-than-rich heiress was not. Okay, so she was married to a financial crook who made the Enron mob look
like a Sunday school class. Okay, so her daddy had gotten word from his overpriced "security consultants" that
Neville Barton was broke and more than likely looking
for a way to get his hands on his wife's money.

And, okay, so Mack was the only detective in the entire Houston Police Department who had a chauffeur's
license—thanks to Uncle Walt. Walter Armstrong owned
Luxurious Limos, and Mack had worked his way through
college driving for his uncle. He still filled in for him
from time to time, so he had kept the license renewed.

Mack had pointed out that a chauffeur's license was
not needed to drive around someone like Cecily Barton—
a garden-variety license would do. Captain Morris had
not been swayed. Deeds, no doubt acting on orders
from Cyrus Culpepper, had insisted on that require-
ment.

Morris had told him that forging a license—an argument Mack hadn't even thought of—would take too
long because the assignment started today.

He still thought it was a bogus assignment. The chances
that a slick operator like Neville Barton was going to
show up on his wife's doorstep anytime soon were slim
to none. Waiting around for nothing to happen was not
the kind police work he enjoyed. Collecting evidence,
solving puzzles, chasing bad guys—he wanted active in-
volvement, not sitting behind the wheel of a Rolls-
Royce with nothing in the rearview mirror but a useless
piece of blond fluff.

Mack sighed and let go of his bad temper. Driving
Mrs. Barton would probably turn out to be a waste of
time, but it was his job. If he looked on it as the same
kind of butt-numbing surveillance he'd done in the
past, he'd be able to stand it.

It wouldn't kill him to do the job right.

But damned if he was going to take any grief from Mrs. Barton while doing it. Mack grinned. If she annoyed him, or if things got boring, he could always try a little insubordination. Cecily Barton struck him as the kind of pampered princess who expected all ordinary mortals to cater to her every whim. If he decided to bail out on this assignment, a little judicious insolence would probably get him fired.

Mack reluctantly abandoned that plan. He had never evaded or avoided an unpleasant assignment before. He wasn't going to start now, no matter how bored he got. He'd just grit his teeth and bear it—and pray fervently that the case was over by Christmas.

The Culpepper mansion came into view, and Mack stopped to look it over. His new home looked like a Spanish hacienda—red tile roof, stucco painted the color of adobe, lots of arches and small balconies. Old oak trees and newer palm trees surrounded the house, along with a lot of expensive-looking shrubbery. He recognized the camellias—his mother had a couple of camellia bushes.

Mack followed the curving driveway to the back of the house. The drive ended in a courtyard, which separated the four-car garage from the house. There were two cars in the garage: a Cadillac Escalade and a candy-apple red Camaro Z28 convertible. According to the police report Captain Morris had given him, Cecily Barton had been driving a red convertible when she had been arrested for reckless endangerment, speeding, and various other traffic no-nos.

Parking the pickup in one of the two empty spaces, Mack got out. The garage was immaculate. No oil stains on the cement floor, no tools hanging from the walls— walls that were painted a pristine white. The windows in the garage sported both blinds and curtains. If the cars hadn't been there, he might have mistaken it for some sort of meeting room.

There were a couple of garbage cans tucked discreetly into one corner of the garage. Mack grinned. Even people as rich as the Culpeppers had garbage.

He walked across the courtyard to the back door and rang the doorbell. A good-looking woman opened the door. Mack pegged her age at forty, give or take. She had brown hair, brown eyes, and a warm smile. She was wearing an apron that read, *Kiss the Cook.*

"Yes?" she asked.

Mack stuck out his hand. "I'm Mack Armstrong, the new chauffeur. Mr. Culpepper told me to come on over and get settled in the apartment."

She took his hand and gave it a firm shake. "Come in, Mack. I'm Iris Wilson, chief cook and bottle-washer around here. Can I get you something to eat? Coffee?"

"No, thanks. I had a bite when I went home to pack. I'd like to get settled." Mack looked around the large kitchen. Lots of marble counters, hardwood floors—there was even a fireplace in one corner, with a couple of overstuffed chairs in front of it. A large round table with six chairs sat in an alcove.

"Okay. I'll get the keys for you." She walked to a built-in desk and opened a drawer. "While I'm collecting the keys, I'll tell you the schedule. Meals are here in the kitchen. I fix breakfast between seven and eight in the morning. Lunch at noon. Dinner at seven. Let me know if you'll be eating elsewhere."

Mack's brows shot up. "I'll eat here? Isn't there a kitchen in the chauffeur's apartment?"

"Yes, and it's fully equipped. I checked it this morning while the cleaning crew were there. The garage apartment hasn't been lived in for quite a few years, not since the days when Cecily had a nanny."

Nanny? Mack managed not to sneer.

Iris found a set of keys. "Don't worry. The apartment is still in good shape."

"Is there a microwave?" He didn't relish the idea of sharing meals with a bunch of servants.

"Yes. It's not the most recent model, though. If you want a new one, let me know." Iris looked him up and down. "You must eat something besides frozen dinners. Otherwise, you wouldn't look so . . . healthy."

"I can fry anything."

"Now, that you will have to do for yourself. No fried foods here—heart-healthy is the menu at Chez Culpepper." Under her breath she added, "At least as long as I'm in charge."

"I don't like my own cooking all that much," Mack said, backpedaling when it occurred to him that he might pick up some interesting information at the kitchen table. "I won't mind eating in the kitchen with the rest of the servants."

Iris laughed. "You and I are it, bucko. No upstairs maids or downstairs butlers in residence.

"You take care of this big place all alone?"

"We have a cleaning service that comes in twice a week. Gardening service, ditto. Otherwise, Cecily and I take care of things—things being Cyrus. He's high-maintenance."

"Do you live here, too?"

"Yes. I've got a bedroom and a sitting room behind the kitchen." Iris pointed to a door next to the fireplace. "Cecily has her own self-contained suite on the third floor. I'll give you a tour of the place if you want."

"Maybe later. Cecily. She's the one I'll be driving. What's she like?"

"She's an angel—with just enough devil in her to keep things interesting." Iris winked at him. "Meals are here in the kitchen unless they're having a dinner party.

Then you and I get out of the way and let the caterers have the kitchen. I usually have a pizza delivered."

"Does that happen often?"

"No. But with the holidays coming, there will be more entertaining. Cecily takes care of those arrangements."

"How long have you worked for the Culpeppers?"

"Almost twenty years. I started when Cecily was eight years old. Poor little thing. I'll never forget—"

"Poor?" Mack scoffed.

Iris raised a brow. "You heard me. She was still missing her mother—and the woman had been gone for six years. And Cyrus was working day and night, proving he could double or triple the fortune his daddy left him. Cecily had nannies and cooks and maids, but she was alone a lot until I got here."

"Her mother died when she was two?"

"Oh, Marjorie didn't die. She's alive and well and living in Venice. Dumped Cyrus, married an Italian count."

"She left her daughter? Or did Cyrus win a custody suit?"

"Marjorie didn't ask for custody. A two-year-old would have interfered with her lifestyle."

Mack had heard the term "poor little rich girl," but he'd never actually believed there was such an animal. After hearing the story of Cecily's childhood, he might have to reevaluate. "I guess I'd better go unpack. Mr. Culpepper said a telephone man would be coming by to hook up the phone and the intercom."

"Really? I didn't realize the phones in the apartment had been shut off." Iris handed him the keys she'd been collecting. "Here are the keys to the cars: the SUV, Cecily's convertible, and Cyrus's Lincoln. He's driving the Lincoln today. This is the key to the apartment, and this is a key to the house."

"No alarm system?"

"Oh, yes. I almost forgot about that." She opened another drawer and took out a folder. "Here's the information about the alarm system, including the security codes. Come on, I'll show you the way."

"Thanks."

Mack followed Iris across the courtyard and into the garage. "I was surprised at the cars," he said as they passed the SUV and the convertible. "I was expecting a Rolls or two—at least a Mercedes."

"Cyrus believes in buying American," said Iris, opening a door at the rear of the garage. A flight of stairs ended in a small landing on the second floor. There was one floor-to-ceiling window opposite a door. "You've got the key," said Iris. "It's the brass one."

Mack unlocked the door and pushed it open, allowing Iris to enter first. A small foyer opened into a large living room furnished with leather sofas, mahogany tables, and a big-screen television set. There was a fireplace.

After showing him the bedroom—also large, with a second fireplace and a king-size bed, Iris showed him the kitchen. "That door leads to an outside staircase," she said. "Same key fits that lock."

Mack followed her back into the living room. Even though the apartment had not been lived in for years, it did not have the impersonal feel of a hotel room. Warm colors on the walls, and the comfortable furniture probably had a lot to do with it.

Mack looked around again. "Nice place—except for that." He pointed to the painting hanging over the fireplace. Dark globs of oil paint formed a montage of gloom. It was the only jarring note in the whole apartment. "That is one ugly picture."

Iris glanced at the painting. "Isn't it? You can take it down, if you want."

"I may have to. I don't think I'd like seeing that every time I walk through the door."

"Neither did Cecily. That's why she moved it from her bedroom to the apartment."

"Why didn't she just throw it away? Or burn it?"

"Cecily would never do that—she has a soft spot for artists, even bad ones. She was an art major in college. But I don't think she'd mind if you put it in a closet. Well, I'll leave you to it. I've got to get a chicken in the oven to roast. Did I tell you dinner is at seven?"

"Yeah. When will I meet the boss?"

"I thought you met Cyrus—oh, you mean Cecily. She went shopping this morning. She'll call when she's ready for you to pick her up. If the phone's not working before then, I'll let you know."

Mack walked Iris down the stairs and retrieved his suitcase and a hanging bag from his pickup.

After he unpacked, he grabbed the folder Cyrus had given him. Culpepper had given him copies of the reports on Neville Barton, and information about a middle-of-the-night telephone call his daughter had received from her husband. Cecily Culpepper did not know that her father had tapped her telephone. And Daddy didn't want his little girl to know that there was a policeman on the premises, either. The Culpeppers had an obvious communication problem, and now he was in the middle of it.

Mack stared at the ugly painting over the fireplace. Some family—an eccentric zillionaire, a fugitive son-in-law, and a ditzy blond heiress. Sounded like the cast of a midseason replacement sitcom, with him tossed in for comic relief.

With a disgusted shake of his head, Mack sat down on the sofa and opened the folder Cyrus had given him.

An hour later, a knock at the apartment door came

as a welcome interruption. A man could read only so many surveillance reports without going cross-eyed. When Mack opened the door, Smitty Allgood, a police tech agent adept at installing bugs, wires, and other electronic surveillance equipment, entered carrying a toolkit and a large case. He put the case on the floor and opened it and a dark blue file folder. "Hey, Mack, I'm here to hook up your wire." He handed Mack the folder. "This is for you."

"What is it? I've got Cecily Barton's criminal file."

"A little something Media Relations put together for you. She's a criminal? I thought her husband was the bad guy." Smitty snapped his fingers. "Oh, yeah. Her license was yanked last year, right? Because of some stunt she pulled with a race car driver?"

"She challenged Lance Ebersol to a race," said Mack.

"Pretty nervy of her, considering Ebersol is a Grand Prix winner."

"Pretty dumb of her. She got busted for speeding and various other traffic offenses. As a result, her license was yanked."

"And you get to drive her around? I've seen pictures of her." Smitty let out a wolf whistle. "Lucky bastard."

"Yeah. I'm jumping for joy. Shouldn't you get started? I'm not sure how long before I get a call to pick up Mrs. Barton."

"Okay. Where do you want the wire set up?"

"In the bedroom. Barton made his call in the middle of the night the first time." Mack tossed the folder on top of the reports on Barton and followed Smitty into the other room.

"How did you get picked for this gig?" asked Smitty. "I thought Adkins was the lead detective on the Barton case."

"Yeah, he is. But Mrs. Barton knows what he looks

like. Adkins arrested her husband at their wedding reception."

"Oh, yeah. I forgot. You're undercover. Think you'll make it under the covers with her?" Smitty laughed at his own joke, but sobered when he saw Mack's scowl. "Hey, I was kidding around. I know that's against the rules."

"Are you done yet?" asked Mack.

"Almost. I still say this is a cushy assignment."

"Maybe, but it's interfering with my life. The perfect house may come on the market while I'm stuck here."

"Oh, yeah. Your partner told me you were house hunting. What brought that on? Ready to settle down? That would be good. Give the rest of us a chance with the ladies."

Mack's scowl deepened. Smitty wasn't the first one to jump to that conclusion—apparently, bachelors were not supposed to be home owners. Everyone from his mother to his partner had guessed his motive for house hunting—and they all guessed wrong. Marriage was not on his mind or on his agenda. "Ready to build some equity instead of pissing rent away."

"Don't forget the tax break. I guess it does pay to own instead of rent. Maybe I'll look into it. When I get a little older. Okay, look here." Smitty opened the door on the bedside table cabinet, revealing a wire recorder. "The recorder is wired into Cecily Barton's private line. It's voice-activated—the recorder will buzz when there is a conversation on her line, and this red button will light up." Smitty pointed to the telephone on the bedside table. "Or, if you're here at the time, you can listen in on this phone—it will ring whenever she gets a call. I rigged it as an extension to her private line. The other telephones—the one in the kitchen and the one in the living room—are hooked up to the main line into the Culpepper house."

"What if she makes a call on her private line?"

"The wire recorder will pick that up. If you're out when she gets or makes a call, you can rewind and listen to every word. Where do you want the earphones?"

"In the cabinet is okay. Thanks, Smitty. Now, get out of here before someone sees you and starts asking questions."

"I'm gone. Good luck."

Mack walked Smitty to the door, then flopped onto the couch. He shoved the blue folder aside and picked up the manila folder. He stretched out on the comfortable sofa and continued reading the International Operatives reports on Neville Barton.

The reports showed that Barton was even more of a scumbag than Mack had thought. He had pissed away his stolen money on an obscenely extravagant lifestyle: houses, including a mansion in São Paolo and a penthouse in Rio; cars—a Lamborghini and a Ferrari. He also spent a bundle on wine, parties, and women. Having a wife—even a wife like Cecily—had not interfered with his pursuit of pleasure.

Why hadn't Barton asked Cecily to join him? If they were still married three years after their wedding day, it seemed odd that they had not gotten together at some point. Mack flashed on the mug shot of Cecily that he'd seen in the police file. Even in black and white, holding a number under her chin, Cecily Barton had glowed with sensual appeal. If Neville was dumb enough to leave her behind, maybe he was dumb enough to come back for her.

Neville Barton had stolen bags-full of money from the citizens of Houston, and he'd made fools of the department by successfully fleeing the jurisdiction with his ill-gotten gains. Barton was a crook worth going after. Mack decided, if his part in bringing Neville Barton to justice was to keep an eye on the dumb

blonde he'd married, so be it. It might not be the kind
of assignment he would have volunteered for, but it was
police work after all.

Mack replaced the reports in the manila folder and
looked for a place to stash it. There was a desk in one
corner of the living room. He put the folder in the middle drawer and closed it. He stretched, then walked
around the apartment. When would he hear from his
new boss? She'd been shopping since morning, and it
was now almost three. How could anyone waste so
much time doing something so useless?

The second folder on the coffee table reminded him
that he hadn't finished his homework. He could see the
edges of newspaper clippings peeking out of the folder.
Mack did not want to read a bunch of society page nonsense—superficial people doing frivolous things did
not interest him. With a groan, he picked up the folder
and opened it.

As he opened the file, a glossy print of Cecily's wedding photograph fell out of the packet. It wasn't your
typical picture of the bride. No demure smile for Cecily—
she was laughing out loud, obviously delighted. Her
blond hair was swept up and away from her face, and
her blue eyes sparkled with joy . . . or mischief. Mack
found himself grinning at her picture.

The grin faded as he realized the photo must have
been taken days before the wedding. Cecily hadn't known
what was coming. Suppressing an unprofessional twinge
of sympathy, Mack carefully replaced the photograph in
the folder and took out the first newspaper article.
Another photograph had him grinning again—a younger
Cecily standing in a fountain, dripping wet and laughing about it.

He flipped through the file, looking for other pictures. The Media Relations Department had included
another copy of her mug shot with the police reports of

her arrest. Mack could feel his body reacting to her photograph.

Uh-oh. Not good. He could not be attracted to Cecily Barton. That would not be smart, not when she was the subject of his assignment. Mack closed the blue folder and tossed it onto the coffee table, then walked into the bedroom. After a moment's reflection, he laughed out loud.

As if police department rules were the only thing making Cecily off limits. She would be out of reach for a guy like him no matter what. In the ordinary course of events, he never would have gotten within shouting distance of her. For starters, he did not have a yacht or a race car or a portfolio jammed with dividend-paying stocks.

So she was photogenic, so what? That could be good lighting and better makeup. Once he met her in the flesh, any fleeting attraction would die a natural death. Cecily Barton might be rich and beautiful, but he preferred women who were smart and sensible—attributes she obviously did not possess. He would forget whatever fantasy her pictures had inspired the minute she opened her mouth.

Mack glanced at his watch. According to her father, Cecily had been shopping since nine o'clock that morning. For what? She had to have everything anyone could possibly want. What a useless way to spend time— searching for one more thing to buy. Mack tossed the folder onto the coffee table and closed his eyes.

He hated waiting. He hadn't even met her, and already she had a lot to answer for. He groaned.

When was she going to call?

Five

Shortly after three o'clock, Olivia called Cecily on her cell phone and told her she had time to take a break. Finally. Cecily took the elevator to the tower floors of the Penn building, where the executive offices were located. Olivia's office was a cubicle with no door. Nepotism may have gotten her the job, but once in the door, Olivia had been treated like any other employee. That meant no corner office and no door until she had earned it.

Cecily knocked on the partition. Olivia motioned her into her office. She was on the telephone. "What's up?" she mouthed.

"Neville called," Cecily mouthed back.

Olivia hung up the phone, then stared at it. "Golly gosh. I just hung up on Ralph Lauren."

"Sorry."

"It's okay. I'll call back later and tell him the line went dead or something. I can't believe Neville actually called you."

"Well, he did." Aware of the people in the cubicles on either side of Olivia's, Cecily lowered her voice. "But

I can't talk about it here," she hissed. "Can we go some-where more private?"

"Sure. How about the Starbucks on the first floor? It's not private, but it's noisy enough that no one will pay attention to us. Leave your shopping bag here." Olivia raised a brow. "Only one? You filled two shop-ping bags at Neiman's."

"I couldn't concentrate," Cecily admitted. "I'll do better next time, I promise."

A crowded elevator prevented any conversation on the way down. Once they reached the ground floor, Cecily followed Olivia into the coffee shop. She stood in line and ordered their lattes while Olivia found a table in an almost secluded corner.

As soon as Cecily put the paper cups on the table, Olivia said, "Sit down and tell me all about it. When did Neville call?"

"Last night. Two o'clock this morning, to be precise. He asked me to meet him."

"Get out. Where?"

"He didn't specify. Except to exclude the entire United States."

Olivia snorted. "I guess so. You're not going to do it."

Cecily didn't answer immediately.

Olivia drew her auburn brows together in a frown.

"Olivia? You're frowning. Botox looms."

"I don't care," said Olivia, continuing to scowl. "You're not going to meet that snake you married, are you? Did you tell Cyrus?"

"No, of course not." Cecily lowered her voice. "And I'm not going to tell him that Neville called. It would only upset him, and he's already upset about some-thing. Cyrus fired Jenkins this morning for no good rea-son. At least, no reason that made sense."

"When has Cyrus ever had to have a reason for what he does? Face it, Cecily. Your daddy can be something of an eccentric at times. Prime example: he *tries* to look like old Saint Nick. That is more than a teensy bit weird."

"I know." Cecily grinned. "But it's kind of fun, living with Santa Claus."

"He may be Santa to you, but he's Scrooge to everyone else."

"That's what Iris called him," said Cecily. "But he wasn't. He gave Jenkins a generous termination package—and the man was retired before he started driving for me, remember?"

"What reason did Scrooge give for firing Jenkins?"

"He said he wanted a driver with a chauffeur's license, and someone who would live in the garage apartment."

"After a year? That's odd."

"Isn't it? I'm pretty sure I know what he's up to. He made a pointed reference to my uselessness this morning at breakfast . . ."

"I don't believe that. What did he say?"

"He asked me if I had anything important to do today."

"That's it? You think he thinks you're useless based on that?" Olivia shot a skeptical look over the rim of her cup.

"And he said it was a good thing that I wasn't in the headlines."

"Well, what's wrong with that? You want to stay out of the headlines, too, don't you? What's the connection with firing Jenkins?"

"It's the time of year—I think Cyrus looked at the calendar and decided to do something about me. I'm pretty sure my new chauffeur's duties are going to include keeping me out of trouble this holiday season." Cecily sighed. "Olivia, don't you get it? Cyrus is hiring a baby-sitter for me."

"A baby-sitter? How does that make you feel?"

"Like a baby." Cecily made a moue of disgust. "What do you think?"

"You could be right. I wouldn't put it past Cyrus to do that—for your own good, though. Not to keep you out of the *Snoop*. I don't think Cyrus gives two hoots about that silly newspaper. But he wants to keep you safe—because he didn't save you from Neville. You could say you brought this on yourself with that crazy stunt last year. You might have been seriously hurt."

Cecily winced. "I know. But I don't want a baby-sitter. I want to keep myself safe. I can do it. I think."

"I *know* you can take care of yourself. Tell Cyrus to back off and let you."

Cecily shook her head. "I can't confront him, not until I am absolutely positive my new driver is more than a chauffeur. I could be wrong, you know. Maybe Cyrus fired Jenkins for a completely different reason that has nothing to do with me."

"Unlikely. You know, Cecily, you protect Cyrus as much or more than he tries to protect you. I wish you would just talk to him. He's not going to have a heart attack if you bring up an unpleasant subject."

"He might. I'm not ready to take that kind of risk. Cyrus is the only family I've got—the only one who didn't run away and leave me behind. Except for Iris, of course. I wish Cyrus would marry her—I'm tired of pretending I don't know what's going on between the two of them."

"Why pretend? If you said something, it might shock Cyrus into making an honest woman out of her. Iris is perfect for your father—she doesn't have any trouble telling Cyrus what she thinks about his more outrageous moves. He'll figure it out sooner or later."

"It's already later. Their affair has lasted years longer than Daddy's marriage lasted. I'm not saying anything about that to Iris, either. It would embarrass her."

"You're just too softhearted for your own good."
Olivia looked around the coffee shop. "This might not
be the best place for us to have a private conversation.
The *Snoop* has eyes everywhere. And ears. They probably have someone here."

After making a quick survey of the tables closest to
theirs, Cecily said, "No one is paying attention to us.
And I need to tell you about it. You're the only one I
can talk to about the call." Taking a deep breath, she
continued, "In a nutshell, Neville apologized for not
getting in touch with me sooner. Being Neville, he
sounded sincerely contrite. And charming."

"Contrite? Charming? *Sincere?* Give me a big, fat break.
The man let you and Cyrus post his bail—one million
smackeroos—and then he left town. Cecily Culpepper,
tell me you're not going to forgive him."

"Have a little faith, Olly. I may have been stupid to
fall for Neville Barton in the first place, but I'm not stupid enough to believe he's really sorry."

"You weren't stupid. Trusting, yes. Gullible, possibly.
Don't forget, Cecily, you were not the only one who fell
for Neville's charming ways. He fooled all those people
who threw buckets of money at him, too." Olivia sipped
her latte.

"Neville also said he'd tried to stay out of my life, to
save me from the embarrassment of being married to a
man accused of robbing half the people in Texas."

Olivia got a thoughtful look on her face. "Not to
speak well of the rat, but Neville does have one redeeming virtue. He robbed only from the rich. Just like
Robin Hood."

Cecily raised her brow. "Robin Hood gave to the poor.
Neville never gave anyone anything but a hard time."

"True."

"And he had to rob the rich—they are the ones with
money, Olivia."

Olivia nodded. "Right. No redeeming virtues. I don't know what I was thinking. What else did he have to say?"

"Neville told me he tried, but he can't live without me. He said he needs me. He used his *very* sincere voice."

Olivia narrowed her eyes. "I know what's happened. Neville must be out of money. He needs your bank account."

Cecily gave a decisive nod. "That's what I think, too. You'd think thirty million dollars would last longer, wouldn't you?"

The second frown of the day wrinkled Olivia's brow. "Oh, I don't know. Buy a mansion or two, a yacht, three or four really expensive cars—before you know it, you're down to your last million."

"When you put it that way . . . too bad. I had this cool scenario going where someone—preferably a female someone—conned Neville out of his ill-gotten gains. That would be poetic justice."

"Which would be the only justice Neville Barton will ever face. The police gave up on finding him the minute he crossed the border."

"What would you expect from a police department that arrests people at wedding receptions?" Cecily paused for a beat, then said, "I did think . . . maybe I could lure Neville into some kind of trap. If I agreed to meet him, that is."

"Cecily Culpepper. Don't you dare. Neville is a rat, and cornered rats are dangerous. It's not your job to put him behind bars. If he's really out of money, that will be punishment enough."

"I wouldn't really meet him. Just agree to a meeting place where the cops could grab him. Even if Neville is broke, that isn't nearly the punishment he deserves. He almost killed Cyrus."

"You don't really think you could convince him to meet you somewhere, do you? Neville has a strong sense of self-preservation. Plus, lying is not one of your strong suits."

"I can lie. Only this morning I lied to Iris and Cyrus about why I couldn't sleep last night. If I can lie to people I love, I can tell the biggest whopper in the world to my dear, departed husband."

"You're going to do it, aren't you? You're going to try to lure Neville back to Houston. Cecily, forget about it. Tell the police."

"No. I don't owe the police any favors—not after the way they ruined my wedding day. Even if I told them about the call, they wouldn't do anything. They certainly haven't done much to capture Neville for the past three years."

"They haven't, have they? I guess you're right, Cecily. It was only one phone call. What could the police do with that? But if he calls again, promise me you won't do anything foolish."

"Olivia, please. Have a little faith." Bringing Neville Barton to justice wouldn't be foolish. It would be brave. Useful. Trust-inspiring. She had never set out to capture a criminal before, but if she succeeded, she would have what she wanted—proof that she could do something that would make Cyrus proud of her. If she could take care of Neville, she could take care of anything, herself included.

"Cecily? You've got a funny look on your face. What are you thinking?"

Her cell phone chirped, saving Cecily from having to tell Olivia about her plan to capture Neville. She answered it.

"Where are you?" asked a familiar voice.

"Hello, Daddy. I'm at the Starbucks in the Penn building, having a latte with Olivia. Why?"

"Call home when you're ready to leave. The new chauffeur will come pick you up."

"New chauffeur? Already?"

"Yes. He should be at the apartment now, moving his stuff in. His name is Mack Armstrong."

"How did you find someone so quickly?"

"We'll talk about it later. I've got to go." Cyrus ended the call.

"Well," said Cecily, staring at her phone. "Curiouser and curiouser. I've got a new chauffeur. He's moving into the garage apartment at this very moment."

"I heard. That was fast."

"Too fast."

"There's no way he could know about Neville's call, is there? Ooooh!" Olivia's eyes rounded. "Maybe Neville called Cyrus, too."

"That thought occurred to me, too, but Neville wouldn't do that. He knows how Cyrus feels about him. And Cyrus couldn't know about Neville's call to me—it came in on my private line." Cecily tapped her nails on the table, thinking. "Olivia, you know Cyrus never hires anyone before he's gotten a complete background check on them. Normally, that takes a week. A day or two, if there's a rush and he really puts the pressure on. But what if Cyrus hired someone he already knew—like one of the people who do his background checks, for instance. That wouldn't take any time at all, now, would it?"

"By Jove, I think you've got it. He *has* hired a private eye to baby-sit you. Or to guard your body. Speaking of bodies . . ."

Cecily held up a hand. "Let's not."

"Well, then. Let's see what this baby-sitter looks like. Call him."

Cecily picked up her phone and hit the speed-dial button for home.

"Culpepper residence."

"Iris? It's me, Cecily. Have you met the new chauffeur?"

"I sure have. Whoooeee. He's a hottie."

"A hottie?" Cecily grinned at Olivia. "Iris Wilson! I'm shocked."

"Why? I may be past the first bloom of youth, but I'm not dead. Far from it. If I didn't know better, I'd think Cyrus had made prior experience with Chippendales one of the qualifications for the job. The man has muscles you wouldn't believe. Your new chauffeur is a hunk and a half."

"Goodness. What does a hunk and a half look like?"

"He's tall, two or three inches over six feet, sandy-colored hair. Soulful brown eyes. Oh, and he's got the cutest dimple in his right cheek."

"Did he show you his chauffeur's license?"

"No. I didn't ask to see it. But I'm sure Cyrus did—you know your daddy."

"I want to see it, too. I'm at the Penn building. Tell him I'll be at the front entrance in twenty minutes. Oh, and tell him to use my car, will you? It's easier to spot the convertible than the SUV."

"Right away."

"Thanks, Iris." Cecily ended the call.

Olivia was bouncing up and down in her seat. "A hottie? Cyrus hired you a hottie. Cecily, this is perfect."

"What's perfect about it? He *is* a bodyguard. Iris said he's got muscles. What would a chauffeur need muscles for? Jenkins didn't have muscles."

"Bodyguard, baby-sitter, chauffeur. What difference does it make? He's a man. He's good-looking. He's perfect."

"You said that before. Why are you bouncing up and down?"

"He's the perfect man for your affair. He's even convenient—right next door, so to speak. So close you won't have to worry about the *Snoop*. It will be easy for you to be discreet."

"Olivia, has anyone ever told you you're crazy?"

"Only my family. And you. This isn't crazy. It's *perfect.*"

"Stop saying that. We don't know anything about him. And I never said I was going to have an affair."

"You said you would think about it."

"No, I didn't." Olivia looked so disappointed, Cecily felt obligated to add, "All right. I will *think* about having an affair. After the holidays. And after I get a divorce."

"Why wait?"

"What's the rush? I've waited three years. One more month won't matter." Neither would two or three months. The idea of letting another man get close to her made Cecily's stomach knot.

"The new guy may leave after Christmas. If all Cyrus hired him for was to get you through the holidays . . . strike now while the . . . hottie is hot. You need to do something for you. Before Christmas. To get the taste of Neville out of your mouth."

"Neville hasn't been in my mouth in years," Cecily protested.

"All right, then. To give you something to do besides plotting Neville's downfall. An affair is safe. Catching criminals is dangerous—that's why policemen have guns."

"I never said I was going to catch Neville."

"You didn't have to say it. I know you. You were thinking about it."

That was the problem of having the same best friend since kindergarten—Olivia knew her too well. "Just thinking, that's all. And affairs can so be dangerous. Remember Jean-Claude."

"Doesn't count. Jean-Claude was French. It's a well-known fact, which I had to learn the hard way, that Frenchmen are coldhearted bastards. Besides, it only hurt for a little while."

"I don't want to hurt at all. Not over a man. Not again."

"Well, if you're only in it for the sex, there's not much chance of that. Think of this man—do you know his name?"

"Armstrong. Mack Armstrong."

"Think of Mack as a life-size vibrator. No one ever got hurt by a vibrator."

"Not true! In college. Jo Ann Allison." Cecily gave a delicate shudder.

Olivia paled. "Oh, I forgot about her. But that wasn't a vibrator; it was a kitchen appliance. That's what happens when you're too cheap to buy the real thing."

"Enough! I need to get my packages from your office and go meet my new chauffeur."

"I'll help you carry your—"

"Bag? There's only one. I think I can handle it."

Olivia pouted. "I want to see him, too. I'm coming with you."

"All right. But no more talk about affairs. As much as I do love to shop, I'm not in the market for a man."

Cecily and Olivia retrieved her shopping bag and made their way to the main entrance. Standing inside the glass doors, they waited for Cecily's new driver.

"There's your car," said Olivia, pointing. "Darn. He's wearing a hat. I didn't get a good look at him when he drove by."

Cecily pushed the glass door open and walked out onto the sidewalk. Olivia followed. They watched as the driver found a parking place halfway down the block, stopped the car, and got out.

"Oh, my," sighed Olivia. "I want one of those for Christmas, please."

Cecily didn't say anything. She couldn't. Her mouth had fallen open the minute Mack came into view. Every demure and decorous thought she'd ever had flew out of her brain. One look at her new chauffeur/body-guard and Cecily felt reckless, impetuous. Wild.

And all he'd done so far was walk toward her.

Olivia kept babbling away—Olivia was not a babbler, so Mack must be the reason she was talking so fast. "I guess Iris does know a hottie when she sees one after all." Louder she said, "Mr. Armstrong? Over here." She must have noticed Cecily's silence, because she nudged her in the ribs with an elbow. "Cecily. Close your mouth."

Cecily closed her mouth. "He's not a chauffeur," she hissed. "He's too . . ."

"Tall," said Olivia. "No, too cocky. Look at the way he walks—like a John. Wayne or Travolta, take your pick."

A shiver slid down Cecily's spine. She had felt a jolt the minute Mack Armstrong had come into view. A familiar jolt. She'd felt the very same sensation the first time she had seen Neville Barton. Sexual attraction. That's what she was feeling. For the first time in three years.

It was all Olivia's fault, talking about affairs and hot bodies.

As Mack approached, Olivia kept up a running commentary. "Look at those broad shoulders, those narrow hips, those long, muscular legs. I wish he'd turn around. I bet he's got tight buns, too." Olivia must have realized that Cecily hadn't said anything. "Are you all right?"

"Fine." But she wasn't. Cecily felt dizzy. Her knees were shaking, and her pulse was racing. "Except I'm having trouble breathing."

"Who wouldn't?" asked Olivia. "Look at how he's looking at you—if he had a spoon, he'd eat you up. He's perfect."

"Olly, shut up. He'll hear you."

"Mrs. Barton?"

"That would be me," said Cecily, taking one step forward. "Except I don't go by that name. I'm Cecily Culpepper. You must be Mack Armstrong?"

"In person," he said, grinning. He held out his hand.

"Ooooh. Dimple." Olivia nudged her in the ribs again. "Cecily, he's got a dimple."

"I see it," sighed Cecily, placing her hand in his.

"Hello, there, Mack," said Olivia. "I'm Olivia Penn, Cecily's oldest and best friend. I'm sure we're going to be friends, too."

"Ma'am," said Mack, touching the brim of his hat.

"Sexy voice, too," Olivia hissed in her ear.

"I heard. Olivia, give me my shopping bag and go away."

"I'll take it," said Mack, reaching for it with the hand that wasn't holding Cecily's. If he heard Olivia's sotto voce remarks, he didn't show it. He gaze was fixed on her.

Cecily looked down at their joined hands, then back at Mack's face. "Sorry. Forgot to let go," he said, giving her hand one firm shake and dropping it. "I'll put this in the trunk."

While Mack was occupied with the shopping bag, Olivia said to Cecily, "I think your Christmas curse is about to be laid to rest—emphasis on the *laid*. You just got the best present a girl could wish for."

"Olivia, I think we're both making a big mistake. Judging a book by its cover. Just like I did with Neville. Mack could be less than he appears."

"Or more."

"I don't think he likes me. Now that I think about it, that grin was more of a sneer."

"Don't be ridiculous. I saw the way he looked at

you—the poor man was in a daze. And he couldn't let go of your hand, remember? He's attracted. You're attracted," Olivia hissed. "Don't try to deny it."

Mack walked across the wide sidewalk. "One shopping bag, safely stowed. Is that it?" he asked.

"That's it," said Cecily. "I didn't get as far down on my shopping list as I'd planned—I was distracted this morning. Bye, Olly. Thanks for the latte."

"Anytime—especially when you pick up the check. Nice to meet you, Mack. I hope you have a long and illustrious career as Cecily's chauffeur."

"Thanks," said Mack, opening the rear door of the Camaro.

"Bye, Cecily. Call me later," said Olivia.

Cecily waved Olivia away, then told Mack, "I don't ride in the backseat. I get carsick."

"Sorry. I didn't know." He opened the front door, and Cecily slid in. Mack closed the door and walked around the front of the car.

Once he was in the driver's seat, he asked, "Where to?"

"Home. Please."

Mack started the engine and pulled into traffic. After a few minutes of silence, during which Cecily managed to get her breathing more or less automatic, she said, "You don't have to wear a uniform."

"I'm a professional chauffeur. Professionals wear uniforms." He kept his eyes on the road, not looking at her. And his voice was cool. She'd been right. Her new chauffeur didn't like her.

Cecily decided not to care. "Well, if you don't mind. You have a chauffeur's license, then?"

"Naturally. Plus ten years experience driving for Luxurious Limos. Your father checked my qualifications and my résumé thoroughly."

"I'm sure he did," Cecily said. Hearing the quivering

sigh in her voice made her tear her gaze away from Mack's profile. She had to stop drooling and get serious, or Mack was going to walk all over her. "I'll want to check them, too. Right away, as soon as we're home. You're going to live in the garage apartment?"

"Yeah. I moved in this afternoon. Nice apartment— except for that painting over the fireplace. That is one ugly painting."

"It was a wedding gift. I forgot it was there. If you don't like it—and there's no reason why you should— you can get rid of it. It *is* ugly."

"A wedding present, huh? Won't whoever gave it to you expect to see it when they visit?"

"My husband gave it to me. He doesn't visit." Cecily loosened the seat belt and turned sideways in the seat. "My husband is Neville Barton—I assume Cyrus told you all about him."

"No, your father didn't mention your husband. But I know the story. I read the *Scoop*. Occasionally. While standing in line at the grocery store."

"It's amazing that paper is still in business, considering no one ever actually buys a copy."

Mack grinned. A small grin—she thought it looked like a reluctant grin, but it was enough to flash his dimple. Another sigh escaped from Cecily's half-open mouth.

"Tighten your seat belt, Mrs. Barton—Ms. Culpepper," Mack ordered.

Her new driver certainly was bossy—some of his remarks had bordered on insolent, too. She'd have to do something about that. "Cecily. Call me Cecily." She adjusted the seat belt, then looked to see where they were. "Oh, we're home already."

Mack pulled into the driveway and got out of the car.

She watched as he came around to open the passenger door. He held out a hand and helped Cecily out of the car. "Would you like to see my license now?"

"Yes. And your résumé."

Taking a slim wallet from his back pocket, Mack flipped it open. Cecily looked at the license. It looked real enough, but she supposed those things could be faked. "Thank you. Now, your résumé?"

"I don't carry that on me." His condescending tone made Cecily bristle.

"I didn't think you did. Where is it?

Mack jerked his head in the direction of the stairs. "Up in the apartment. I'll get it and bring it to you later."

Cecily stuck out her chin. It was time to show Mr. Armstrong who was in charge here. "I want to see it now."

"Fine," said Mack. He motioned toward the staircase. "After you."

Cecily started up the narrow stairway. For no particular reason, she let her hips sway a little more than absolutely necessary.

Six

Mack followed Cecily up the stairs. Slowly. He had a sinking feeling that he was in big trouble. Cecily Barton—Cecily Culpepper—was sexier in person than in newsprint. No photograph could capture her scent, subtle and intriguing, or her voice, soft and husky. Having her next to him in the Camaro had almost done him in. Watching her heart-shaped derriere wiggle up the stairs was undermining his resolve to be the consummate professional.

Cecily reached the landing outside the apartment door. Her hand went to the doorknob. "Oh, it's locked." She stepped back from the door, bumping into Mack as she did.

His hands went to her waist. He told himself it was an automatic reflex that made him grab her. He wasn't sure why he wasn't letting her go. "Steady," he said.

"Unlock it, please," she said. Her voice sounded breathless. That had to be from climbing the narrow stairs—she couldn't be feeling what he was feeling. Whatever that was.

Mack fumbled with the key ring until he found the

brass key. With one hand still on her waist, he slid the key into the lock and turned it. The door swung open.

The sensual haze he'd been wallowing in cleared the second Mack saw the folder he'd left on the coffee table—the folder with *H.P.D. Media Relations Department* plastered on the front of it, the folder containing newspaper clippings about the woman in front of him.

Cecily's view of the coffee table was still blocked by the half-open door. Mack whirled her around, wrapped both arms around her, and kissed her.

Clinging to his broad shoulders, Cecily tried to orient herself. It felt like her chauffeur was kissing her, but that couldn't be right. She must be dreaming. That's what it was—she had fallen asleep in the car on the way home. Understandable, since she'd been up half the night.

Mack's hot mouth on hers didn't feel like a dream.

He wanted her to . . . move. Mack was pushing her through the tiny foyer into the apartment. Cecily forced her eyes open. He wanted her on the sofa. She began to panic. Twisting her head, she broke the kiss. "What—"

Mack clamped his mouth on hers again, bending her backward over one strong arm. But not before Cecily glimpsed a folder on the coffee table. A dark blue folder. He wasn't assaulting her—he was trying to keep her from seeing that folder. She relaxed.

And kissed him back.

Sure enough, with his free arm Mack reached for the folder. Once he had it in his hand, he sat down on the sofa, taking Cecily with him. While she sprawled across his lap, he tucked the blue folder between the sofa cushions.

Up until then, Mack had only vaguely been aware of the effect his kiss was having on Cecily. Once the folder was out of sight, he discovered that her arms were wound around his neck, that her bottom was nestled between his thighs.

And that she was kissing him back.

"Cecily?" he muttered, their lips still touching.

"Hmmmm?" Her tongue traced his lower lip.

With a groan, Mack deepened the kiss once again. Cecily wriggled on his lap, pushing against his chest with one hand while the other hand clasped his nape. Mack fell back, and Cecily settled herself on top of him.

"What are you hiding?" she murmured. One hand slid behind him, between the cushion and the arm of the sofa.

She was reaching for the folder.

Mack sat up quickly, taking her with him.

Cecily ended up facing him, her legs around his waist. She had the folder in one hand—he could feel the stiff cardboard between his shoulder blades—but that hand was behind his back. She couldn't see it. Yet. "What's this?" she asked.

"What?" Mack tried to kiss her again.

Turning her head, Cecily tried to bring the folder under his arm. Mack trapped her hand in his armpit, nuzzling her neck at the same time. "Kiss me, Cecily."

"In a minute," she muttered. Using only wrist action, Cecily tossed the folder into the air. It opened. Newspaper articles flew out.

The folder landed facedown on the coffee table.

Cecily pushed out of his arms and wiggled off his lap. Sitting next to him on the sofa, she stared at the *Houston Scoop* clippings littering the carpet. "Well, what do you know? I was right. You're not a chauffeur."

"I've got the license," Mack protested. Weakly. He had messed up. Big-time.

"I'm sure you do. And the right kind of résumé, too. Cyrus would have insisted on the proper credentials.

But I know why you're really here. My father hired you to keep me out of trouble, didn't he? That kind of trouble." She pointed to the stack of clippings from the *Scoop*. "You're not a chauffeur—you're a bodyguard. And a liar."

Mack closed his eyes and breathed a quick sigh of relief. His cover was tattered but not completely blown. She didn't know he was a cop. "Yeah. I'm a bodyguard. But I am a chauffeur, too. My uncle Walt really does own Luxurious Limos. And I drive for him occasionally."

"And that makes you what? Half a liar? Why did you kiss me?"

"I was trying to keep you from seeing the dossier the agency prepared for me." Mack leaned over and picked up a couple of the newspaper articles and put them on top of the blue folder on the coffee table. "I'm really sorry, Ms. Culpepper. I should not have done that. Are you going to tell your father?"

"What? That I know who you are, or that you kissed me?"

"Either. Both. Are you?"

Cecily leaned back against the sofa cushions. "I don't know. If I tell him, he'll probably fire you."

"Yeah." Mack didn't have to fake the disgusted look on his face. He thought he caught a flash of pity in Cecily's eyes before she turned away.

"Do you work for that agency that Cyrus uses to do background checks on people? International something or other?"

"You're right again. I work for International Operatives, Inc. I should say I used to work for them. They won't like it that I blew my cover the first day on the job. The only reason I got this assignment was because I have a chauffeur's license. I don't usually do field work." Mack attempted a pitiful sigh.

"You're an office worker?"

"Yeah. Mostly I do computer checks on people. But I was ready for something a little more exciting, so when this assignment came up, I took it."

"Humph. I guess after you read about me in the *Snoop* you thought things were going to be a lot more exciting. No telling what kind of antics a dumb blonde with a rich daddy might get up to. And you would have stopped me?"

"I would have tried."

Cecily gave him an assessing look. Her eyes narrowed. "Maybe we can come to an arrangement."

"What kind of arrangement?"

"I won't tell on you if you don't tell on me."

"I'm not sure what that means," Mack said cautiously. "Are you planning to do something you don't want your father to know about?" Like take a pot of Daddy's money to her husband, for instance—Mack kept that thought to himself.

"Maybe. It *is* that time of year. If I am, do you agree not to tell Cyrus?"

"I don't know. Like you said, I was hired to keep you out of trouble. If I let you get away with something, I will have failed at my job."

"You already failed," Cecily pointed out ruthlessly. "If you promise not to tell my daddy what I'm up to, I'll fix it so you don't get blamed for anything I do."

"In that case, yes. I accept your proposition."

Cecily smiled. "Good."

"What are you planning to do?" asked Mack. "Does it have anything to do with your husband?"

"Neville? Why would you think that? I haven't seen him in three years."

"I'm supposed to keep you out of trouble. Your husband sounds like trouble—from what I read in the *Scoop*."

"My husband is thousands of miles away. And, as I told you, he doesn't visit. You don't need to know my holiday plans—yet." Cecily got up, straightened her clothes, and headed for the door. Once there, she turned back. "I think this arrangement is going to work out well, Mack. At some point, I may need professional assistance. Do you have a gun?"

"A gun?" Mack started to stand, quickly changed his mind, and remained seated. With his legs crossed. "Are you planning to shoot someone?"

"Only if necessary. Do you have a gun?"

"Not with me. I didn't think I would need to be armed for this job."

"Do you know karate?"

"I can hold my own in a fight. I'm not liking the sound of this. What's going on? What are you planning?"

"You'll know when you need to. Until then, do your job—your chauffeur's job." With triumphant smile, Cecily swept from the room.

Mack sat frozen with shock. He had never screwed up a case so bad, so fast. The buzz of the wire recorder made him jump guiltily. He got up and went to the bedroom. Carefully, he opened the cabinet door and took out the earphones. He put them on.

". . . a bodyguard or a chauffeur?"

Mack recognized Olivia Penn's voice.

"Oh, he is definitely a bodyguard," Cecily said. Her smug tone had Mack wincing.

"You sound awfully sure of yourself."

"He admitted it—he had to. Mack had a dossier on me, full of *Houston Snoop* clippings. And I think I saw a copy of my wedding photo, so they must have given him the *Houston Chronicle* stories, too."

"A dossier? How did you happen to see it?"

"He left it on the coffee table. In plain sight. Or it

would have been, if he hadn't tried to hide it while he was kissing me, but I—"

"Whoa, there. Back up. He was *kissing* you?"

"Only to distract me. It didn't mean anything."

Olivia made a noise that sounded a lot like a pig's squeal. Mack held the phone away from his ear until she finished.

"Cecily, no man has sullied your lips since your wedding day. That means something. How did you end up in the chauffeur's apartment, anyway? You skipped over that part."

"When we got home, I asked to see his résumé . . ."

"Résumé? What a good idea. More practical than asking to see his etchings. Most men don't have etchings these days. But everyone has a résumé."

"Olivia, I was checking his chauffeur story. The résumé was in the apartment, or so he said. Come to think of it, I never did get to look at it. But it doesn't matter now. I found out what I needed to know. He may have a license, but he is more than a chauffeur."

"Is he a good kisser?"

"Oh, I guess you could say he's adequate."

Mack winced.

"Of course, he wasn't really kissing me—that was a diversion. Even so, I had forgotten . . ."

"How good a kiss can be?"

"Something like that."

"What happened after the kiss?"

"I saw him stuff a folder between the sofa cushions—"

"You were on the sofa? How did that happen?"

"He sort of manhandled me there. So he could move the folder from the coffee table to the sofa without me seeing it."

"But you saw it anyway."

"Yes. And I must say that rolling around with him on the couch was very . . . stimulating."

Another squeal. "Cecily Jeanne Culpepper! You're having too much fun."

"I don't know about fun, but it was exciting." Cecily paused. "You know, Olly, I don't think Mack is very good at his job. I mean, he shouldn't have left something that incriminating just lying around."

Mack winced again.

"He doesn't have to be good at his job—as long as he's good in bed. But, in his defense, Mack obviously didn't expect anyone to visit him. Especially not you."

"I guess not. And he did say that this was his first undercover assignment—he was picked because he has a real chauffeur's license. Usually, he does office work—computer research, that kind of thing. Mack begged me not to fire him."

Mack bit his tongue to keep from arguing that point. He had not *begged*.

Olivia sucked in a noisy breath. "Don't you dare fire him. He's the first man in three years who has made your hormones sit up and take notice. You can't waste an opportunity like this."

"That's exactly the conclusion I came to. Even if the kiss was only so-so, Mack is too good to waste. I figured that much out when we were wrestling over the dossier. He does have muscles, but he didn't use them to overpower me—well, he did, but only because he wanted to get to the sofa. Giving him the benefit of the doubt, I'm sure he would kiss better if he'd been concentrating on me instead of on his job."

"Plus, he's got that dimple." Olivia sighed.

"The dimple is killer," said Cecily. "The dimple is what convinced me he's perfect. It *is* time I forgot about my wedding vows. Three years is too long to go without a man. I am ready to make merry this Christmas."

"About time," Olivia agreed. "Mack can be your transition man."

"What's that?"

"The man who's the bridge between being married and being single again. And you won't have any trouble with the *Scoop*—he's right there, practically in your house."

"Right. I will not be in danger of seeing my name linked with Mack's in the newspapers. Can you imagine the headline? *Cecily Shags Chauffeur.*"

Olivia giggled. "Or *Mrs. Barton Boinks Bodyguard.*"

Cecily laughed. "Olivia, you're going to think I'm weird, but what I really like best about Mack is not the muscles or the dimple, or even his proximity. What is most arousing is that I'm in charge. He has to do whatever I want him to do, or risk losing his job." She paused. "I never knew how intoxicating power could be."

"That's not weird. What woman wouldn't want to have a strong, sexy male in her control? What have you made him do so far?"

"I forced him to agree that he wouldn't tell Cyrus what I'm up to. In return, I'm not going to tell Cyrus that I know he's more than a chauffeur. As long as Mack does what I tell him to do, his career as an undercover operative is safe."

"What you're up to? I knew it. I really don't think that's a good idea, Cecily. It could be dangerous."

"Not if I'm smart. And now I have Mack to help me."

"True. You are so lucky." Olivia's sigh sounded envious.

"I know. But I'm shallow, too, don't you think? I mean, only last Friday I vowed to be demure and decorous—but that's not at all what I want to be with Mack. I want to be . . . indecent and improper."

"You go, girl. When are you going to tell him about his other duties?"

Cecily laughed. "Soon."

Indecent? Improper? And soon? Mack felt his face heat up. And what dangerous stunt did she have planned for this holiday season?

"How soon? When will you see Mack again?" asked Olivia.

"At dinner. Which is only thirty minutes away. I'd better go see if Iris needs any help. Good-bye, Olly. I'll talk to you tomorrow."

As soon as he heard the dial tone, Mack carefully replaced the receiver. His hand was shaking, he could feel sweat beading on his forehead, and his knees felt like rubber. He sat down on the edge of the bed. Why did women do that? Say their most intimate thoughts out loud?

He reached for the telephone again. He would call Captain Morris and tell him he was not the right man for this assignment. It needed someone older. Someone married. Happily married. Someone who wouldn't leave evidence of his deception in plain view. Someone capable of resisting a blonde heiress who wasn't dumb at all. Cecily Culpepper was smart enough to have guessed that he was more than a chauffeur even before she'd seen the folder of newspaper clippings.

And she was ruthless enough to take advantage of his stupidity.

Mack groaned. He couldn't tell his boss that he had screwed up a simple assignment like driving Cecily, not without risking permanent assignment as a school-crossing guard. He was a cop, with almost ten years' experience. He'd been face-to-face with armed robbers, rapists, and murderers, and he'd survived. He could handle one little woman.

He had to. He had a job to do, and allowing Cecily to seduce him was not on the agenda. That would violate both departmental guidelines for undercover behavior and his own sense of fair play. If he could resist her, it would go a long way toward restoring his shredded self-esteem.

By sheer luck—the H.P.D. folder had landed face-down—Cecily hadn't connected him to the police department. And she hadn't cottoned to the fact that her daddy knew about her husband's telephone call—that call hadn't figured in her conversation with Olivia at all. She didn't know he was a cop, and she didn't know her phone was tapped.

He might make it, after all.

Mack picked up the blue folder, retrieved the International Ops folder from the desk drawer, and took them both downstairs and locked them in his truck.

He started back upstairs, then glanced at his watch and changed direction. Almost dinnertime—dinner was at seven, Iris had said. Maybe if he could start acting like a cop instead of a lust-crazed male, he would be able to get some useful information from the cook. Iris might be able to shed some light on Cecily's feelings for her husband—and her propensity for seducing unsuspecting males.

Mack knocked on the kitchen door a couple of minutes before seven. He was surprised when Cecily opened the door.

"Hi, Mack. Come on in. Iris is carving the chicken. Have a seat at the table—anywhere but there." She pointed to a chair. "That's where Cyrus sits."

Mack sat down. The round table was set for four. "I didn't know I'd be eating with you and your father."

"We almost always eat in the kitchen. The dining room is too big for two or three people."

Iris set a platter of chicken on the table. "Call Cyrus, will you, Cecily? Tell him dinner is on the table."

Cecily picked up the phone and punched in a two-digit number. "Daddy? You'd better come on. We're all waiting on you." She hung up. "He's on his way."

Cecily took the seat next to Mack. Her knee brushed his as she scooted her chair closer to the table. Mack stiffened. She wasn't going to play footsie with him under her daddy's nose, was she? Cyrus entered the kitchen just as Mack felt silky toes sliding under the hem of his jeans. She was.

Taking his seat, Cyrus said, "Hello, Mack. Settled in, are you?"

Mack had to clear his throat before he could answer. "I moved the necessities—I'll get the rest of my stuff later."

"Where were you living before?" asked Cecily. She had managed to get her whole foot inside his pant leg. She wiggled her toes against his bare calf.

"I had an apartment," Mack said through clenched teeth.

"Did you have any trouble getting out of your lease?" Iris asked.

"No. Mr. Culpepper paid it off."

"No big deal. The lease was up in a month," said Cyrus. "Walt—that's the owner of Luxurious Limos, Iris, where Mack worked before—Walt told me that you're house hunting. What are you looking for?"

"A fixer-upper in a good neighborhood. I'm partial to Craftsman-designed homes."

Iris spoke up. "I like Victorian myself. If you're house hunting, you must be getting ready to settle down, start a family."

The toes stopped wiggling against his calf.

"Why does everyone assume that?" asked Mack, taking the bowl of mashed potatoes Iris handed him. "I'm buying a house because I want a house. No other reason."

"You don't want a family?" asked Cecily.

"Got one," said Mack, concentrating on placing a heaping spoonful of mashed potatoes on his plate.

"You're married?" asked Iris.

The toes slid completely away. "No. Mother, father, older brother. That family."

"Oh. Gravy's in that pitcher," said Iris, pointing.

Cecily passed him the gravy. "So you're not involved with anyone at the moment?"

"Cecily. That's rather a personal question, don't you think?" Cyrus said.

"If Mack has a girlfriend, he'll probably want the weekends off. That's the only reason I asked." Cecily turned to Mack. "Do you want the weekends off?"

"No," he said, mesmerized by her blue eyes. As soon as she looked away, he gave himself a mental kick. He should have said yes—Cecily's retreating toes showed that she had scruples about teasing another woman's man. "Although my mother expects me to show up for Sunday dinner occasionally."

"That won't be a problem," said Cyrus. "I can drive Cecily anywhere she needs to go on Sunday."

"So, you don't have a steady girl?" asked Iris.

Cyrus rolled his eyes but didn't chastise the cook as he had his daughter.

"No, ma'am. Not at the moment." Mack bit his tongue. Why hadn't he said he was engaged? He'd missed another chance to keep Cecily at a distance. Her silky toes rubbing his leg must have fried his brain.

"I didn't think so," said Cecily, smiling.

The toes were back. Mack stretched his leg out, dislodging Cecily's foot.

"Chicken." Cecily pushed the plate of carved chicken closer to Mack's plate. Under the table, she hooked her ankle around his calf and pulled his leg back into toe range.

"What did you do today, C. J.?" Cyrus asked.

"I shopped. At Penn's. I found the perfect gift for Mr. Seaton. A red silk cummerbund and a matching red bow tie."

"Good choice—he'll think red will make him dashing. Seaton was one of my first customers," Cyrus explained. "He fancies himself a clotheshorse. C. J. does all my Christmas shopping for me. She's good at it, too. Always finds the perfect gift."

"That's something I can't seem to get the hang of—finding the right gift," Mack admitted.

"Do you have your Christmas shopping done?" asked Cecily, taking her toes away.

Mack breathed a sigh of relief. Too soon. He felt a hand on his thigh. "Uh, I'm a last-minute shopper, I'm afraid. I try to think of something to buy, but I usually end up on Christmas Eve getting gift certificates."

"Gift certificates?" Cecily wrinkled her nose. "That's awful."

"Cecily! What is it with you and Mack? You're being rude again."

"Well, gift certificates *are* awful," said Cecily. She patted him on his thigh. "You might as well give a person money."

"I give you money," said Cyrus, scowling.

"Exactly," said Cecily, giving her father a saucy wink. She turned to Mack. "You would think someone who goes out of his way to look like Santa Claus could do better, wouldn't you?"

Mack shrugged.

"Maybe you could help Mack out," said Iris. "He'll be with you while you shop anyway."

"That's a good idea," said Cecily. "Who do you buy gifts for? Your girlfriends?" She stroked his thigh.

"He said he didn't have one," said Cyrus. He sounded exasperated.

Mack could understand that. Cecily was the most exasperating female—he grabbed her hand before she got closer to finding out how her little games were affecting him.

"He doesn't have a special girl. I heard. But that doesn't mean he doesn't have *any* girlfriends. He could have lots of not-so-special friends." She flashed a speculative look his way.

A lifeline had been offered, and Mack took it. "I do. That is, I have several women . . . friends. I'm not ready to limit myself to one woman—I don't think I ever will be. My future sister-in-law says I have commitment issues."

Cecily withdrew her hand. Mack grinned. He'd managed to turn her off. Finally. He sneaked a peek at her. She was frowning.

"You must have a long list, then," said Iris. She had a twinkle in her eye.

Mack shook his head. "Not so long. If you buy a woman a gift, she thinks it means you're serious—I learned that lesson a long time ago. So I buy gifts only for my immediate family. And this year I drew Aunt Opal's name—we draw names at Thanksgiving so that everyone doesn't have to buy gifts for the whole family."

"Got a large family?" asked Iris.

"Yeah, pretty large. My mother has two brothers and a sister. Her brothers are married; the sister is a widow. Dad has one brother and a sister. I have eight cousins, and a couple of them are married with children. Joe— my brother—is engaged, so I guess I'll give Sarah a gift this year, too."

Cyrus helped himself to another spoonful of potatoes. "All of them are in Houston?"

"Most of them."

"That's nice," said Cecily. "I always thought a large family would be fun. Not that you aren't fun, Daddy. But there's only one of you."

"You could add to the family tree, if you'd get rid of that scoundrel you're married to and try again."

Cecily scowled. "Daddy, let's not talk about him."

"Listen to her, Cyrus," said Iris. "You want to spoil everyone's dinner?"

"Nothing could spoil this meal—you're a fantastic cook, Ms. Wilson."

"Why thank you, Mack. And call me Iris."

"What's for dessert?" asked Cyrus.

"Apple pie," said Iris.

"Fine." Cyrus stroked his beard. "I want mine á la mode."

"Get out the frozen yogurt, Cecily."

"I want ice cream," Cyrus said. His mustache quivered in indignation.

"We don't have any ice cream, Daddy. The yogurt is good."

"Humph. What about a hunk of cheddar?"

"I think there is some fat-free cheese in the fridge," said Iris.

"Not that. Tastes like rubber. If rubber is tasteless. All right, I'll have the yogurt." Cyrus shook his head. "Bossy women. What's a man supposed to do?"

"Grin and enjoy it," said Iris.

Cecily winked at Mack.

After dessert, everyone got up from the table.

"What time will you need me tomorrow?" Mack asked Cecily.

"I have to be at the Humane Society animal shelter by nine o'clock. It takes about twenty minutes to get there."

"You'll see her at breakfast. You can set the exact time of departure then. Come into my study, Mack. I've got a few forms for you to sign to get you on the payroll—W-four and such."

"Mack? When you're done with Daddy, would you bring me my shopping bag? We left it in the car. I'm on the third floor. Take the elevator if you want."

With a nod, Mack folded his napkin and followed Cyrus out of the kitchen.

As soon as they were out of earshot, Cecily said, "Where's the rest of that mistletoe?"

"What do you need mistletoe for?"

"I just need it. You didn't throw it away, did you?

"No. I wrapped it in wet paper towels and put it in the refrigerator in the butler's pantry. I thought I might take it to my sister's this weekend. But if you need it, I'll get it for you." Iris gave her a curious look.

Cecily took the dishes from the table and put them in the sink while Iris went to the pantry.

Grinning, Iris handed her the bundle of mistletoe. "I figured out why you want this. You're going to use it on Mack. You think Mack is a hottie, too, don't you?"

"I don't know what you're talking about. I just want to add more decorations to the third floor."

"You think he's cute. He is. But he sure was jumpy at the dinner table. You didn't have anything to do with that, I suppose?"

"Of course not. Tell Mack to bring the stepladder when he comes back, will you?" Cecily hurried from the kitchen before Iris could continue her speculations.

Mack followed Cyrus down the wide center hall. Cyrus opened pocket doors and motioned him into a paneled room. He settled himself behind the desk, steepled his fingers, and said, "Well? Found out anything yet?"

"You didn't hear her latest call?"

"No. The extension didn't ring."

"Oh, right. It was an outgoing call. Cecily called her friend, Olivia."

"Don't usually listen to calls from her friends—only the ones from that SOB she married. There's only been one of those, thank God. I am not going to invade her privacy any more than is necessary to keep her safe."

Mack breathed a sigh of relief. At least he didn't have to worry about placating an irate father. "Your daughter thinks I'm a bodyguard."

"Does she? Smart girl. Guess I got rid of Jenkins a little too abruptly. But I didn't want to waste any time. No telling when that snake will call again. She doesn't know I know about Neville's phone call, does she?"

"I don't think so. She seemed to think you hired me to keep her out of trouble—the kind of holiday trouble she's gotten into the past couple of years."

"Thinks you're a bodyguard, not a chauffeur, hey?" At Mack's nod, Cyrus said, "Keep her guessing for as long as possible. It will give her something to think about besides her husband. And it wouldn't be a bad idea for you to try to keep her out of trouble—all kinds, not just whatever Barton is up to. Cecily does tend to get a little wild this time of year."

"I'll do my best, Mr. Culpepper—Cyrus. There's something else you should know—sir." Mack cleared his throat. "I kissed your daughter."

Cyrus drew his white, fluffy brows into a frown. "Did you? Did she like it?"

"I think so. She kissed me back. The thing is, I screwed up. I left the folder about her on the coffee table. I had to do something fast to keep her from seeing it—"

"She went to your apartment?" asked Cyrus.

"Yes. She wanted to see my résumé."

"Ah. So you kissed her to keep her from finding out you're a cop?"

"Yes. Leaving that folder out was careless. Stupid, in fact. I'll understand if you want me off the case."

"Nonsense. You're a fast thinker—kissing her was a good idea. I only wish you had kissed her because you wanted to kiss a pretty girl—maybe if Cecily found you appealing, she'd take steps to get rid of Neville. Ah, well, if you're not attracted to her, don't force it. Go on, now. Cecily is waiting for you."

Yeah, thought Mack. Like a black widow spider, waiting to make a meal off the next male caught in her web.

Seven

Cecily sat at her worktable—a large mahogany table set in a windowed alcove overlooking the backyard. The table was covered with rolls of wrapping paper, assorted spools of ribbon, and various small seasonal items that she used to decorate the packages she wrapped. Several stuffed shopping bags were tucked under the table.

While she waited for Mack, Cecily tied a red ribbon around the stem of the mistletoe. Then she got up and paced. She wasn't usually a pacer, but she wasn't usually so keyed up, either. Having dinner with Mack had been exhilarating, exciting, and . . . scary. She was discovering she could do things she had never dreamed of doing—like teasing Mack under the table.

No matter what the tabloids said about her, she had always thought of herself as a nice girl. A nice girl didn't tease.

A nice girl didn't take pleasure from having a strong, virile male—a male with a very sexy dimple—completely in her power.

A nice *married* girl certainly wouldn't be thinking

about using that power to seduce the strong, virile male.

She was very pleased with her power. And she was not only thinking about seducing Mack, she was actively plotting exactly what she was going to do to him and his sexy dimple as soon as she maneuvered him underneath the light fixture.

Ergo, she wasn't nice.

She was ruthless, reckless, and a little bit wild.

After another few minutes' reflection, Cecily decided she could live with that—but it was lucky for her that Mack did not have a special woman in his life. She wasn't *that* ruthless.

Taking off all her clothes and ordering Mack to join her in bed would be the most expedient route to what historical romance novels referred to as "ruin." But instant gratification was not what she was after. She wanted something . . . less than love but more than sex. She wanted an exciting, sensual, *romantic* affair.

She wanted Mack to want that, too—and that might take some doing. So far, all she had accomplished was to make him noticeably nervous—"twitchy," as Iris had put it.

Although it was fun being the aggressor, she wanted to be sure Mack wasn't repulsed by her advances before they took the ultimate step together. She didn't think she repulsed him—Mack had kissed her first, and even though the kiss had an ulterior purpose, he hadn't gagged or anything. She didn't really want to make Mack do something he found repulsive, did she? No, came the prompt answer.

He did not find her repulsive.

When they'd been rolling around on the couch, she was almost sure he had been aroused. Almost. Just to be sure, she wouldn't kiss him tonight. She would try getting Mack to kiss her. The mistletoe would give him the traditional holiday excuse to plant one on her. If that worked, she would move slowly, one kiss at a time, until she and Mack were both so ready for each other . . .

Cecily shivered in anticipation.

She heard the elevator begin its ascent. Slipping out of her shoes, she walked across the room to the wide hall and waited.

Mack stepped off the elevator carrying the shopping bag and the kitchen stepladder. "Where do you want the ladder?" he asked. His expression could only be called wary.

She stifled a grin—the big, bad bodyguard was scared of her. "In here," she said, motioning him into her living room.

"Isn't it a little chilly to be going barefooted?" Mack stared at her naked feet. Was he remembering that her bare toes had tormented and teased him all through dinner?

"Not with carpet and central heat. Just put the ladder under the ceiling fan, please."

Mack set the shopping bag on the floor and put the ladder where she had indicated. "Do you need a bulb changed?"

"No. I want to hang some mistletoe from the light fixture."

"Mistletoe?" Mack paled visibly. "Why?"

"Because it's Christmas. I've decorated my tree, and I've hung garlands on the fireplace, but I forgot the mistletoe."

He might have groaned. "I'll do it. Where's the mistletoe?"

"I'll get it." She walked over to her worktable and picked up the sprig of mistletoe. As she started toward him, Mack climbed the ladder.

"Here," she said, reaching up to hand him the mistletoe. When her fingers brushed his, Mack wobbled on the ladder. He *was* afraid of her. "Careful," said Cecily, grabbing his knees. "Don't fall."

"I am not going to fall, Ms. Culpepper," Mack said through clenched teeth. "Take your hands off me. Please."

Cecily removed her hands. It took Mack longer than it should have to tie the mistletoe to the light fixture—his hands appeared to be shaking. Once he'd managed to anchor the mistletoe, he backed down the ladder.

When he turned, Cecily was waiting for him. With a shocked look, Mack took a step back and hit the ladder. The ladder threatened to topple, but Cecily reached around him and steadied it. She put her hands on his waist and moved closer.

They were only centimeters apart. Mack sucked in a breath and held it.

Cecily looked at him, her blue eyes full of . . . mischief.

"What are you doing?" asked Mack, resisting a strong urge to cut and run. He was a trained law enforcement officer, used to dealing with people a lot more dangerous than one not-so-dumb blonde. He held his ground.

"Waiting."

"For what?"

"We're under the mistletoe, Mack. What do you think I'm waiting for?"

"Uh. You want me to kiss you?"

Her lower lip came out in a sexy semi-pout. "It is traditional. I'm very big on holiday traditions. Aren't you?"

"I don't want to kiss you," lied Mack.

Cecily slowly licked her pouty lower lip. "You don't?" The mischief disappeared from her amazing blue eyes, replaced by something that looked like hurt. "Don't you like me, Mack?"

Mack groaned. "I like you. I don't want to kiss you, that's all. There's something you need to know about me, Cecily. I won't be good for you."

"You don't have to be good, Mack. Bad works for me."

"Cecily. Pay attention here. I'm trying to tell you—I have commitment issues."

"Not a problem. I have commitment issues, too. My issues are bigger than your issues. I'm married, remember?"

He tried again. "You would be one of many."

"Many women?" A tiny frown appeared between her eyebrows. "Is that what you're talking about?"

"Yeah. I've got a different woman for every night of the week. My little black book is the envy of every man I know."

"Is it, really? Maybe you should sell it, then—no, auction it off. A valuable collection like that would probably bring a tidy sum on eBay."

"Cecily—"

Her fingers on his mouth stopped whatever inane excuse he'd been about to spout.

"Hush, Mack. I think you're forgetting something. Now you work for me. Exclusively. You brought this on yourself, you know. You kissed me this afternoon."

"That wasn't a kiss. That was a ploy."

"A ploy? Oh. To keep me from seeing the clippings from the *Snoop*. But it was a kiss, too, Mack. A real kiss. And I seem to recall there was more than one." She closed her eyes and tilted her face up. Her lips parted slightly.

"Cecily, this is not a good idea."

Her eyes remained shut. "Yes, it is. It's the best idea I've had in years. You're not going to make me order you to kiss me, are you?"

Lowering his head, Mack stopped himself right before his lips touched hers. Cecily sighed. He inhaled the sigh that escaped from her parted lips. Her breath mingling with his drove him over the edge. He kissed her.

Mack could have tried for a quick brush of lips and a quicker escape. But once his mouth was on hers, his brain—the little he had left—ceased to function.

Primitive and powerful, instinct took over. Mack's arms went around Cecily, and he jerked her against him. A noise somewhere between a moan and a purr sounded deep in her throat. Mack swallowed that, too, and all the other small gasps and sighs coming from her delicious mouth.

A second before he would have pushed her to the floor and fallen on top of her, Cecily pulled away.

"My. That certainly kept the tradition alive." Her cheeks were pink, and her breaths came in short gasps.

"Tradition?" Mack said, his mind blank.

Cecily pointed overhead. "The mistletoe, remember?"

He looked up. "Oh . . . yeah. Mistletoe."

"You can take the ladder back to the kitchen. Thanks for your help. Good night, Mack."

As soon as the elevator doors closed, Cecily sank onto the sofa. Fanning her face with her hand, she relived the kiss. "Wow," she murmured. "I've got to tell Olivia about this."

She picked up the portable phone and dialed Olivia's number. When she answered, Cecily said, "I maligned him before. Mack is an outstanding kisser."

"Is he? Tell me more."

"I had him hang up some mistletoe—

"Mistletoe was my idea," Olivia said, her tone smug.

"And an outstanding idea it was. Anyway, under the mistletoe, he kissed me. Although . . . he tried not to."

"What was that?" asked Olivia.

"What?"

"A clicking noise, like someone picking up another phone."

"I didn't hear anything. Where was I? Oh, yes. I wanted the kiss to be Mack's idea. Power over another human being can be misused, you know. I didn't want to force Mack to do anything that repulsed him."

"Of course not," Olivia murmured. "How did he try not to kiss you?"

"He told me he wouldn't be good for me—said he had commitment issues."

"Yeah, right. Him and ninety percent of the male sex. They all have commitment issues until they meet the right woman,"

"I don't want to be Mack's right woman—I just want to be his right-for-now woman. I'd better make that clear before this goes any further—I am not looking for forever. Anyway, Mack gave up arguing and he kissed me. I thought I was going to have to order him to do it, but I didn't. And it wasn't the mistletoe, either. Mack *wanted* to kiss me."

"As well he should. Well? Don't stop now. What was it like? Gentle? Hard? Were tongues involved?"

"Hard. Hot. Definitely tongues. I had to stop or I would have ended up a puddle at his feet."

"You stopped? Why?"

"Because. I want this—whatever it is I'm feeling—to last. So I'm going to take it slow—if you can call two kissing sessions plus what happened under the table slow. Olivia, do you realize that I met Mack only a few hours ago?"

"Under the table? What table? What happened under it?"

Cecily told her. "I decided I am not a nice girl."

Olivia giggled. "More of a hussy than I ever thought you could be. Are you having fun?"

"Yes. I am. I'm having a wonderful time."

"Good. What's next on the agenda?"

"I'm not sure. I'll have to think about it. Tomorrow is my day at the animal shelter, so I will have time to think." She paused. "One thing for sure: I need more mistletoe."

Tuesday morning, Mack almost called Iris and told her he'd be having breakfast in his apartment. He'd spent half the night fantasizing about what he would to Cecily if she put her hands—or her mouth—on him one more time, and the other half trying to come up with ways to keep out of her reach.

Telling her about his other women—the exaggerated version—hadn't stopped her. She had commitment issues, she'd said. That was probably the truth—he could see how being married to a crook could turn a woman off to the whole idea of marriage. She had said as much to Olivia.

Too bad she hadn't mentioned sooner the part about not wanting to take her seduction plan any further if she thought she repulsed him. It was a little late to fake disgust with her now, assuming he was that good an actor, which he most likely wasn't.

Mack stared at the telephone. If he had to listen to one more telephone call between Olivia and Cecily, he might explode. His kiss had almost made Cecily melt into a puddle at his feet—he did not need to know that. It made him want to try again. Or run.

Running away wasn't an option. He had job to do, and hiding from Cecily wasn't going to get it done. Resigned to his fate, Mack put on his chauffeur's uniform. Before leaving the apartment, he called the Burglary and Theft Command office and asked to speak to Captain Morris. He reported that International Ops had traced Neville Barton to the Cayman Islands.

He also told his boss that Cecily thought he was a body-guard.

"How did she get that idea?" asked the captain.

"Something about the abrupt way her father changed chauffeurs made her suspicious. She thinks her father hired me to keep her out of trouble this Christmas."

"Smart girl. Well, I don't think it matters much what she thinks about you. The important thing is for you to stay close to her. If Barton is on the move, her father may be right. He could be coming after her."

"Yes, sir." Close to Cecily. But not too close. That woman was downright dangerous to his career. And his freedom.

Mack headed for the main house. Having someone besides his mother cook breakfast for him would be a novel experience. Not that several women of his acquaintance hadn't offered, but Mack knew better than to take advantage of those kinds of offers. Too many strings. He laughed out loud. What he wouldn't give for a few familiar strings—the kind he knew how to avoid.

Cecily Culpepper knew how to tie a man in knots without strings. No telling what antics she would be up to this morning. Maybe he could arrange it so he wasn't within groping reach at this meal. And if he could figure out a way to get her to ride in the backseat of the Camaro, he'd be able to make it through the day.

Mack knocked on the kitchen door and opened it. "Morning, everyone," he said, taking off his hat.

"Good morning," chorused Iris and Cecily.

Cecily looked him over from head to toe, her gaze smoldering. "I wish you wouldn't wear that uniform. It makes me feel underdressed."

Cecily was wearing well-worn jeans that molded to her body like a lover's caress. Mack shook his head. *Lover's caress?* That kind of thinking was off limits. He moved his gaze upward, to the baggy burnt-orange University of Texas sweatshirt. Which was not baggy enough to conceal her soft, round breasts. Mack shifted his gaze again, this time to her forehead.

"What do you want me to wear?" he asked.

"Oh, I don't know. Something a little more color-ful—velvet tights and a codpiece might be interesting," said Cecily with a saucy grin.

"Cecily Jeanne!" said Iris. "Stop that. You're embar-rassing the boy."

She sobered immediately. "Oh. Sorry, Mack. You can wear whatever makes you comfortable. But not the hat. I really don't like the hat."

"Yes, ma'am. I'll leave the hat here."

"Just hang it on the hall tree," said Iris. "You can take it back to the apartment when you come home. Will you two be home for lunch?"

"Yes," said Cecily. "At least I will. After cleaning out the dog cages, I'll need to shower and change before going anywhere else today. How about you?"

"I thought I might grab an early lunch with my brother," said Mack. "Didn't you say you'd be busy until around one o'clock?"

"Yes. What does your brother do?" asked Cecily.

"Joe's an FBI agent."

"Really? And he's engaged, you said. I guess that means he doesn't have commitment issues."

"He did. He got over them when he met Sarah."

"That's sweet," said Iris. "When's the wedding?"

"They haven't set a date yet." Joe still had time to come to his senses, although he didn't seem to be look-ing for an escape route.

Iris handed Mack a steaming mug of coffee. "Cream? Sugar?"

"No, thanks. Black is fine."

"What do you want for breakfast? Cecily is having French toast."

"Sounds good to me."

"We try to have things that Daddy can have, too. Iris makes his with Eggbeaters. He acts so sad when he can't eat what everyone else is eating."

"Is he on a diet?"

"Not to lose weight, although he could drop a pound or two. Heart-healthy is what he's supposed to eat. He had a heart attack few years back," said Iris.

"Right after my wedding," added Cecily, her expression grimmer than he'd seen before. "We have to watch him every minute, or he would be eating steak and eggs for breakfast."

"Smoking, too. He'll try to get you to smuggle him cigars, Mack. Whiskey, too. Don't do it. He can't smoke, and he can't drink. Except wine. He can have a glass of wine with dinner," said Iris.

"Wine is for sissies. Bourbon and branch water is a man's drink," said Cyrus, entering the kitchen.

"Good morning, Daddy. Bourbon isn't good for you."

"Maybe not, but at least I would die happy."

"We don't want you to die."

"Glad to hear it, Pumpkin." Cyrus kissed the top of Cecily's head as he passed her chair. "Morning, Iris. How's it going, Mack?"

"Fine.

Cyrus sat down and opened the newspaper. The paper lowered. "What's on the agenda for today?"

"It's my community service day, Daddy," said Cecily. "You ought to know that by now."

"Your community service ended weeks ago. You're still going to the animal shelter because you want to play with the animals. I'm surprised you haven't brought one home yet."

"One?" said Iris. "We're lucky she hasn't moved the whole kit and kaboodle here."

"I'm looking for the right one," said Cecily, gazing at Mack. "Actually, I think I've found him."

After breakfast, Mack escorted Cecily outside and opened the passenger door to the Camaro. Instead of getting in the car, Cecily turned to face him.

She ran her hand through his hair. "The hat messed it up," she explained. That didn't explain why she kept one hand on the side of his neck for longer than two seconds.

Sliding both hands from his shoulders to his chest, she murmured, "But the tie has to go."

Mack stood still—except for the occasional twitch—while Cecily untied his tie. When she started unbuttoning his shirt, he covered her hands with his. "What are you doing?"

"Undressing you. One button at a time. Only one this morning. More later." She gave his chest a pat, then slid into the car and buckled her seat belt. "Well? Aren't you going to close the door?"

Mack closed his mouth first. It had fallen open on the "more later" promise. He shut the door and walked stiffly around the car.

Once they were en route, he told her, "Do not touch me while I'm driving. I have a perfect driving record and I do not want to blow it."

"All right. I wouldn't want you to lose your license. Then Cyrus would have to fire you. Do you know where the Humane Society animal shelter is?"

"Yeah."

"Take your time with your brother—I'm usually finished by one o'clock, but there are always things that need doing. It won't matter if you're not back right at one."

"Yes, ma'am," said Mack, still thinking about Cecily's button-by-button remark. With an effort, he blocked that image from his overheated brain. "Will you be going out this afternoon?"

"I may do some more Christmas shopping."

"You do a lot of shopping."

"Is that a criticism?" she asked.

"No. An observation."

"It's not that I don't want to do something useful. But I'm not qualified for anything. Except cleaning up dog poop."

"Wouldn't your father give you a job? He owns his own business, doesn't he? Uncle Walt said Cyrus was a venture capitalist."

"Yes, but Culpepper Enterprises is really just Cyrus. He has clerks and research people and a secretary, but he's the one who does the real work of the company."

"What does a venture capitalist do, exactly?"

"He gives people money to start businesses, or to develop products. If they succeed, he gets a piece of the action. If they fail, he loses his investment in them. He doesn't fail very often."

"Would he give you money to start a business?"

"Only if I could think of something to do that would make money."

"You worked at that art gallery."

"Objet d'Art, yes. How did you know that? Oh, from the *Scoop*. They mentioned it because that's where I met Neville. He came in to buy a painting."

"So you do have a job skill—sales."

"Not really. I was more of a lure than a saleswoman. The owner hired me because he thought all my friends would patronize the gallery if I worked there."

"Was he right?"

"I guess." She sighed.

Mack almost halted the interrogation—his questions were making Cecily uncomfortable. Gritting his teeth, he made himself continue. "Why did you stop working there?"

"Because I thought I was going to have a full-time job as a wife and mother." Cecily turned her head to look out the passenger window. "That didn't work out."

"You wanted a family?"

"Of course. Don't you?"

"No. Not that I've got anything against families, you understand. But I like variety."

"Ah. All those women in your little black book—that kind of variety?"

"Exactly. Why are you still married?" Mack asked.

"Because." She turned her head and met his gaze in the rearview mirror. "I'm scared to get a divorce. I made a horrible mistake when I married Neville Barton—the same kind of mistake Cyrus made when he married Marjorie. The Culpeppers are not good at choosing spouses. I had this idea that staying married—even if it's only a paper marriage—would keep me from making another bad choice if nothing else, but—oh, here we are."

Mack brought the car to a stop.

"Don't bother getting out," said Cecily, opening her door. "I'll see you at one, or later."

"Wait." Mack got out of the car and followed her. "But what?"

"Huh?"

"You said staying married keeps you from making another mistake, *but*. But what?"

"Oh. But now I've changed my mind." She stood on tiptoe and kissed him on the cheek. "Thanks to you."

Mack watched her disappear into the building, rooted to the spot where she'd left him. What was it about her? Okay, so she was beautiful, if classic features, big blue eyes, and a body fit for a goddess defined beauty. Okay, so she loved her father, and she was kind to animals.

Okay, so she wasn't a dumb blonde, after all. That didn't mean he had to go weak in the knees—and the head— every time she kissed him.

Mack got in the car, took his cell phone out of his jacket pocket, and called the Houston FBI office. When his brother came on the line, he asked, "How about lunch?"

"It's a little early for lunch. What's up?"

"I need some brotherly advice," said Mack.

Eight

While Cecily wielded the pooper-scooper, she thought about Mack. After only one day, which had included one night's worth of hot dreams, she was positive he was exactly the right man for—what had Olivia called him? Oh, yes. Her transition man. She wrinkled her nose. *Transition* sounded so . . . cold and calculating.

But she was absolutely sure that Mack *was* the right man to take her from married to single again—if for no other reason than that she was in control. She stopped in mid-wield, furrowing her brow. Something about that didn't feel right, but what other reason could there be? It wasn't as if she'd fallen in love with him at first sight, after all.

She stared at Rex, the old English sheepdog whose cage she was cleaning. "I don't believe in love at first sight. Although, I did fall for you hard and fast."

Rex thumped his tail on the cement floor.

A dog was one thing. A man was something completely different. She could not have fallen in love with Mack yesterday—his dimple was potent, but not that potent. Love at first sight did not happen to Culpeppers—

she had only to look at Cyrus and Iris to know that kind of romantic fantasy was not in her genes.

Iris had worked for them for almost ten years before Cyrus had noticed what an attractive, sexy woman she was. It would probably take her father another ten years to realize he was in love with the cook.

"What's love got to do with it?" she asked Rex.

He cocked his head to one side and let his tongue loll out.

"Nothing, that's what," said Cecily, answering her own question. What she had in mind was much more elemental. Mack was a man. She was a woman—a sex-starved, horny woman. No sane man would turn down an offer from a lusty lady. She had something else going for her—she was safe. Mack couldn't think that a married woman would be much of a threat to his bachelor status. There was that bodyguard ethics thing, but she could talk him around that hurdle. She was the seducer, not him.

All in all, she was the perfect woman for a brief, no-strings affair.

"So why is he resisting me, Rex?"

Rex put his paws over his nose.

Grinning, Cecily dumped the last load into the plastic garbage bag. She coaxed Rex out of his kennel with a dog bone, then got the hose. As she sprayed the kennel floor, she tried to come up with a reason for Mack's attitude. He did not find her repulsive. When he had kissed her under the mistletoe last night, he'd been very aroused. He wanted her. She wanted him.

Maybe he didn't like aggressive women, but he had started the kissing business. And he was the one who had initiated the kiss last night, too—after she had maneuvered him under the mistletoe. Maybe Mack didn't like being manipulated.

Or maybe he felt sexually harassed.

Was she making him feel like a victim? She had threatened to tell Cyrus and his bosses that he'd blown his chauffeur cover his first day on the job. Of course, she would never do anything to get him fired.

But he didn't know that.

"Well. Darn. If I let him know I won't tattle on him, I'll lose control. If I don't, I may lose him. I'm between a rock and a hard place, Rex." She turned off the hose and put it up.

She gave Rex one last pat before putting him back in his clean kennel. "There is only one thing to do. I have to be selfish. Ruthless. I can't afford to worry about Mack's feelings. He is the first man I've wanted since Neville. I'm not letting guilt keep me from—"

Her cell phone chirped. It was Olivia. "Anything new?" she asked.

"Someone brought in five really cute puppies this morning," said Cecily.

"Not with the dogs. With Mack."

"We had a nice talk on the way here. He's really a nice guy, Olivia. I was feeling a little guilty about harassing him into an affair, but—"

"Cecily! Don't you dare—"

". . . I got over it. He is the first man in three years who I've wanted to get naked with. That must mean something."

"It means Mack Armstrong is going to be the happy recipient of thirty-six months of pent-up lust. Why would you feel guilty about that?"

"Well, when you put it that way . . ."

"Exactly. Now, I called because I got an invitation to the opening of that new supper club, Millennia. You must have gotten one, too."

"I don't know. The mail hadn't come when we left home this morning. A supper club? Isn't that kind of old-fashioned?"

"That's the point. Elegant dining, sophisticated entertainment, and dancing to a real band—just like the good old days. The private opening is this Friday; the club doesn't open to the public until Saturday. I'm going with Rory, my new guy. You could order Mack to take you."

"What a good idea! Especially the dancing part." Cecily shivered at the thought of being in Mack's arms.

"*Slow* dancing. Vertical foreplay, in other words," said Olivia.

"I'll ask him," said Cecily.

"What do you mean, ask? You *tell* Mack he has to be your date Friday night. Don't go soft and mushy now, Cecily."

"Right. Ruthless—that's me. Do you want a puppy?"

"No. Petruchio would go into a decline if I brought another dog home." Petruchio was Olivia's ten-year-old Irish setter. "Why don't you take one?"

"I had my heart set on Rex, but someone else is adopting him this week. Probably just as well—he's so big, and he's got all that hair. I'm pretty sure Iris wouldn't have been thrilled about him. Rex sheds. Anyway, right now I don't have time for a puppy or a dog." With a fugitive husband to catch and a bodyguard to seduce, her plate was full.

Cecily kissed Rex good-bye and moved to the next cage, humming to herself and day-dreaming about dancing with Mack. She couldn't wait to ask—order him to take her to the club opening. She stopped in mid-hum. She hadn't felt so confident in years. It had to be the control thing.

On the way to meet Joe, Mack could not make his brain get off thinking about what Cecily had said about her marriage. A horrible mistake, she'd called it. A paper marriage. And she had decided to do something about it. Something involving him, if her thank-you kiss meant what he thought it did.

Maybe he was overreacting. She could be planning something that had nothing to do with him. Yeah, right. Who had she talked about with Olivia? Him or Barton?

Okay. She'd talked about both of them. But he had to remember that she might have plans for her husband *and* for him. She had made it clear what she wanted from him. What could she want from Barton? To get a divorce, maybe. Or—and this was the possibility he needed to keep constantly in mind—she might be planning to join Barton and make their paper marriage the real thing.

Mack burped. The idea of Cecily with Neville Barton had given him a queasy stomach.

Nah. That wasn't what had done it. Whether Cecily and her husband got together for a wedding night would only matter if it meant he missed a chance to arrest Barton. Speculating about Cecily's sex life hadn't upset his stomach—anticipating her under-the-table games at breakfast had made him gulp down his French toast too fast.

Could Cecily be playing him? Maybe she had seen the H.P.D. logo on the blue folder. In that case, her sexy talk and her groping could be designed to distract him. She could be plotting to clean out her bank account and fly off to the Cayman Islands for all he knew.

He didn't believe that for a minute.

There was something too . . . *nice* about her. Even if she was taking advantage of him.

After killing a couple of hours talking to his mother and his uncle—he reminded Walt to spread the word to the other drivers that he was undercover—Mack drove to the restaurant. Joe was waiting for him. The waiter put a basket of chips and two bowls of salsa on the table, took their order, and left.

"What's up?" asked Joe, munching on a chip.

"I'm in trouble." Mack quickly summarized what had gone on between him and Cecily.

"What was in the folder?" asked Joe.

"Police reports on the Bartons, plus newspaper articles about them—mostly about her. The thing is, the folder had an H.P.D. logo on the front. If she'd seen that, my cover would have been completely blown."

"Yeah, you did screw up there. But you saved the day with quick thinking. Or quick smooching." Joe grinned and took another chip from the basket. "Tell me this, Mack. How is working for Cecily Barton going to help you catch her husband? Is he coming home?"

"Only if he's stupid. But Cyrus Culpepper put the screws to our esteemed DA, and I'm stuck with being a chauffeur for a couple of weeks. I called Mom this morning and told her to tell the rest of the family not to mention that I'm a cop if they see me around."

"Like the Armstrongs run in those circles—but it never hurts to be careful. Which brings up a question. Why weren't you careful with the folder?"

Mack winced. "Damned if I know."

"Hmmm. Maybe I should come to visit you at Chez Culpepper—I'd like to see how the other half lives. Hey, if you keep up the kisses, maybe Cecily will fall for you. You could marry her and never have to work again." Joe crunched another chip.

"I like working. And I'm nowhere near ready to get married. Even if I was—which I am not—Cecily is married, remember?"

"Right. She is. I wonder why. I would have thought she'd have divorced the crook by now."

"She hasn't."

"Too bad. She's a babe."

"She's a target. And I kissed her." Mack hung his head. "There are rules against getting too friendly with a target."

"You had a pretty good reason for kissing her. And switching your cover story from chauffeur to bodyguard was a good idea. That's a better story, considering you want to stay close to her. You might have bent the rule a little, but you didn't break it."

Mack raised his head and looked Joe in the eyes. "That's not the problem. The problem is, I want to break the rules. She wants me to break the rules."

"She doesn't know about the rules," said Joe.

"She knows I want her. She wants me back. I don't know why, but she does."

"How do you know she does? Just because she didn't slap your face doesn't mean she's ready to jump in the sack with you,"

"I know because she tells her friend everything." Mack looked around the restaurant, then lowered his voice. "Cecily Culpepper is planning to seduce me."

"Oh. I see." Joe's lips twitched.

"Are you laughing? Because if you're laughing, I'm going to have to hit you. Hard."

"I'm not laughing." Joe took a drink of water. "Any chance she's pulling your leg? Maybe she knows you're listening."

"Not a chance. Do you think I should ask Captain Morris to take me off the case? Before I get in any deeper?"

Joe choked, giving Mack an excuse to slap him on the back. Hard. When he'd recovered, Joe said, "You don't need to run and hide; nothing's happened yet. You can handle this. You've had women come after you before."

"Not women like her. She's different." Mack almost

told Joe about the way Cecily made him weak in the knees with a look—never mind what her kisses did to him. He stopped himself. He'd never hear the end of it if Joe found out Cecily could make him sweat.

"How is she different? It's not because she's rich, is it?"

"No. I don't care about her money. Or her daddy's money."

Joe shot a speculative look his way. "You could be falling in love."

This time Mack choked on a chip. "Love? Are you crazy? I met her on Monday. This is Tuesday." Mack glanced at the calendar on the wall to make sure. It did seem as though he'd known Cecily for longer than one day. It must be because he knew so much about her from the reports and newspaper stories.

"It can happen that fast," said Joe. "I took one look at Sarah and knew she was the one for me."

Mack gave Joe a pitying look. "I know. You poor sap. But Cecily is not the one for me—like you said, Armstrongs don't move in those circles. I don't want to marry her. I just want to . . ."

"I know what you want to do to her. Don't."

"That's it? That's your advice? Resist temptation?"

"That's it. Except I think you may be in denial about the love thing."

"You wish. Just because you went and got yourself engaged doesn't mean I'm ready to give up my freedom."

"You're looking to buy a house." Joe cocked his head to one side. "That could be construed as a sign you're looking for a wife. Just like the birds—first you build a nest; then you find a girlie bird to share it with."

"I am not a bird. I want a house. For me. Only me. Why does everyone jump to the wrong conclusion when a single guy goes house hunting? Why did you? You *know* me."

"Yeah, I do. And I know you fit the profile—thirty, bored with the dating scene. Plus, ever since you hired that real estate agent, you've spent your days off looking at houses. You haven't had a date in six weeks. From the way you've neglected your current crop of women, I deduce that the girlie bird you're looking for is not in your little black book."

"Jeez, Joe. Leave deduction to Sherlock Holmes. You're not even close. I'm house hunting for the tax break."

"Yeah. Right. Keep on telling yourself that—right up until you carry an armful of woman over the threshold of your new house. You may not know it yet, but your subconscious thinks you're ready to settle down. That's why you got a sudden urge to buy a house." Joe held up a hand, stopping Mack's protest. "And that's why you left that folder in plain view—so you would have an excuse to kiss Cecily Culpepper."

"You *are* nuts. Does the FBI know you're nuts? What kind of behavioral-science babble is that?"

"Everything happens for a reason," Joe said. "You left that folder out when you know very well how to secure sensitive material. You didn't have to kiss her to distract her. You could have told her to wait outside while you straightened up the apartment. She might have thought you were the kind of slob who leaves his dirty underwear on the coffee table, but she wouldn't have seen the file. You *wanted* to kiss her."

"Not that time."

Joe's brows shot up. "There's been another time?"

"Last night. Mistletoe. She had me hang mistletoe for her. When I climbed down the ladder, she was right there under it."

"So you kissed her again?"

"Yeah. Mistletoe. Tradition." Mack smiled weakly. "You know."

Joe just looked at him.

The waiter appeared with their enchiladas. "Enjoy," he said, and left.

Mack buttered a corn tortilla. "So, I should forget about the kiss—kisses. And not do it again."

"You didn't need me to tell you that."

"I guess not. I know better than to get involved with a target."

"Maybe you thought I would know of a loophole."

"Maybe I did. Isn't that what lawyers do? Even lawyers who are FBI agents?"

"Well, if I had to come up with one . . ." Joe paused while he ate a big bite of enchilada.

"What? Not that I'm looking for a loophole, you understand. But what?"

Joe swallowed. "The reason for the rule against hanky-panky between undercover agent and target is to keep a defendant from using it as a defense. Sleeping with a target could be a form of entrapment. So, the first question is, is Cecily really a target? Do you think she's going to be a defendant?"

"I don't know yet. She could be an accessory if she helps her husband avoid arrest—by giving him more money, for instance."

"Or by warning him that a police detective is waiting for him to show up."

Mack nodded. "That, too."

"So find out how she feels about her husband."

"I can do that."

"And if you find out she's completely innocent, what then? Will you let yourself be seduced?"

"No. I can't do that. The rule isn't the only problem. There is also the fact that I'm listening to her conversations. I know what she thinks about me, what she plans to do to me. That gives me the shakes. But it also gives me an unfair advantage."

Joe shook his head. "Mack, Mack, Mack. What I

wouldn't give to be in your shoes—if Sarah was in Cecily's place, I mean. You, a man, have the opportunity to find out exactly what a woman wants."

"I know what she wants. I can't give it to her." Mack looked at his watch. "I'd better be going. She'll be waiting for me. Thanks. For not much, but thanks."

"Anytime. I haven't had such a good time in weeks. Keep me posted. I want to live vicariously."

"Not a chance. From now on, I'm handling this assignment strictly by the book. That means no talking to people outside the department about it. And it also means not getting too close to Cecily."

"Not getting too close too soon you mean. Once she's in the clear, it could be clear sailing for you—I think she's the one."

"You're pitiful, you know that? I am not ready to follow in your footsteps, Joe. I am a bachelor, and I intend to stay that way for a long, long time. If I've been neglecting the women in my little black book, it's only because most of them have gotten to the state where they want some kind of commitment—like an engagement ring." Mack shuddered. "Why do women do that? Even women who swear all they want is a good time?"

"Maybe you'll find out—you and your wiretap. Personally, I think it's programmed into their psyches. Something to do with survival of the species. Men are programmed that way, too. You'll find out once you meet the right woman. Which I think you have. Cecily sure has you in a tizzy."

"I am not in a tizzy." He had told Joe too much—he should never have confessed that Cecily gave him the shakes. "I am concerned about my career. I'm up for promotion soon. I don't want to blow my chances by getting too friendly with a target."

Joe tossed his napkin onto the table. "Come on, Mack. She's not a target. No one can seriously think she's aiding and abetting Barton—her father wouldn't have gotten a cop to act as chauffeur if there was the slightest chance his little girl would be arrested. You don't think she's a target, do you?" He didn't give Mack time to answer. "You're hiding behind departmental rules because you're afraid you've met your match—the woman you want to spend the rest of your life with. You just aren't ready to admit it."

"You are wrong. I'm not hiding, and I'm not scared of her." At Joe's skeptical look, Mack insisted, "I'm not! If she's not a target, what is she?"

"A potential victim. Someone you're supposed to protect"—Joe snickered—"and serve."

Nine

Mack was waiting for her, leaning against the front fender of the Camaro, when she exited the animal shelter. He stood up straight when he saw her and grinned, flashing his dimple.

Cecily swallowed a sigh—that dimple was going to get her in trouble, she just knew it. Once she was in the car, she said, "Home, Mack. I'm starving. You must be hungry, too."

"Nope. I already ate," said Mack.

"Oh, right. You had lunch with your brother. How is he?"

"Joe's fine. Will you be needing me this afternoon?"

"I would like to go shopping this afternoon. We could get a start on your Christmas list."

"It's too soon."

"Twenty-two shopping days until Christmas—that is not too soon, Mack. Let's see." She began ticking off people on her fingers. "On your list we have your mother and father, your brother, and his fiancée—is that it?"

"Aunt Opal. I drew her name at Thanksgiving. That's

a family tradition. We draw names for Christmas at the family Thanksgiving get-together."

"Tell me about the Armstrongs' other Christmas traditions."

"Mom and Dad have an open house for the family on Christmas Eve. Everyone brings food, Mom makes dessert—something different every year—Dad makes his famous eggnog, and we all eat, drink, and sing Christmas carols. It can get pretty rowdy at times."

"That sounds nice," Cecily said wistfully. She'd always envied people with large, rambunctious families.

"What do you do?" asked Mack.

"Order pizza so Iris doesn't have to cook. Then we watch some version of *A Christmas Carol*. My favorite is the one with George C. Scott, and this is my year to choose."

"That sounds nice, too. Cozy."

"Well, it's pretty hard to get rowdy with only three people."

"Doesn't sound madcap."

"No, it doesn't, does it? Oh, we have another tradition—we open one present on Christmas Eve. The rest on Christmas morning. And Cyrus cooks breakfast—broiled trout, scrambled eggs, and cottage-fried potatoes."

"Every year?"

"Yes. I think those are the only three things he knows how to cook. Luckily, the doctor said he could have the eggs and the fried potatoes in moderation—once a year is not a problem."

"You worry about him a lot, don't you?"

"I guess I do. He is my only relative, you know."

"What about your mother? Iris said she was still living."

"She doesn't count. I haven't seen her in years, not since I was two. I don't know her."

"Have you ever thought about visiting her?"

"I used to. When I was sixteen, I ran away. I got as far as Rome."

"What happened in Rome?"

"Cyrus caught up with me."

"He didn't want you to see your mother?"

"He knew she wouldn't want to see me. He was right about that—I had called her before Cyrus got there. Marjorie told me not to come to Venice, because she was on her way to Paris. She didn't ask me to meet her there."

"Oh." Mack glanced at her in the rearview mirror.

When she saw the expression on his face, Cecily scowled at him. "You're not feeling sorry for me, are you? I hate it when people get that pity-the-poor-little-rich-girl look. I don't have a mother. No big deal. Lots of people don't have a mother. Most of them don't have a father as generous as Cyrus. And Iris is better than a mother. My family may be small, but it's choice."

"Family is important to you." Mack sounded surprised.

"Well, yeah. Isn't it to you?"

"Yes."

"Then you should spend a little more thought on what you give them for Christmas."

"You're right. I will. If you'll help me—that won't be too much trouble, will it?"

"Five gifts? Piece of cake. With Cyrus's business gifts and gifts for his employees, our friends, plus multiple gifts for Cyrus and Iris, I have at least fifty presents to buy—and I'm more than halfway done."

"Fifty? *Fifty?* That's . . . a lot of presents."

"Yes. Tell me about your family. I need to know something about them if I'm going to help you find exactly the right present."

"You don't have to do this, Cecily. I can take care of buying my own presents."

"Oh, really? What did you get your mother last year?"

"Uh . . . a Penn's gift certificate."

"Olivia will be happy to hear that. What did your mother use the certificate for?"

"She got herself a new vacuum cleaner."

Cecily groaned. "Oh, Mack. That's awful! You broke two rules of giving with one present."

"Rules? I didn't know there were rules. What rules?"

"Rule number one: no gift certificates. Rule number two: no appliances. A gift should be something someone wants . . ."

"Mom *wanted* a new vacuum cleaner," Mack protested.

". . . that they wouldn't buy for themselves. Tell me about your mother. What does she do?"

"She does what mothers do. Mom—her name is Betty, by the way—cooks and cleans and takes care of my father. She still takes care of Joe and me, too, whenever she gets a chance."

"What does she do for herself?"

Mack drew his brows together. "I don't know what you mean."

"Does she have a hobby? Play a sport? Visit with her friends?"

"She collects cookbooks. No sports, but she takes a walk every day. She says she needs to keep in shape. And she plays cards once a week with her girlfriends— the same night my dad plays poker with his friends."

"What about beauty? Does she go to the salon often?"

"I don't know. I think she has her hair cut every couple of months. Mom has nice hair—brown, thick. It always looks nice."

"Does she wear makeup?"

"I've seen her powder her nose and put on lipstick. She's a pretty woman—she doesn't need much makeup."

"Hmmm. I see. Okay, how about this? A visit to a

day spa, complete with facial, massage, hairstyling and makeup?"

"Wouldn't that involve a gift certificate?"

"Yes. But not a generic gift certificate."

"You said there was a rule against certificates."

Cecily scowled. "There is. This is an exception. Do you think Betty would like it?"

"Yeah. I do. How much would something like that cost?"

"Not more than two hundred dollars or so. How much do you have to spend?"

"I have a Christmas club account at my credit union— about a thousand."

"That will be more than enough. Now. Stocking stuffers. We'll get a couple of small things for stocking stuffers—you do hang up Christmas stockings, don't you?"

"Sure. Mom made them, years ago. Oh, I forgot. Mom sews. She knits, too. Joe and I usually get a new sweater or scarf every Christmas."

"That's good. We could get her something like yarn or material or a book of patterns. Or a cookbook. Which ones does she have?"

"I don't know. There are dozens of them. One has red and white checks."

"I don't suppose you know what knitting pattern books she has, either."

"No. Can't say that I do."

"Never mind. Let's stick with things she wouldn't buy for herself. What size is she?"

Mack slanted a glance her way. "About your size. Except she's a couple of inches shorter, and a little wider. Maybe."

Cecily rolled her eyes. "Forget about clothes. Maybe we'll get her a pretty scarf. How about jewelry? Does she buy jewelry for herself?"

"No, but Dad does. He usually gets her earrings for Christmas."

"Good for him. Does she wear perfume?"

"I guess so. She always smells good."

"You're not a lot of help. I would have thought you would be more observant. Isn't that something a bodyguard should be good at? Observing other people?"

"I'll observe her the next time I go home—which will have to be soon. I need to move the rest of my stuff out of my old apartment some time this week. I thought I'd leave the boxes in my old room at my parents' house."

"Why not move them to the garage apartment?"

"Because I won't be staying there, not after . . ."

"The holidays?" She'd been right. Cyrus had hired Mack for the Christmas season only. Once the holidays were over, Jenkins would probably reappear. Cecily felt a pain in her chest. Not heartache, not because an affair that hadn't started already had an ending in sight. She must be hungry.

"Right. Once the holidays are over, it will be back to the office for me."

Cecily got out of the car before Mack had the engine off. "Why don't you go move your stuff this afternoon? I changed my mind; I don't want to go shopping today." She had to rethink her plan—so far she'd only worried about the consequences for Mack. She hadn't given any thought to what might happen to her if Olivia was right. Maybe she wasn't as sophisticated as a madcap heiress ought to be. Maybe, even after Neville, she still believed that love had to enter into it. Whatever "it" was.

He got out of the car and walked with her to the kitchen door. "Look, Cecily, you don't have to help me shop."

"I want to help. I do. But tomorrow will be better for

that—we'll get an early start. I forgot that I've got presents to wrap, and I haven't finished with the decorations."

That much was true—she needed to hang up a lot more mistletoe.

"All right, then," said Mack. "I'll see you later."

Cecily walked into the house alone.

"Where's Mack?" asked Iris.

"He's gone to move the rest of his things from his old apartment."

"Without lunch?"

"He had an early lunch with his brother while I was at the Humane Society. I'm not very hungry, Iris. You don't have to fix anything for me, either."

"What's wrong?"

"Nothing."

"Cecily Jeanne, I know when something's bothering you. Now, what is it? Did Mack do something to upset you?"

"No. I managed to do that all by myself." Cecily sat down at the kitchen table. "Oh, Iris, I like Mack."

"I do, too. What's not to like?"

"No. I mean I really, really like him."

"It's about time you noticed another man. I was beginning to think that you were going to grieve over Neville forever."

"Grieve? I wouldn't call how I feel about Neville grief."

"What else would you call it? Because of him, you lost your innocence—and I don't mean your virginity. You lost your ability to trust yourself and others. Especially other men. That's why you've stayed married, isn't it?"

"You're so smart. I don't see why Cyrus doesn't—"

"Marry me? Neither do I. I've waited five years for him to pop the question. I may have to take things into my own hands and propose."

"Oh, Iris! Would you? That would be so . . . so right!" She threw her arms around Iris and gave her a big hug.

Iris smiled broadly. "I take it you wouldn't object."

"Object? I'll give away the bride. I'll dance at your wedding. I'll—"

"Stay at home by yourself while we go on a honeymoon?"

"Definitely. Will you really ask him?"

"I'm giving him one more chance. When he asks me what I want for Christmas, I'm telling him I want an engagement ring." Iris frowned. "Unless . . . I hope it doesn't shock him into another heart attack."

"It won't. I think Cyrus is tougher than we give him credit for."

"You're right about that. He hides his toughness around us—that man likes pampering as much as the next man. More. He may complain about us being the cholesterol cops, but trust me, Cyrus basks in our attention."

"Pampering. Is that the way to a man's heart?"

"Man or woman. Everyone likes being taken care of, don't you think?"

"Hmmm. That's something else to think about. I'm going upstairs."

"Not until you've eaten something."

"I've got peanut butter and jelly in my kitchen. I'll fix myself a sandwich after I shower and change."

After she'd washed the doggy smells off, Cecily sat at her dressing table blow-drying her hair.

This morning she'd been worried about Mack's skittishness. Now she was feeling spooked, too. Sex was scary, no doubt about it. Getting that close to Mack might satisfy an urge, but it would also leave her open and vulnerable to . . . what? Falling in love again? Hadn't she learned her lesson with Neville?

"Maybe not," she murmured to her reflection.

She turned off the hair dryer and laid it on the table.

Opening her jewel box, she rummaged around until she found the small velvet box. She opened it. The two rings winked at her—her diamond solitaire engagement ring and the diamond band she'd worn for only a week. She'd taken both rings off the day Neville had fled, leaving her behind.

That had hurt. Not just her pride. Her heart had ached—a real, physical ache in her chest. Another person who should have loved her had left her. Compounding the hurt had been the fear that she would lose Cyrus, too.

It had taken months for the pain to fade, then years before she'd begun to feel good about herself again.

Was she ready to risk getting hurt again?

Mack loaded up the boxes he'd left at his old apartment and drove to his parents' house.

"Mom? You here?"

"In the kitchen."

"What are you doing?"

"Making fruitcake."

"Why? No one likes fruitcake."

"*You* don't like fruitcake. Don't project your opinion on the whole world. You might like this fruitcake—it's made with dried fruits that I've been soaking in rum since Halloween. What are you doing here?"

"Aren't you glad to see me?" He picked her up and swung her around.

"Put me down, Mack."

Mack sniffed his mother's neck as he set her down. "You smell good. What perfume are you wearing?"

"*Eau de* cinnamon. I'm not wearing perfume. I never wear perfume."

"I didn't know that. How do you manage to smell so good all the time?"

"I use lavender soap."

"Lavender. Is that what that smell is? I never knew that."

"You didn't come by during your workday to smell my neck. Why are you here?"

"I came to drop off the stuff from my old apartment."

"You found a house? Where? How many bedrooms—"

"Hey! Don't get so excited. House hunting is on hold for the time being. I'm living over the garage at the Culpeppers'. Didn't Joe tell you?"

"He told me you were working undercover as Cecily Culpepper's chauffeur. He didn't say you had moved."

"The job comes with an apartment—a nice one."

"Imagine driving a madcap heiress around. What's she like?"

"Madcap heiress? I didn't know you read the *Scoop.*"

"I don't. Sometimes I might glance at a headline when I'm in line at the grocery store. Joe said you like her."

"Did he?"

"Do you?"

"She's okay. For a madcap heiress. She's married, you know."

"Oh, yes. The poor girl. Imagine having your husband arrested on your wedding day. Has she gotten over it?"

"I believe she has. She kissed me under the mistletoe." Mack winced. He shouldn't have told his mother that. And why had he put the blame on Cecily? He had kissed her.

"You kissed her?"

What was it with mothers? How did they do that?

"Yeah, Mom. I kissed her."

"Does she know you're a policeman? I thought you weren't supposed to do that. Your father always told me—"

"She thinks I'm a bodyguard. And she's not the target of the investigation. Her husband is."

"That makes a difference?"

"Yeah, I think so. Ask Dad."

"I will. I want to meet her."

"Why?"

"If she's going to be my daughter-in-law, I should meet her. Bring her to dinner on Sunday. Joe and Sarah will be here. We'll all pretend you're a chauffeur."

"Slow down, Mom. How did you get from a kiss under the mistletoe to marriage? That's a leap even for you."

"You're buying a house. You kissed her under the mistletoe. And Joe said you were smitten."

"Joe was teasing, Mom. I'm not smitten."

"If you can't come to Sunday dinner, invite her to the open house."

"We're not dating, Mom. I can't date Cecily Culpepper. I'm going to arrest her husband."

"You can kiss her, but you can't date her? I don't understand that."

"Neither do I."

"You're going to arrest that crook she married? I thought he ran off."

"He did."

"He's baaaaack?" His mother gave a credible imitation of Arnold Schwarzenegger.

"I can't talk about it." He should have used that line sooner.

"Pish-tosh. Of course you can talk about it. I'm your mother. You can tell me anything, anything at all."

"Not today, Mom. I've got to get back to work."

"What does someone rich and beautiful do all day?"

"She shops. Her best friend is Olivia Penn."

"Of the Penn department store Penns?"

"You got it." Mack kissed his mom on the cheek. "Bye, now."

"You'll be here Christmas Eve, won't you?"

"Only one thing could keep me away: Neville Barton. But I'm pretty sure he'll show up well before then."

"Oh, dear. You're not in any danger, are you?"

"No, Mom. Barton is a con man and a thief—no history of violence. He never hurt anyone."

"Except his bride. She must have been devastated. Is she over him? Oh, she must be if she's kissing you. Well, if you expect Barton soon, there's no reason you can't bring Cecily to the open house, is there?"

"Mom. Cecily Culpepper is not my girlfriend. She is my assignment. I am around her only because I'm a policeman with a job to do."

"That's what your father said when he gave me that speeding ticket for going thirty-two in a thirty-mile zone. But he asked for my license *and* my telephone number."

"Yeah, but . . ." He couldn't think of a but.

His mother drew her brows together. "Oh. I see what the problem is. You're going to arrest Cecily's husband. She might not like that. Why is she still married to him? Is she in love with her husband?"

"I don't think so. But I'm not sure."

"She kissed you."

"I kissed her first. There's a difference."

"Yes, there is. I'm not sure I want you getting involved with a married woman."

"So, the invitation to Sunday dinner is withdrawn?"

"No. I'd like to meet her. If I see her, I'll be able to tell how she feels about her husband. And you."

"How?"

"I will. Bring her on over."

"Maybe I will."

His mother patted him on the cheek. "Go on, now. Put up those boxes. I've got to get these fruitcakes in the oven."

Ten

Neville Barton paid the captain of the *Wanderer*, a charter boat out of Perdido Key, Florida, the agreed-upon fee and disembarked. He had no luggage except for a battered leather briefcase. Neville had dressed for his fishing trip in white duck pants, a blue-and-white striped knit shirt, and a navy windbreaker. After spending the night on the boat on the tedious trip from Grand Cayman Island to the shores of Alabama, he was a long way from his usual fastidious appearance.

Nevertheless, he looked the way he wanted to look—like a sport fisherman returning from a long day fishing in the Gulf of Mexico. His clothes might be wrinkled and dirty, but his money was crisp and clean. Neville used several of the bills, along with a fake driver's license in the name of Bill Smith, to rent a car, a nondescript sedan. Once he had transportation, he drove to a mall in Pensacola and purchased new clothes and a suitcase, then went to a drugstore for a toothbrush, a razor, and other supplies. He used the drugstore's pay phone to call a rental agency in Gulf Shores, Alabama.

"Hello, this is Michael Waters. I rented a condo at South Shore for the week, but I'll be late arriving."

Neville listened as the clerk explained that the office closed at seven o'clock, and that the keys to his condominium unit would be left in an after-hours pickup slot. He waited until eight o'clock, using the time to get a quick and anonymous meal at a fast-food drive-through. After he ate, he drove to the rental office and retrieved the keys to his condo.

Once there, Neville opened the briefcase and took out a driver's license and a bank book in the name of Michael Waters. He replaced the Bill Smith identification in the briefcase and closed and locked it. He took his other purchases out of their bags, hanging up the clothes and putting the toiletries in the bathroom.

Neville showered and washed the brown dye out of his hair, revealing his bleached blond crew cut. He removed the contacts that turned his green eyes brown, and reviewed the results in the bathroom mirror as he shaved off two days' stubble. Not bad. He might not be as handsome as he was with his natural coloring, but that was to his advantage.

He wanted to be nondescript. Forgettable.

Even if Cyrus Culpepper's hirelings found the *Wanderer* and its slightly shady captain, it wouldn't do them any good. If anyone showed the captain a photograph of Neville Barton, the skipper would not connect the man he knew as Bill Smith with the fugitive from Houston. He would describe his recent passenger as a brown-haired, brown-eyed man with a scar on his right cheek— the scar that was slowly disappearing as Neville shaved. When he'd finished, Bill Smith was no more.

No one at the rental office or the condominium would see Michael Waters. He would leave Gulf Shores before dawn. By the time they realized the unit was empty, he would be out of the country once again, with enough money to continue the lifestyle to which he had grown accustomed. Neville already had a purchaser lined up to buy the very valuable item he'd left with his darling wife.

Cecily. Strange that she was still his wife. When things had gone so horribly wrong on their wedding day, he had assumed that she would divorce him as soon as possible. Even if she had some romantic idea about joining him, Neville had thought surely Cyrus would insist on it. If Cecily had defied her father, she must really love him.

The fact that he was still her husband had made him speculate about taking advantage of the legal ties that bound them together. But it hadn't taken long for him to abandon any hope of cashing in on their marital status. It wouldn't do any good to have Cecily killed—he had no way of knowing if he was the beneficiary of her will. More to the point, Cecily wouldn't have any real money until Cyrus was history. Killing two people on the off chance that he might benefit was not worth the risk. He would be the prime suspect, after all.

After dressing in the silk pajamas he had purchased at the mall, Neville turned back the sheets—no more than 250 count, he sneered—and slid between them. Too bad Cecily hadn't jumped at the chance to meet him. But then, he hadn't really expected her to—that would have been almost too easy. His plan to reenter the United States had been in place before he'd telephoned her.

In hindsight, Neville wished he had kept in touch with his bride, at least enough to keep her charmed and in love with him. But he hadn't expected his millions to melt away so quickly. When he'd discovered that she hadn't divorced him, he'd thought he might have a chance of talking her into bringing him what he wanted—that awful painting he'd given her as a wedding present.

He hadn't worried overmuch that she would destroy the painting—Cecily would never destroy a work of art, no matter how dismal it was. It had occurred to him that she might give it away, and that had given him more than one sleepless night. That had led him to take the step of calling her. If she had given Alejandro's daubs to someone else, he would have had two choices: steal the painting from its new owner, or steal Cecily away from Cyrus.

Cyrus would pay any sum he asked to get his darling daughter back.

But that wouldn't be necessary—Cecily had said the painting was on the premises. "Not executed, sire, but banished," she'd said.

No longer hanging over the fireplace in her bedroom, then. But the painting was still in the house—probably in one of the seldom-used guest rooms. Cecily had said so, and Cecily, poor girl, didn't know how to tell anything but the most innocuous social lie.

In any event, Cecily had refused to meet him. And she hadn't been as overjoyed to hear from him as she might have been. But then, who could blame her? He had made no attempt to contact her for three years. Of course, she'd been surprised by his call. Shocked, even. And hurt.

She still loved him, though. Cecily was a true romantic—she believed in happy-ever-after. He'd figured that out right away, and he'd used the insight to make her fall in love with him. Flowers, poetry, soulful sighs, all the silly trappings of a pulp romance novel—he'd used them all in his courtship. Successfully.

Poor girl. Destined to pine away for him once she realized he'd only come back for the painting, not for her.

The first step toward his goal had been successfully completed. He was back in the USA.

He would make one more telephone call before getting closer to Houston—Cecily might still be persuaded to meet him and bring him the painting. Perhaps she longed for the wedding night she had missed—a loss he'd be happy to correct. But if not, he would accomplish his goal another way. Sooner or later, he always got what he wanted.

This time, once his Swiss bank account was healthy again, he would do a better job of holding on to his wealth. His first purchase would be a new face—his current disguises were good enough for a quick trip in and out of the country. His future plans would require a more permanent change in appearance. South America and the various island countries without extradition treaties with the United States bored him.

He needed more sophisticated surroundings. That left out Houston, of course. Neville smirked at the idea of any city in Texas being urbane enough for him. Not even New York or San Francisco, the only two American cities offering the kind of society worthy of him. London, Paris, or Rome was more his style.

Once he had money enough, and a new face, he would be able to go wherever he wanted, with no problem at all. But first things first. Neville smiled. "Houston, *you* have a problem."

Eleven

Three days on the job, and Mack felt as if he'd been riding endlessly on the Texas Cyclone—his young cousins' favorite Astroworld roller coaster. After driving him nuts on Monday and Tuesday, Cecily had stopped teasing and tormenting him on Wednesday, even though Wednesday was the day mistletoe had sprouted all over the house. She had even hung a sprig on the garage door opener. But she hadn't taken advantage of the greenery, and he had stood in harm's way a couple of times.

Strictly by accident, of course.

He had to conclude that Cecily had lost interest in him. Mack knew he ought to be relieved. Instead, he was pissed. What kind of woman drove a man wild with under-the-table touches and under-the-mistletoe kisses and then just stopped? Cold turkey. No tapering off, no explanation. No calls to Olivia. Mack had no idea what was going on under those silky blond curls.

He could ask her.

But she had pretty much stopped talking to him, too. Here it was Thursday, and she hadn't even shown up for breakfast. Iris had told him and Cyrus that Cecily had decided to eat her Wheaties in her third-floor mini-kitchen. Neither Iris nor Cyrus had seemed surprised by Cecily's absence.

If he hadn't been sure Barton was in the United States and on his way to Houston, Mack would have asked to be taken off the job. He should ask anyway, before he lost it completely and demanded that Cecily continue trying to get inside his Jockeys.

But he couldn't bring himself to leave her. The idea of some other man taking his place as her protector made him nuts. What if she transferred her seduction plan to his successor? Some other man might not be so scrupulous about resisting her. And he would have resisted her, if she had given him the chance.

Captain Morris had predicted the case would be over by Christmas. That seemed likely. If Barton actually made it to the United States, he wouldn't want to remain any longer than necessary to accomplish whatever he planned to do. But that presupposed that he would manage to return. He'd have to have a powerful incentive to risk it.

Cyrus was convinced that Barton intended to kidnap Cecily and hold her for ransom. Mack hadn't come up with a better reason for the man to risk arrest. In fact, the only other reason he could think of was that Barton had left something valuable behind, something that would replenish his depleted Swiss bank account.

But according to her father, the only items Barton had left with Cecily were her engagement and wedding rings, which she no longer wore, and the ugly painting hanging over the fireplace. The rings were worth a couple of hundred thousand—a lot to most people, but chump change to a man like Barton. The painting was worth much less—Cecily had said the artist's paintings never sold for more than two or three thousand dollars.

It was possible that Barton had left money or jewels or bearer bonds in a safety deposit box in Houston, and that his call to Cecily had been nothing more than a cruel joke. Possible, but unlikely. Barton's finances had been under close scrutiny for months before his arrest. Adkins and his team had known of Barton's wire transfers from Texas banks to accounts in Switzerland, the Isle of Man, and the Caymans before Barton's arrest.

If he had remained in custody, Barton would have been pressured to repatriate his accounts to the United States, where the funds would have been used to reimburse his victims. Restitution would have been a way— probably the only way—for Barton to negotiate a favorable plea bargain. As it was, he had no bargaining chip left—he had squandered his victims' money, and he had no known assets in the United States. If he got himself arrested again, he would be facing years in the state penitentiary.

Cyrus had to be right—Neville was coming after Cecily. Cecily, and Cyrus's hefty bank account.

Cyrus knew that Cecily was being coy about her plans should her husband show up, but he would not admit that there was a chance she would actually agree to meet Barton somewhere. Mack wasn't so sure. As much as he did not want to think that was a possibility, he had to face facts. Cecily didn't act like she was still in love with the bastard, but something was going on behind those big, blue eyes. She planned to do something this Christmas, something she didn't want Cyrus—or him—to know about.

What if Barton had called her on her cell phone? They could be planning a rendezvous right under his nose, and he would have no way of knowing. Mack growled in frustration.

The telephone rang, and he almost tripped over his own feet in his haste to answer it. "Cecily?"

"No," said Cyrus. "Cecily's father. Listen, Mack. When I got to the office this morning, I had a message from International Operatives. The man watching Neville reported in this morning. Bad news. He lost him."

"What? How did that happen?"

"After leaving Panama, Neville went to the Cayman Islands—George Town on Grand Cayman, to be exact. Yesterday he chartered a fishing boat for a day trip. When the boat returned, Neville wasn't on it."

"Did your private detective talk to the boat captain?"

"Yeah. He said another boat met them and took Neville on board."

"Did the International Ops guy have any idea where Neville is headed?" asked Mack.

"I didn't ask—I know the answer. Neville is on his way to Houston. He's coming after Cecily, just as I predicted. I'm glad you're in place, Mack. You wouldn't be here if Neville hadn't been careless enough to make that phone call to Cecily. The son of a bitch came up with a pretty clever way to get into the country—come in on a charter somewhere he wouldn't be noticed."

"The Florida Keys, maybe," said Mack. "Or Grand Isle. Some place without a huge Border Patrol or Customs presence."

"I told International Ops to canvass charter boat companies from here to Florida. And to put pressure on that boat captain from George Town. He knows more than he's told them so far—like the name of the boat that met them."

"Good. Barton must have some funds left. Chartering boats and paying the captains to keep their mouths shut can't come cheap."

"Best we can figure, he's down to his last million—practically a pauper." Cyrus's laugh was harsh. "I'm sure that's what Neville thinks."

"I've been meaning to ask you something. Is there

any possibility that Barton has another reason for returning to Houston? Could he be coming back for a stash of money he left here?"

"Where? I thought the police searched his apartment and office after he skipped town."

"Barton might have a safety deposit box, or he might have left something with Cecily. Something besides her rings and that ugly painting." Mack stared at the offensive work of art as he waited for Cyrus's answer.

"I don't think he did. Why don't you ask her?"

"Why don't you?" Cyrus and Cecily's communication problem was beginning to irritate him.

"She's more likely to talk to you about Neville—she refuses to discuss him with me." Cyrus sounded more rueful than indignant.

"Why is that?"

"She thinks it upsets me—she's afraid I'll have another heart attack if she mentions his name in my presence. I won't. But try to convince her of that."

"I think we should tell her that Barton may be on his way here, especially now that he's not under surveillance."

"Not yet. If we do that, we'll have to explain how we know. I don't want to spoil her Christmas. She hasn't had a good Christmas in three years. You'll just have to stay close to her."

Cyrus would have some other explaining to do, too. He obviously didn't want to admit he'd been spying on his daughter for years—that might ruin his Christmas, and a few other holidays, too. Like Father's Day, for instance. Mack kept that opinion to himself. "Yeah. Close."

As soon as he ended the call from Cyrus, Mack dialed the number of the Burglary and Theft Command office and asked to speak to Captain Morris. After passing on the information about Barton's mysterious disappearance somewhere between the Carribean and the Gulf of Mexico, Mack asked, "Adkins doesn't know of any valuable asset that Barton might have left behind, does he?"

"No. Barton dealt in cash. He didn't own any real estate or other hard assets that Adkins and his team ever found. He leased everything—his office, his car, his condo."

"That's what I thought. Well, then, it looks like Cyrus was right—Neville must be coming after Cecily."

"Yeah. Do you know yet if she's going to join him willingly? Or are we looking at a potential kidnapping?"

"I'm almost one hundred percent sure it's the latter."

"You'd better stick close to her, then. I'll get an APB out on Barton. If he's in the country, he's probably headed this way."

Mack hung up the telephone. Both his bosses—the permanent one and the temporary—had ordered him to stay close to Cecily. He could do it. He could stay close—not too close, but close enough to protect her from Barton.

Assuming she wanted to be protected. Exactly how Cecily felt about her fugitive husband was something he needed to find out, and soon. Neville could have contacted her again, on her cell phone. Maybe that was why she'd forgotten her seduction plan—she had arranged to meet her husband. That would also explain why she had avoided him and Cyrus at breakfast.

He ought to go drag her out of her aerie and shake some sense into her. Neville Barton was a con man, a crook, and a womanizer. Barton was not the right man for Cecily.

He was.

Mack's mouth dropped open. Where had that come from? He was *not* the right man for Cecily. Not short-term or long-term. He wasn't the right man for any woman. Not now. A few years down the road, maybe. But this was not the time. He had things to do, people to meet, places to go before he could begin to think about looking for that special woman.

Groaning, Mack shifted his train of thought to a different track. He needed to focus on the reason he'd been assigned to the Barton case. Concentrating on keeping Cecily safe might keep him from daydreaming about resisting Cecily's seduction attempts.

Yeah. Right. He shouldn't lie, even to himself. Resisting was not a big part of his daydreams. Succumbing to Cecily's charms was the preferred plot in his private fantasyland.

Even after discussing his problem with Joe, even after giving his boss an expurgated version of his screw-up, Mack still felt guilty. He was an officer of the law, assigned to protect Cecily Culpepper. He should not be obsessing about making love with her.

Never mind that it had been her idea.

That was not an acceptable excuse for unprofessional behavior. Even if he was 99 percent certain that the only feelings Cecily had for Neville Barton were disgust and anger, he could not ignore that 1 percent of uncertainty. He had to face the fact that he might have to arrest her. If she aided Barton in any way, she would be an accomplice to 347 counts of theft.

The buzzer sounded, indicating an incoming call on Cecily's private line. Mack put on the headphones.

"Cecily? What's going on?" It was Olivia's voice.

"Nothing," Cecily sighed.

"Nothing? You're not getting cold feet, are you? I thought you had decided to be ruthless."

"Yesterday I decided to ruthlessly back off."

"That sounds like you're going in the wrong direction."

"Things were moving too fast."

So that was why things had come to a screeching halt. After making him hot all over, Cecily had gotten cold feet.

"Too fast for Mack? Or for you?"

"Him. Me. Both of us." Another sigh.

"You're scared, aren't you? Scared you'll be hurt again."

"Well . . . yes. Once burned . . ."

"Mack is not Neville."

Mack swallowed a snort.

"I know. Mack is a good man, a man I can trust. Not at all like Neville."

Cecily *trusted* him—that made him squirm.

"Right. So what's the problem?"

"Oh, Olly, don't you see? He could hurt me a lot worse than Neville."

"How?"

"Lots of ways."

"Name one."

"What if I fell in love with him and he didn't love me back?" She said the words very fast.

Mack's mouth dropped open. Love? She was thinking about him and love at the same time? He hadn't gotten past thinking about her and sex simultaneously.

"Cecily, you've got to get over this obsession with love and marriage. Mack is your transition man, remember? A fun fuck—that's all he'll be. Trust me. You're not going to fall in love with him."

"Are you sure?"

"Positive. Mack is cute and sexy and available. But he's *so* not second-husband material—not for you, anyway. What do you have in common with a bodyguard?"

Silence. Mack willed Cecily to say something.

"Uh . . ."

That was all she said. *Uh.* Like they had absolutely

nothing in common. For some reason, that pissed him off. He could point out several—

"Not anything, Cecily," said Olivia, interrupting his thoughts. "So stop being Miss Doom-and-gloom. Take a page from your madcap-heiress book and do something wild and crazy just for you."

"I don't want a second husband."

Cecily sounded like someone who wanted to be positive but couldn't quite manage it.

"I knew that. Have you figured out what it is you do want?" asked Olivia. "Besides Mack, that is."

"No. I don't know what I want. Including Mack. Not that he isn't wantable—he is. But I'm still not sure I should take advantage of him." She paused. "It must be that time of year—it is the season when people leave."

There was another pause; then Olivia said, "Marjorie left Cyrus in December, didn't she? I'd forgotten about that. Then there was the fiasco with Neville. But I thought this Christmas was going to be different. Oh, Lord. Did Neville call again? Is that what's got you feeling blue?"

"No. He didn't call. But he will. He said he would. I wish he would hurry up and get it over with. Maybe that's why I'm in a bad mood—waiting for his call has me a little crazy."

"You're not still thinking about trying to catch him, are you?"

What was that? Cecily was going to try to catch Barton? Mack pressed the earphones tight against his ears.

"Well . . ."

"Cecily, don't. The man is dangerous."

"Yes, but now I've got Mack to help me. He knows karate. And I think he may have a gun."

"Does Mack know what you're planning?"

"No. I'll tell him when he needs to know—which

won't be until I know where Neville is. If I tell Mack now, he'll tell Cyrus."

"No, he won't. Not if you threaten to tell Cyrus you know he's not a chauffeur—he'll lose his job."

"I wouldn't do that really."

"He doesn't know that."

"Yes, but I think he'd tell Cyrus anyway. Mack has a thing about duty, and he thinks it's his duty to keep me out of trouble."

"Neville could be trouble, all right. What about Friday? Have you told Mack he's escorting you to the Millennia opening?"

"No. He's not going to like it."

"He will, too. What's not to like? You, good food, good music, good company—that would be me. Tell him."

"I will . . . I guess."

"What *is* wrong with you, Cecily? You're not sick, are you? If Neville hasn't called, has something else happened to upset you?"

"No. I'm not sick. Nothing has happened to upset me. I'm just . . . brooding."

"About Mack?"

"About Mack and the holidays and Cyrus and Iris and my whole life. I still feel useless."

Olivia made a protesting kind of noise.

"Maybe 'useless' is the wrong word. I feel . . . uncertain." Cecily sighed—a mournful sound that squeezed Mack's heart. "I wish I could decide what I want to be when I grow up."

"How about starting with becoming a divorced woman? I found out who handled Bunny Kravitz's divorce—Ann Roberts. As long as you're half-ass married, you're in a weird kind of limbo. Once you're single again, you'll have all sorts of opportunities—and I'm not just talking about men. You've spent the last

three years being Neville Barton's abandoned wife. Get
over it."

Cecily laughed. "You really know how to puncture a
person's self-pity balloon."

"Well." Olivia sounded embarrassed. "That might
have been a little harsh, even for me. But, Cecily, you
got over Marjorie. Having your mother leave you had to
be a lot worse than being left by that criminal you mar-
ied."

"You're right. I have spent too much time lately feeling sorry for myself—over Neville. What was I thinking?
Neville Barton does not have the right to make me feel
bad about myself. I shouldn't give him that kind of
power over me."

"No, you shouldn't. Why don't you pay Mack a visit?"

"Good idea. Chasing him around the apartment will
cheer me up. If I'm lucky, maybe he'll let me catch
him."

"What makes you think he'll run away? He did kiss
you under the mistletoe, didn't he?"

"Yes, he did. And there's a lot more mistletoe around
here."

"Then go take advantage of it . . . and Mack. Love in
the afternoon is always good for a pick-me-up."

"I thought love didn't enter into it."

"Right. No fancy frills, no romantic furbelows, just
good and dirty, sweaty sex. And don't tell me I'm ob-
sessed with sex."

"Okay," Cecily chuckled. "But you are."

"It's a very healthy obsession. I recommend it highly.
Trust; you're sure to like it—especially with a man like
Mack. Remember that dimple."

"If he dimples at me, I won't be responsible for what
happens next."

"Then make the man grin. I want you to feel better."

"I feel better already. Before I go to see Mack, I'm

going to call Ann Roberts and make an appointment. It's time I got over being married. Thanks, Olivia."

"What are best friends for? I'll talk to you later."

Mack took off the headphones and replaced them in the cabinet. As usual after listening to one of her calls, his hands were shaking. This time his knees felt wobbly, and his thighs were quivering, too. As if he had just gotten off a roller-coaster ride.

Cecily was getting a divorce—that was a high point. Then the swoop to the bottom—he wasn't in the running for second-husband honors. Why the hell not?

He wasn't buying the nothing-in-common excuse. They had a lot in common—they both wanted to catch Neville Barton. Catch Barton? Good God. Cecily had some idiotic plan to trap Neville. What was wrong with her? Was she nuts? She was a civilian, untrained and unarmed.

She was counting on him to help her.

With more than capturing her husband. Cecily wanted him for hot and sweaty sex. The bottom fell out of his stomach, worse than the final loop on the Texas Cyclone.

It was his fault. He had tempted the gods by wishing for another chance to resist her.

Cecily had sounded so sad at first. She'd blamed it on the time of year. Some people did get depressed around the holidays, or so he'd heard. If anyone had a right to feel sorry for herself in December, Cecily did. She'd lost her mother and her husband at Christmastime.

And she was expecting him to make her feel better. With sex.

He couldn't do that. Daydreams were one thing, but there was no way he could make those dreams reality, not without betraying his principles and losing all respect for himself.

On the other hand . . . What would rejection do to her?

Mack snorted. Great. He would make love with Cecily solely in the interest of cheering her up? How damn noble of him.

He looked around the apartment. He had to do something to ensure that he wouldn't do anything he'd regret later. Hearing Cecily say she was on her way to see him had him more than half aroused.

His gaze landed on the telephone. Quickly Mack dialed Joe's office number. When he got him on the line, he said, "I need you to call me in fifteen minutes. No—make that half an hour. If a woman answers, tell her you're my boss at International Ops. Say you have to see me right away."

"What's going on?"

"She's coming after me. I need an escape route." Joe laughed. "Are you sure?"

"Positive. I heard her say so—she wants me for a fun fuck."

"You poor guy." Joe did not sound at all sympathetic. "Imagine having no-strings sex with a gorgeous woman—every red-blooded bachelor's dream."

"Not this bachelor's. You will call, won't you?" Mack could imagine Joe leaving him to his fate. "Swear."

"I swear. I will call you at . . . one-fifteen. But a lot can happen in thirty minutes. Is she there yet?"

"No. She's calling a divorce lawyer to make an appointment before she comes after me."

"She's getting a divorce? Interesting. She stayed with her fugitive husband for three years after any sensible woman would have ended the marriage, but three days after she meets an Armstrong male, she decides to become a free woman."

"Yeah. I'm irresistible. It's the dimple."

"Is that what does it? I always wondered. I'm better looking. Taller. More experienced. But I don't have a dimple."

"Call me. Don't forget."

"I won't forget. But I might be a few minutes late. I'm expecting a call from an informant—that will take precedence. Talk to you later." Joe hung up before Mack could get him to swear again.

Mack was pretty sure his brother had been snickering as he hung up the telephone.

Once Cecily had made an appointment with the divorce attorney, she felt much better. She was in control. No longer waiting around for something to happen, she had taken action. She felt all-powerful, like an Amazon warrior.

And this Amazon had another conquest to make. Today. Right now. As soon as she changed clothes and freshened her makeup—spruced up her armor and shined up her weapons, so to speak.

When she knocked on Mack's door, he opened it immediately, as if he'd been standing and waiting for her on the other side. He opened it only a fraction, enough so that she could see one of his eyes. The eye was glaring at her.

That couldn't be right. She hadn't done anything to him since Tuesday. She gave the door a little push. "Hello, Mack. May I come in?"

"Why?" His voice sounded strange—strangled.

"I want to . . . to talk to you."

"About?"

"Are you going to let me in or not?" Cecily gave the door another, harder push. Mack opened the door a little wider. "Please? Let me in?"

"Oh, all right." He stood aside and let her enter.

She walked to the sofa and flopped down. "What's wrong with you?"

"Not one damn thing. I'm perfect."

"Gee, Mack. Maybe you should work on your self-esteem. If you're perfect, why are you grouchy?"

He rubbed his forehead. "Headache. I've got a headache."

"Oh, I'm sorry. Have you taken anything for it?"

"Excedrin. It hasn't kicked in yet."

Cecily patted the sofa next to her. "Come here and I'll massage your temples."

Mack stayed by the door. "Do you need me to drive you someplace?"

"Not this minute. We could go shopping together. Later. Right now I want you to . . . talk to me."

"I thought you were finished Christmas shopping."

"I'm not. I haven't gotten anything for Olivia yet, and I need a few more stocking stuffers for Cyrus and Iris. Then there are your gifts. Have you even started on your list yet?"

"Christmas is weeks away. It's too soon."

Cecily rolled her eyes. "For gift certificates, maybe. But not for real gifts. We'll start finding the perfect gifts for your family, too." She patted the sofa cushion again. "Come here, Mack."

"Now that you mention it, shopping is a good idea. Fresh air would probably help with the headache. Let's go." Mack walked to the coat closet next to the door and took out a jacket.

Cecily got up and followed him to the closet. "Mack, I think you're forgetting something."

"What? It's not cold enough for gloves and a scarf, is it?"

She puffed out a breath, making the curls on her forehead bounce. "It isn't cold at all. Put your jacket back in the closet."

"Or what? You'll tell your daddy that you know I'm not a chauffeur?" His lip curled in a sneer. "Maybe I don't care. Maybe I don't like being ordered around by you. Maybe . . . I don't like you, period. Did you ever think of that?" He turned his back to her and hung the jacket up.

"Yes, yes, I did." Cecily slid her arms around his waist and rested her cheek between his shoulder blades. She could feel his muscles tense. "You may not like me ordering you around. But you like me. You kissed me under the mistletoe."

Mack shrugged. "That was a mistake. I'm here for one purpose, and one purpose only: to keep you from doing something wild and crazy this Christmas. That includes keeping you from starting an affair with a stranger."

"What stranger?" She let go of Mack.

"Me." He turned around and faced her.

"You're not a stranger. And who said anything about an affair?"

"An affair is what all the mistletoe is leading up to, isn't it? And I am a stranger. We met three—four days ago. You don't know anything about me."

"I do, too. I know you take your job seriously. I know how you feel about your family. I know you have a fear of commitment—oh! Is that what this is about? You're afraid I'll expect more than mistletoe kisses from you? Well, you're wrong. The last thing I want is another committed relationship. I'm still not out of the first one, remember."

"That's another thing—I have a rule against getting involved with married women."

"Good for you. But I just made an appointment with a divorce lawyer. And I'm not married, not in any real sense of the institution."

"You're legally married."

"Legally. But not emotionally. I got over Neville years ago."

"Then why do you do something stupid every Christmas?"

She raised her brow. Mack's bad temper had her rethinking what she'd come for—this might not be the best time to launch her seduction ship. "I don't know. The things I did seemed like good ideas at the time."

"And this year you've decided ordering me to take you to bed is a good idea?"

"There you are, bringing up sex again." Cecily frowned. It was almost as if he knew what she'd come for. "I came to talk. That's all."

"Yeah? What did you want to talk to me about?"

"Tomorrow night. A new club is having a private opening. It's called Millennia. Have you heard of it?"

"No. Do you need me to drive you there?"

"More than drive—I want you to take me there. Millennia is an old-fashioned supper club. Dinner, soft music, dancing—that sort of thing. I need an escort." She took a breath. "Will you be my escort tomorrow night?"

"Do I have a choice?"

"No." Cecily took his face in her hands. "Where does it hurt?"

Mack gave her a blank look. "What?"

"Your head. Where does it hurt?"

"It doesn't."

"I thought you had a headache." She touched his forehead.

"Oh, right. It's gone. The Excedrin must have taken effect."

"Good. Then you can kiss me."

"I'm not going to kiss you. It's unprofessional."

"All right. I'll kiss you. I don't have a profession. No profession, no professional ethics. There are advantages to being unemployed." She smiled at him.

He smiled back.

"Ooooh. That dimple gets me hot."

Mack immediately sobered. "What time is it?"

"Who cares?" Cecily touched her lips to his. With her mouth clinging to his, she wrapped her arms around his neck. She backed up, pulling him toward the couch. When she felt the sofa hit the back of her knees, she let herself fall.

Mack fell on top of her, just as she'd planned. "Ooof," she said.

"Sorry," said Mack, straddling her. He wasn't trying to get off her, though. He was nuzzling her neck. She nuzzled back.

"Touch me, Mack," she said, arching her back.

"Where?" he asked, moving his left hand to her breast.

"There. But wait." She arched her back and pulled her sweater up to her collarbone. She hadn't bothered with a bra. "Now. Touch me again." She lay back on the sofa cushions and closed her eyes.

She heard Mack groan and felt his palms on her bare breasts.

The telephone rang.

"Don't answer it," Cecily ordered, her mouth on his.

"Have to—might be my boss. Or my mother. They're the only ones who have this number." Mack reached over her head and grabbed the telephone as if it were a lifeline.

Cecily sat up, straightened her clothes, and walked to the door. "I've got your number, too, Mack Armstrong. You're afraid of me."

Mack answered the phone.

"Need help?" asked Joe.

"Oh, yeah. I do." To Cecily he said, "I need to take this call, Cecily. In private."

She stuck out her tongue. "Scaredy-cat." She grinned at him and waved good-bye.

Mack breathed a sigh of relief. "Thanks, Joe. I owe you one."

"I'll collect, don't worry. Any word on Barton?"

"Yeah. They found the boat that brought him in—a fishing charter out of Perdido Key, Florida. But no trace of him after that."

"He is heading your way, though."

"Yeah. Cyrus was right. He's coming after Cecily."

Twelve

Mack skipped breakfast with the Culpeppers Friday morning. After his narrow escape Thursday, he wasn't risking another encounter with Cecily so soon. He needed time to build up his defenses. At ten o'clock, he checked with Iris, who told him that Cyrus had taken Cecily to the Galleria.

"She said she'd be home for lunch, so she'll be calling you to pick her up in an hour or so. Where were you this morning? Don't you like my cooking?"

"I love your cooking, but my mother called. She needed me to run a couple of errands for her. I had breakfast with her."

"Well, for that, you're excused. I'll see you at lunch."

While he waited for Cecily's summons, Mack called Cyrus at his office. "Did you tell Cecily that Barton is probably on his way to Houston?"

"No. She would have wanted to know how I found out. It's one thing for her to think I hired you to keep her out of trouble. And a whole other thing if she finds out I've been spying on her and Neville for three years—I'm not opening that can of worms."

"What about having the police call and tell Cecily that Barton has been spotted en route to Houston? That would put her on guard without implicating you."

"Good idea. All right. Make sure it's your boss who calls, though. Him or the chief. I don't want to take any chances on someone else exposing you as a cop. Cecily would know for sure that I had something to do with getting you set up as her driver."

"I'll get Captain Morris to call Cecily right away."

"Fine. Iris tells me you and Cecily aren't joining us for dinner tonight."

"Yeah. She's meeting Olivia at some new restaurant—Millennia, I think it's called. She asked me to be her escort, so I'll be with her."

"Good. Keep a close eye on her. This is the first time she's gone out at night in several weeks."

"Yes, sir," said Mack. He consoled himself with the thought that with International Ops and the state and local police forces on the lookout for Barton, it was only a matter of time before he was captured.

Cecily called him around two. When he met her, she was carrying two shopping bags. "More Christmas presents?"

"No. I wanted a new dress for our date this evening. Then I had to buy new shoes and lingerie to go with the dress."

"Lingerie?" Mack blinked to clear his vision. His eyes had glazed over at the thought of Cecily's underwear.

"Yes. I had to—the dress is too low-cut for a regular bra, so I got these . . . well, you'll see. Later." She winked at him.

"I am not going to see your underwear. Not tonight. Not ever."

"It's so cute the way you play hard-to-get. Did you know that you dimple when you sulk? I think I mentioned what that dimple does to me."

"I am not sulking. I am telling you how the cow ate the cabbage. We are not going to be lovers, Cecily. Get that out of your head."

"How the cow ate the cabbage? What a quaint turn of phrase. And there you go again, talking about sex. I don't know why you think I'm trying to get inside your pants."

"I'll tell you why—every time I turn around you're kissing me. Or talking about kissing me."

"Kissing isn't sex."

"Kissing leads to sex."

"Really? Like marijuana leads to cocaine leads to heroin?"

"Yeah. Exactly like that."

"I never knew that. What are you going to wear this evening? Do you need a new suit?"

"No."

"Well, I bought you new underwear, too. Just in case." She took a small paper bag out of one of the shopping bags.

"I don't need new underwear."

"Men always need new underwear."

At a stoplight, Mack opened the bag. "All I see is tissue paper. No way do I need any kind of underwear that gets wrapped in tissue paper." He closed the bag and handed it back to Cecily.

"Golly gee, but you're a grump. Someone brings you a perfectly innocent gift, and you won't even open it. And another thing—you don't seem the least bit excited about our date. If you don't watch out, you're going to hurt my feelings."

Mack didn't bother arguing about whether their . . . appointment later that night qualified as a date. He pulled into the Culpeppers' driveway, parked, and got out of the car. So he could stay out of reach, he retrieved the shopping bags from the backseat, letting Cecily get out of the front seat all by herself. She had the paper bag, which she handed to him again. "You forgot this," she said.

"Thanks," he mumbled, taking the bag. "What time will you be needing me tonight?"

"All night long." She sang the words, wiggling her eyebrows suggestively.

"Cecily!"

"Oh. You meant for our date. Eight. You won't be driving, by the way. Olivia and her date will pick us up— Olly is renting a limousine. I told her to use Luxurious Limos." She took the shopping bags from him, stood on tiptoe, and kissed him on the cheek. "See you later. I can't wait until eight o'clock."

Mack retreated upstairs. He called his Uncle Walt and told him to make sure the driver that evening would not expose him as a cop.

There was a knock on Mack's door at seven-fifteen, just as he was about to get into the shower. He pulled on his jeans and opened the door. It was Cecily, of course. Her new dress was black and slinky, but not low-cut—she must have said that just to get his hormones hopping. Her hair was piled on top of her head, held there with something sparkly. A few strands curled on her cheeks and nape.

"What?" asked Mack. "I thought we weren't leaving until eight. You're early."

"I wanted to see what you were wearing. Jeans won't do." She eyed his bare chest. "Although I like the topless bit."

"I was shaving. I intend to wear a shirt. And a suit."

"Good." She scooted past him into the bedroom. The paper bag she'd given him was on the bed, unopened. "You haven't opened your present." Cecily looked genuinely disappointed. "Don't you like presents?"

"Yeah. I like presents."

"Well, then, open it.

Mack opened the bag and dumped the contents on the bed. "Good . . . Lord." Leopard-skin briefs—extremely brief briefs—fell out of the tissue paper. He recoiled in shock.

"You don't like them."

"It's not that. I'm a boxer man."

"You are not." She opened the dresser drawer and pulled out a pair of Jockeys. "I checked before I went shopping."

"You went through my underwear drawer?"

"I did. Your closet, too. I had to—to get your sizes."

"Cecily, that's an invasion of privacy."

She looked stricken. For about a millisecond. Then her eyes narrowed. "Yes, well, so are all those *Snoop* stories you collected about me. Turnabout is fair play. Plus, my motives were noble—I had to know your sizes for Christmas shopping purposes. *Your* purposes were . . . nefarious."

"Protecting you is not nefarious."

"Being sneaky about it is. Tell the truth, Mack. If I hadn't seen those clippings, you would have let me go on thinking you were a chauffeur, wouldn't you?"

Mack cleared his throat. "You'd better leave now. If you want me to get ready for . . ."

". . . our date?" she finished.

"We're not dating."

"Pretend, Mack." She opened the closet and found his suit. "Is this what you were planning on wearing? It will do. Do you want me to help you change?"

"Good God, no."

"You're right. We'd probably get distracted somewhere between what you've got on and what you're going to wear to the Millennia. We might end up having our date right here."

"We'll get there," said Mack. "But it's not a date."

"Yes. It is. You're my escort on a Friday evening—
Friday *is* one of the two premier date nights, you know.
We're both dressing up. We're going to a party where
there will be music and dancing and food and drink.
This is a date."

"We're not dating," Mack repeated. If he said it often
enough, she might believe it. *He* might believe it.

"Tonight we are. Olivia is bringing her current
boyfriend, and I'm bringing you. It's a *double* date."

"I want to register a protest," said Mack. "This is not
in my job description."

"Of course it is. Cyrus always includes 'other duties as
assigned' in any job description he prepares. This is one
of those other duties."

"Fine. Then it's a job duty, not a date. Leave and let
me change."

"It is a date," she muttered. "I'm not leaving. I want
to watch you change."

"Voyeur."

"Prude."

"Cecily, go away. I'll be with you in ten minutes."

"Spoilsport."

"Tyrant."

She grinned at him and left the bedroom.

Mack unclenched his fists and took his hands out of
his pockets. He had stashed his hands so he couldn't
use them to grab Cecily, toss her on the bed, and . . .

She had wanted to watch him undress.

He should have let her. Maybe a strip would have
scared her off. He had to do something to cool her down.

Cool her down? He was the one sweating.

The bedroom door was open. He could see Cecily
wandering around the living room. Mack closed the
bedroom door.

Cecily opened it. "Don't close the door. We can talk
while you dress."

"You'll peek."

"I won't. I promise." She turned her back to the open door. Her dress didn't have a back.

"I'm going to take a shower." Cold. But she didn't have to know that.

"Okay. I don't suppose you need any help? Washing your back? Or your front?"

"Cecily, stop." Mack grabbed his underwear and socks from the open dresser drawer and took them with him into the bathroom. He locked the door.

When he'd showered and partially dressed—he should have brought the suit in with him, too—he cautiously opened the bathroom door and stuck his head out. She wasn't in sight. He walked into the bedroom. "Cecily?"

No answer.

He finished dressing, then checked the whole apartment. She wasn't there.

Mack called the main house. Iris answered. "Is Cecily there?" he asked.

"Yes. She forgot her coat and came back to get it. She's in the living room, waiting for you. Olivia and her date aren't here yet."

"Tell her I'll be there in a minute, will you?"

When he got to the kitchen, Iris opened the door and let him enter. "My, you look very nice, Mack. I'm glad you asked Cecily out on a date."

"It wasn't my idea," Mack muttered.

"Why not? It's a good one. Cecily needs to regain her confidence where men are concerned."

"She has plenty of confidence," said Mack. "I wish she'd use it on someone else."

Iris bristled. "You don't like her?"

"Oh, I like her. But it's not in the cards." Mack wasn't sure what "it" was, but Iris seemed to understand what he meant.

"Because she's married? Don't let that stop you. That

marriage is a farce, and I happen to know Cecily has an appointment with a divorce lawyer on Monday. About time, in my opinion."

"Yeah. She told me about that."

"Did she? That's interesting. She likes you, too, Mack. This is her first date in three years."

"This is not a date."

"Then what is it?"

"A duty. She ordered me to act as her escort."

Cecily appeared in the doorway carrying a coat over her arm. "Is he here—oh, hi, Mack. The limousine is here."

The hussy had the nerve to look shy.

"Did you take care of that stack of mail that came this afternoon?" asked Iris.

Cecily winced. She'd forgotten all about the mail. "Oh. No. Sorry. It looked like mostly Christmas cards and catalogs, though. I'll do it tomorrow, I promise."

She hadn't done much all day except whip herself into a froth thinking about the evening. And now it was finally here. Mack in a gray suit, white shirt, and red-and-blue striped tie looked . . . good enough to eat. Cecily felt a crowd of butterflies hatch in her stomach. He also looked as though he would rather be anyplace in the world except standing in her kitchen.

Maybe she'd gone too far.

Cecily let Mack help her into her coat. He took her by the elbow—gingerly, as if he were afraid she might bite—and walked her down the hall to the foyer, where a limo driver waited.

When they were seated in the limousine, Olivia's escort stuck out his hand. "Evenin' folks. I'm Rory Austin. You must be Cecily," he said.

"That's right."

"Mack Armstrong." He took Rory's outstretched hand and shook it.

"Olivia was telling me about this place we're going to tonight. Sounds interesting."

"Millennia is supposed to be an old-fashioned supper club. Food, entertainment, and dancing," said Cecily. She turned to face Mack. "You do dance, don't you?"

"I can do the Texas two-step."

"That will do."

The limousine deposited them in front of the club. Mack put his hand on Cecily's back and steered her toward the line of people waiting to be admitted. "Have you got the invitation?" he asked.

"Yes, right here." Cecily took the invitation out of her coat pocket and handed it to him.

Olivia gave hers to Rory. "This is the place to be tonight. Look at the crowd."

"Who didn't they invite?" asked Cecily.

"Most of Houston," muttered Mack. "I don't see any of my friends."

"I don't, either," said Rory. "But I will. Most of the team got invitations."

"Rory is a football player for the Texans. Tight end," said Olivia. "Very tight."

Cecily giggled nervously. She should never have told Mack this was a date. She wasn't ready to date. She might never be ready to date. She wanted to go home. "Mack—"

"Wow! Look at this place," said Rory.

The Millennia had formerly been a movie theater—the ornate kind designed to resemble a sultan's palace—before being put out of business by the multiscreen, stadium-seating sort.

The large, plushly carpeted lobby had been completely remodeled. There was a coat-check room on one side of the lobby, and a bar on the other side. In the middle of the lobby, where the concession stand had been, there was a large three-tiered fountain.

"A fountain," moaned Cecily. "Why did there have to be a fountain?"

"What's wrong with fountains?" asked Rory. "I think it's kind of pretty."

"Cecily tends to end up in fountains," explained Olivia. "It's expected of her."

"That's not true. I only ever ended up in one fountain. And that wasn't my fault."

"It wasn't?" asked Mack, remembering the photograph.

"No. Jade Jones pushed me in—and made sure her photographer caught me dripping wet."

"You were laughing," said Mack.

"You remember the photo?" Olivia asked. "That had to be ten years ago."

"Eleven," corrected Cecily. "But Mack saw it again very recently. He has a scrapbook about me."

"How . . . obsessive," said Olivia, raising a brow.

"Hey—I like that. You can start a scrapbook about me," said Rory. "I've got lots of clippings—I'll make copies for you."

"Thank you, Rory. I needed a hobby." Behind his back, Olivia rolled her eyes. "We'd better check our coats."

Mack helped Cecily out of her coat, exposing her bare back. "Are you sure you don't want to keep this on? You're going to get cold."

"No, I won't. You'll keep me warm."

After the women's coats were checked, the foursome showed their invitations and passed through double doors into the club proper. The Millennia did not resemble a sultan's palace any longer. The new owners had decorated the club in art nouveau—black and white and silver. Three levels of horseshoe-shaped booths upholstered in white leather were arranged in a semicircle around a large dance floor, opposite a bandstand. At the moment, the only music came from a sound system.

Mack allowed Cecily to slide into the booth next to Olivia.

"Oh, look. The *Snoop* is here," said Olivia.

"What? Where?" Cecily scanned the tables.

"Over there," said Olivia, pointing to the far end of the tables. "Jade Jones and a photographer are cruising the tables, interviewing people and taking pictures. The restaurant critic from the *Chronicle* is supposed to be here, too."

"Darn," hissed Cecily.

"Don't you like the press, Miss Cecily?" asked Rory.

"Not particularly. Especially not the *Snoop*."

Rory's brow wrinkled. "*Snoop?* Would that be the *Houston Scoop?*"

"Yeah," said Mack. "The grocery store tabloid. Cecily, I need to talk to you." He jerked his head in the direction of the *Scoop* reporter. "About that."

"I don't read it—they don't have a sports page," said Rory.

"Mack," said Cecily, "maybe we should leave."

"Leave?" said Olivia. "Why? We just got here."

"The *Snoop,*" said Cecily. "I should know better than to go out in public at this time of year."

"Are you ready to leave?" asked Mack.

Cecily nodded. "I've had a bad feeling about this place ever since I saw that fountain."

"How will you get home?" asked Rory. "The limo's not coming back until one o'clock."

Mack got up. "There's a cabstand across the street."

"There's a taxi stand across the street? I didn't see it," said Cecily, putting her hand in Mack's.

He helped her from the booth. "I'm a trained observer, remember?"

"Uh-oh," said Olivia. "Look who's here—and look who he's talking to."

"Oh, no. It's Lance." He was talking to Jade Jones, and they were both looking at her. "I really don't want to see him. He still hasn't forgiven me for last year. He had his license yanked, too."

Mack led Cecily through the crowded tables into the foyer. Some of the crowd milled around the fountain bar, but it wasn't as crowded as the club room.

"Wait here," said Mack, parking Cecily by a column. "I'll get your coat."

Mack had moved a few steps away when an arm grasped her around the waist. A husky male voice said, "C. J., darlin'. I thought that was you. You're not leaving so early, are you?"

Cecily twisted her head around to see whose mouth was next to her ear. "Hello, Lance. How are you?"

"Still grounded. You can't leave yet, honey. The party hasn't gotten started. How about a dance?"

"No, thank you. We're on our way out of here."

"We? You're here with someone?"

"Yes, yes, I am. He's getting my coat. Nice to see you again." Cecily tried to move past Lance.

He tugged her away from the pillar. "We never did get together again after our little race. You owe me, honey."

"I don't owe you anything. Let me go, Lance."

"Aw, Cecily, be a sport. My pit crew is here. They've been wanting to meet the girl who got my license yanked."

"That wasn't my fault."

"No? Whose idea was it to race on a public highway?" He tightened his grip on her arm.

"Mine. But you didn't have to agree. Lance, let me go. I don't want to dance." Their struggle was beginning to attract attention. Cecily tried once more to pull away from Lance. She was seriously thinking about kneeing him in the groin when Mack appeared.

"Take your hand off her, Ebersol," said Mack.

"Do I know you?"

"No."

"I didn't think so. Back off. C. J. and I are old friends."

"Tonight she's with me. And we're leaving."

"Not yet. It's payback time."

Lance swung Cecily into his arms and headed for the fountain. He'd taken two steps when Mack got him in a choke hold. "Let her down, slowly."

Lance dropped her, then grabbed Mack's forearm with both hands.

"Fight!" someone in the crowd yelled.

"What's going on?" asked Mack, keeping his hold on Lance.

"Mack, you can let him go. Lance just wanted to buy me a drink."

"Do you want a drink?"

"No, I don't."

"All right, pal." Mack let Ebersol go. "Tell Cecily good night."

"Not yet." Lance grabbed her arm again and started pulling her toward the fountain. "You can have her back in a minute."

Mack grabbed her other arm and tugged.

"Hey!" said Cecily. "Let me go! Both of you. You're making me feel like a wishbone."

Mack dropped her arm. Lance didn't. Tossing her coat to her, Mack used both hands to grab Lance's lapels. "Let Cecily go, Ebersol. Now."

"Who the hell are you, telling me what to do? I want Cecily to see the fountain. Up close." He giggled like a girl.

Cecily spotted Jade and a photographer standing next to the fountain. "Oh, no. Not again." She dug in her heels and jerked her arm free. "I'm not going to land in another fountain. Jade put you up to this, didn't she?"

"I don't know what you're talking about." Lance grabbed her again.

Mack clipped him on the chin. Lance went down with a crash. "Come on, Cecily. Let's get out of here."

Lance was on his feet, blocking their way. He took a swing at Mack, catching him on the shoulder. Mack shoved Cecily behind him.

"Fight!" someone in the crowd yelled.

A woman pulled Cecily's hair. "Get that thug off of Lance."

"He is not a thug," said Cecily, pushing the woman. She careened into another woman, who took exception and shoved her. Cecily stumbled and fell to her knees, losing one of her shoes in the process.

People began converging on the spot where Mack and Lance were wrestling with each other. Cecily looked for her missing shoe—she spotted it and began crawling toward it.

As she reached for it, someone stepped on her hand. Cecily screamed. The man whose foot had landed on her hand jumped back, bumping into another man.

The second man whirled him around and swung at him.

After that, fighting erupted all around her. Cecily managed to get to her feet. Now she'd lost both her shoes. She looked around for Mack.

He was standing over Lance.

Cecily wiggled her way through the chaos to his side. "I think we should leave now."

"Yeah," said Mack. "I agree."

He took her by the hand and began pulling her toward the exit. Once they were outside, he started across the street.

"Wait," said Cecily. "My shoes. What about my coat?"

"Buy a new one," said Mack. He looked at her bare feet and picked her up, carrying her across the street and stuffing her into a taxi. He gave the driver the address, then leaned back.

"Ohmigod," said Cecily. "You're bleeding."

Mack pulled a handkerchief out of his pocket and pressed it to his eyebrow. "No big deal."

"It *is* a big deal. Driver, take us to the nearest emergency room."

"Driver, take us home," Mack countered. "I don't need a doctor. It's just a scratch." He leaned his head back and closed his eyes.

"I feel awful. This is all my fault."

One eye slitted open. "How do you figure that? It looked to me like Ebersol started it."

"Yes. But he started it because he's still mad at me. He lost his license, too."

"He doesn't need a license to drive on a racecourse. As a pro, he should have known better than to dragrace on a highway. He was going to throw you in the fountain, wasn't he?"

"That was the plan. I'm pretty sure Jade Jones put him up to it—she and a photographer were lurking by the fountain."

"Photographer? Did he take any pictures?"

"I think so—I saw flashes. Maybe he didn't get a good one."

"I hope not. The last thing I need is for the *Snoop* to run a picture of me in the middle of a barroom brawl—I'll lose my job."

"I'm sorry. I never should have forced you to—"

"This is the place," Mack told the taxi driver. "Pay the man, Cecily."

Cecily opened her purse and pulled out a bill. "Keep the change," she said. By the time she got out of the taxi, Mack had disappeared.

She entered the garage and climbed the stairs to Mack's apartment. She knocked on the door. "Mack, let me in. I think you should go to the emergency room."

No answer. She knocked again, harder. "Mack!"

The door opened. "What?" Mack had a wet towel pressed against his eye.

"I think we should go to the emergency room," Cecily repeated. "You might need stitches."

"I don't need stitches."

"Let me get you an ice bag."

"I can take care of myself, Cecily. Go away and leave me alone."

"You're mad at me, aren't you?" Her chin trembled.

Mack sighed. "No, I'm not mad at you. I'm mad at myself. I should know better than to get in a fight."

"You did it for me."

"Yeah, well, I could have gotten us out of there without slugging Lance."

"Why did you hit him, then?"

"Damned if I know."

"You weren't jealous, by any chance?" Cecily felt her heartbeat speed up.

Mack just looked at her with his one good eye. "Good night, Cecily. I'll see you in the morning." He closed the door in her face.

Thirteen

Saturday morning, Cecily dressed in record time and used the elevator to get downstairs. She wanted to see Mack as soon as possible. She needed to be sure he was all right.

When she walked into the kitchen, Cyrus handed her a newspaper. "You're in the *Scoop*," said Cyrus, handing her the paper. "On the front page."

Cecily took the newspaper. The photo showed Lance tugging her by the arm, while Mack, his back to the camera, pulled her in his direction. The headline screamed, *Cecily Causes Commotion at Club.*

"It wasn't my fault," said Cecily. "What is it with the *Snoop* and alliteration? What would they do if my name was Rosemary?"

"*Rosemary Wrecks Restaurant?*" Iris suggested, making Cyrus chuckle.

Cecily wrinkled her nose. "Where did this paper come from, anyway? I didn't know we subscribed to the *Snoop*."

"It was on the doorstep this morning—a complimentary copy, no doubt." Cyrus picked up the *Chronicle.*

"Eeeuw. That means someone from the *Snoop* was snooping around here this morning." Cecily shuddered. "That's an invasion of privacy."

Iris looked over her shoulder at the photograph. "I never liked that Lance fellow. Is that Mack holding on to your other arm? Those shoulders look familiar."

"Yes, and he got hurt saving me from Lance. Lance was going to push me into the fountain."

"There was a fountain?" asked Cyrus, peering over the top edge of the *Chronicle*.

"Uh-huh. In the lobby, where the concession stand was. The Millennia used to be the Majestic Theater. Jade Jones was there, with a photographer. She put Lance up to tossing me in the fountain—Mack stopped him."

"We may have to get a restraining order against that woman," said Cyrus.

"That won't be easy," said Iris. "Freedom of the press and all that. Mack got hurt? How?"

"He was bleeding. Here." Cecily pointed to her eyebrow. "But he wouldn't go to the emergency room, and he wouldn't let me take care of him."

"Sounds like someone else we know and love," said Iris. "Why is it that men can be such babies when they're hurt sometimes, and other times they don't want anyone to touch them?"

"I don't know," said Cecily. "But last night Mack was definitely in the don't-touch-me mode." She sighed.

"The skin around the eyes is thin," said Cyrus. "Boxers quite often get cuts around the eyes." He glared at Iris. "And I have never acted like a baby."

"Oh, no? What about the time—"

Mack entered the kitchen, stopping Iris's tirade. His left eye was swollen almost shut. "Good morning."

"Oh, Mack," said Cecily, half rising out of her chair. "Your eye looks awful."

"Interesting shade of purple," said Cyrus. "Thanks for taking care of Cecily last night."

"You should have put beefsteak on it," said Iris.

"Where would the boy have found a steak in this house?" asked Cyrus. "He'd have had to settle for a chicken breast or a fish fillet."

"Does it hurt?" asked Cecily, wincing.

"No. Just my pride." He squinted at the newspaper on the table. "Is that us on the front page of the *Scoop*?"

"Yes. But they didn't get a picture of your face."

"The story refers to you as Cecily's mystery man," said Cyrus.

"Good. I wouldn't like my family to see me on the front page of the newspaper."

"How about bacon and eggs?" asked Iris. "After such a rough night, you need protein."

"He gets bacon and eggs?" asked Cyrus. "I didn't know we had bacon. I want bacon."

"You can have turkey bacon," Iris said. "But Mack gets the real thing. He's a hero. A wounded hero. He needs to keep up his strength."

"Humph. Some hero. Looks to me like he got clobbered by that race car driver."

"Lance just got in a lucky punch," said Cecily. "He ended up flat on his back. Do you want an ice pack?"

"Too late for that," said Iris. "Why didn't you bring him here last night?"

"I tried," said Cecily. "He wouldn't come with me. Wanted to go to his cave and sulk in private. Mr. Armstrong can be quite stubborn at times."

"Hey, I wasn't sulking. I just didn't want anyone fussing over me. My eye looks a lot worse than it feels."

"What do you have planned for today, Cecily?" asked Cyrus.

"We were going Christmas shopping—Mack hasn't

even started on his list. But I don't think he should drive. Not with only one eye."

"I can drive. I can see fine, out of both eyes."

"No, you rest," said Iris. "Cyrus can take Cecily anywhere she needs to go today. I've got a few more presents to buy, myself."

"Rest? All day long?" Mack looked horrified.

"I'm going to the office," said Cyrus. "I don't have time to be carting Cecily around."

"The office? It's Saturday, remember?" Iris glared at Cyrus.

"I know what day it is. I have work to do. And so does Mack. He can see well enough to drive, can't you?"

Mack nodded. "Sure. No problem."

Obviously, Cyrus intended for Mack to guard her body no matter what kind of shape he was in. Cecily said, "Rest, Mack. I don't need to go anywhere today. We'll hit the mall tomorrow afternoon. Or Monday." She got up. "I'm going to wrap packages."

"I'm going to make fudge," said Iris. "And divinity."

"Oh, yum," said Cecily. "In that case, I'll stay here and help you. I can always wrap packages later."

"Fudge?" said Mack. "With pecans?"

"Of course. Do you like fudge?"

"Yeah. I do. Maybe I'll hang around here for a while, too. If I won't be in the way."

"She'll put you to work," said Cyrus. "Woman has no heart."

"Daddy, Iris has a big heart. She must, if she's put up with you all these years."

"What's that supposed to mean?" asked Cyrus.

Cecily gave her father a wide-eyed look. "Why, only that she's worked for you longer than anyone else."

"Humph," said Cyrus. His cheeks turned a soft shade of pink.

Mack looked from Cyrus to Iris to Cecily. "Oh."

Cecily grinned at him. "I really do love Christmas."

After a day spent on candy-making and Mack-pampering, Cecily retired to her rooms. She had just gotten out of the shower when her telephone rang. She grabbed her terry cloth robe and rushed to the telephone next to her bed. She lifted the receiver. "Mack?"

"Darling. Who is Mack? Your 'mystery man'?"

"Oh, it's you. Hello, Neville." Cecily narrowed her eyes. Neville had read the *Snoop*. How else would he have known about her mystery man? That had to mean he was close by—the *Houston Scoop* only had a local circulation. "How are you?" she asked, making her tone as civil as she could.

"I didn't wake you, did I? I called earlier this time. Who is Mack?"

"No, you didn't wake me. I wasn't asleep. Mack is my chauffeur. What do you want?" She winced. Her impatience had seeped into her voice that time.

"You have a chauffeur? That's a new addition. When did you acquire that symbol of wealth?"

"I've had a chauffeur for over a year—ever since my license was suspended. Neville—"

"And he calls you at this time of night? It's almost ten o'clock, isn't it?"

"It is. You must be in the right time zone this time. What do you want? I was taking a bath and I'm dripping all over the floor."

"Sorry. I know you have every right to be angry with me." Neville was using his contrite voice again.

"Well, yeah. I do." Cecily heard a sound, a familiar sound in the background. She pressed the receiver closer to her ear.

"I am so sorry I hurt you. But you must see that it was unavoidable. I had to leave you."

"I'm not angry. I stopped being angry a long time

ago." About the same time she'd stopped thinking she was in love with him, and that had been shortly after he'd fled. She identified the sound: waves hitting the shore.

Neville sighed. "Thank God. You're too good, Cecily. Thank you for forgiving me."

Forgive? How had he gotten the idea that she had forgiven him? Not bothering to correct his assumption, Cecily asked, "Why did you call?"

"I want to see you. Soon."

Definitely surf, thought Cecily, straining to hear any other background noise that might help her figure out where Neville was calling from. "I'm very busy, Neville. The holiday season, you know? Dinner parties, charity balls. My schedule is full. And I can't leave Cyrus. He needs me." Thanks to you, she added silently.

"I need you, too, sweetheart. A quick trip, a long weekend. That will do for now. We need to discuss our future together."

The thought of a future with Neville had her gagging. Almost. She swallowed and asked, "A trip to where, Neville? Where are you?"

There was a pause. She heard that familiar sound again, and the surf noise grew fainter.

"Tell me you'll come, and I'll get word to you about the destination."

He really expected her to drop everything and run straight into his arms. How arrogant of him. That was a good thing, though. He wouldn't suspect she was setting a trap for him. "Neville, you're so impetuous. But, darling, I can't give you a date right this minute. I have to check my calendar, and it's downstairs in Cyrus's study. But I do need to see you . . . for closure, if nothing else." He wouldn't believe her if she told him she wanted anything more. "Give me your number, and I'll get back to you."

"Check your calendar, then, but make it soon. Have to go now. I'll call again in a day or two."

A dial tone told Cecily that Neville had hung up. She replaced the receiver and did a little dance around the room.

She didn't have to wait for another call. She knew where he was.

Cecily dressed quickly in black slacks and a black sweater. After slipping her feet into a pair of black flats, she walked down the stairs, tiptoeing as she passed the second floor. She turned off the security alarm and went outside by the front door. The kitchen door was too close to Iris's bedroom, and Iris had ears like a bat.

Circling the house to the garage, she didn't open the garage doors—too noisy—but walked to the rear of the garage and up the outside staircase to the door that opened into the apartment kitchen. She knocked on the door.

It opened. "What are you doing here?" asked Mack. He looked her up and down. "And why are you dressed like a cat burglar?"

She slipped by him into the kitchen. "Your eye looks better—not so swollen." Cecily stared at his bare chest. "And I really do like the topless look."

Mack braced himself for a pass. "I was getting ready for bed."

She didn't touch him. Instead she peered at his eye. "Can you see all right?"

"I can see fine." What was she up to? She seemed tense, on edge. Excited. But she wasn't throwing herself at him. Except for that one lascivious look, she hadn't come on to him. Neville's call had to be what had stirred her up.

"Good. Get your shirt on. I want to go for a drive."

Mack squinted at the kitchen clock. "It's after ten."

She couldn't be meeting Neville. He'd heard the entire conversation, and Neville hadn't told her where he was.

"Ten o'clock's not late—it's two whole hours before anyone turns into a pumpkin. I need to go somewhere. Now. If you won't take me, I'll drive myself."

"Without a license? I don't think so. Where do you want to go?" Maybe she and Neville had some kind of code.

"I'll tell you when we're on our way. Hurry up, will you?"

"All right. Give me a minute to get dressed."

She stayed in the living room while he put on a sweatshirt and running shoes. Something must be wrong—she'd been using every opportunity all day long to touch him. Now she paced.

Once they were in the car, Cecily said, "Go to I-forty-five South."

"The interstate? Why? Where are we going?"

"Galveston."

"Galveston? Why would you want to go there?"

She waited a few seconds before answering him. "Mack, I'm going to tell you something, but you have to swear you won't tell Cyrus. It would only upset him, and when he gets upset his blood pressure shoots up. He could have another heart attack or a stroke."

"I swear. Tell me."

"Neville called tonight—that's the second call I've had from him in less than a week."

Mack swallowed a grin and faked surprise. "Your husband called you? What did he want?"

"He asked me to meet him."

"Where is he?" Cecily had confided in him. She trusted him. Mack couldn't hold back a satisfied grin any longer.

"Galveston. What are you grinning about?"

Mack didn't answer that question. "He told you where he was?"

"No. I figured it out for myself from the background noises. I heard surf first—he must have been standing on the deck. Then a sliding glass door opened and closed, and the noise of the waves muted."

"That's it? Cecily, there are a lot of beaches in the world. They have beaches in Brazil—isn't that where he's supposed to be?"

"You don't understand. The sound of the door opening and closing was familiar—the door had a hitch in it, a little bump. Just like the door to our beach house. Iris keeps telling Cyrus to get it fixed, but—"

"What beach house?" Mack asked.

"The Culpepper beach house on Galveston Island. I told you that's where we're going."

"You told me we were going to Galveston. You didn't say anything about a beach house." Mack slowed the car. "Look for a pay phone. We need to call the police," said Mack.

"No. We're not calling anyone, especially not the police. Not until I know for sure that Neville is where I think he is. The sound was very faint. I could be mistaken. And if I'm wrong, can you imagine what the police and the *Houston Scoop* would have to say about me?"

"I still think we should call the police." Mack gritted his teeth. Why hadn't he brought his cell phone along?

Cecily crossed her arms over her chest and stuck out her chin. "No. Absolutely not. We are not calling the police. I'll tell Cyrus and your boss that I know who you are, if you even try. Now, stop poking along. Step on it."

"All right," Mack capitulated. She probably *was* wrong. He'd heard the door open and close, too, but he hadn't heard anything out of the ordinary. A sticking door wasn't all that unusual. "But when we get there, I'm going in first. And alone. You'll wait in the car."

"I will not. Neville is my problem."

"Keeping you safe is my job. If I have to handcuff you to the steering wheel to do it, I will."

"You have handcuffs?"

"No. I was speaking figuratively." He should have had handcuffs, and a gun, and a cell phone. All tools of his trade, and he'd left them behind like the rankest rookie cop. Of course, he hadn't known they were going Barton hunting. But he should have guessed. "If Barton is at the beach house, how would he have gotten in?"

"Keys. Neville has a set of keys. When we were engaged, we met at the beach house a few times."

She had made love with Barton at the beach house. Mack gripped the steering wheel tighter, blinking rapidly to erase that image from his brain. "Is there a security system?"

"Yes, but he knows the codes."

"You didn't change them?"

"No. Once he left the country, there didn't seem to be any reason to do that. Cyrus has a hard time remembering the codes we've got now, and they're based on his birthday."

"Are there any guns at the beach house?"

"No."

"How about spear guns?"

"No. No one spearfishes. The water is too murky. There are knives—kitchen knives, fish-cleaning knives, that sort of thing. Do you have a weapon?"

"No."

"What kind of bodyguard are you? No gun?"

"Guns are dangerous."

"You don't know karate, either, do you?" She sounded disgusted.

"What makes you think that?"

"You didn't use it on Lance. Maybe you were right, Mack. Maybe we should have help."

Now she thought he couldn't take care of her. "Good thinking. Dial nine-one-one."

"I'm not calling the police." She took her cell phone out of her purse. "What's the number of International Operatives? You can get a couple of other agents to meet us."

Mack clenched his jaw. She had him there—he didn't know the number. "Never mind. We're almost there. I can handle Barton. If he's there, which I doubt."

Once they were on the island, Cecily directed him to the beach house. "Stop here. The house is around the next bend."

Mack pulled the car onto the shoulder and cut the engine. "Give me the keys," he said.

"No. I meant it, Mack. I'm going with you." She opened her car door and got out. "You have to take me with you. I have the key and I know the security code. You don't."

"Setting off the alarm might be a good idea," said Mack. "The security firm will call the police and have them here in a matter of minutes."

"No, it wouldn't. If Neville is there, he'd be able to get out of the house the minute he heard the alarm. All the rooms open onto the deck."

"All right, then. Come on. At least promise me you'll stay behind me. Get the key out now. We don't want keys jangling while you search for it."

Cecily did as he asked. They started walking. "Lord, it's dark. Where are the stars and the moon?" she whispered.

"It's cloudy. Hush."

The house was dark. Mack started for the front door. Cecily grabbed the back of his sweatshirt. "Wait!" she hissed. "If we go in through the carport, we'll be on the opposite side of the house from the bedrooms. If he's there, he must be sleeping. None of the lights are on."

Mack veered to the right. He stopped outside the door and held out his hand. Cecily gave him the key. Before he opened the door, Mack put his mouth close to her ear and asked, "Where is the keypad for the alarm system?"

"On the left, right inside the door. I can take care of that."

"What room will we be in?"

"A mudroom. Five steps straight ahead there's another door, to the kitchen."

Cecily felt Mack nod. She heard the faint scrape of the key entering the lock; then the door opened and Mack was inside. The glow from the alarm pad allowed them to see the washer and drier and the kitchen door.

Cecily punched in the numbers while Mack carefully opened the door to the kitchen. "I can't see a thing," he whispered.

"Let me go first. I know where things are."

He held out an arm to keep her in back of him, and her stomach collided with his elbow. "Ooof!" she said.

"Stay behind me, Cecily. Tell me which way to go."

"See that lighter oblong to your right?"

"Yeah. Door?"

"To the living room. That's where the slider with the bump is. The bedrooms are on the other side of the living room. There's a hallway to the left, close to the front door. There's another keypad by the front door, so there may be some light in there."

Mack inched forward toward the door. Cecily grabbed hold of the waistband of his jeans and let him pull her forward.

"Oh, I forgot. There's a butcher block island—"

Mack hit it before she got the warning out. Something on the island crashed to the floor. From the splintering sound, it must have been something breakable.

"Damn!" hissed Mack.

"Sorry," said Cecily. "I forgot about the island. If anyone is here, he must have heard the crash."

"No kidding," said Mack, keeping his voice low. "Be quiet."

For once, she did as she was told. Mack strained but heard nothing but the soft sounds of their breathing. "Is Barton a heavy sleeper?"

"I don't know. I never spent the night with him. I don't think he's here—the house feels empty."

"Stay here while I check it out," said Mack, feeling his way toward the living room door.

Cecily grabbed his belt again. "I'm going with you."

Outside the beach house, Neville watched as lights flashed on in one room after another. He caught a glimpse of Cecily as she walked by the glass doors in the master bedroom. There was a man with her.

Interesting. So that was why she couldn't meet him tonight—Cecily had a prior engagement.

He shouldn't have visited the beach house. But calling Cecily from the bedroom where they'd made love had appealed to his sense of . . . irony.

And he had thought that the painting might be there. Banished, she'd said.

He had been walking away from the house on the narrow road when he had heard a car approaching. He'd raced back to the house and hidden on the far side—the few palms lining the narrow beach road did not afford much cover. Now, standing in the shadow of the boathouse, he followed the progress of Cecily and her companion through the house.

They wouldn't find any sign of his visit. He had left the decanter of brandy on the kitchen island, but that

wouldn't give him away. Cecily wouldn't know it hadn't
been there all along. Of course, if they tested it for fingerprints . . . But why would they? Cecily and her companion would have other things on their minds.

And besides, no one knew he was in Texas.

Neville left the shadows and walked to the beach. His
motel was two miles up the beach. If anyone saw him,
they would think nothing of a man walking on the
beach on such a balmy night. The clouds were dispers-
ing, and the moon shone on the water.

He could use the time thinking about where else the
painting might be. "Not executed, sire, but banished."
Cecily must have moved it to another room in the Culpepper mansion, more than likely to one of the guest
rooms.

The trip to the beach house had not been a waste,
not at all, Neville decided. He had learned that the neither the locks not the security codes had been changed.
And that his wife had not been any more faithful than
he had been—sneaking off to Galveston with another
man.

Another thought occurred to him. They had not
driven all the way to the house. They had parked down
the road, but why? There were no other houses close
by, no nosy neighbors . . .

Neville snapped his fingers.

But there was the *Houston Scoop*, and the story that
morning had referred to her mystery man. Cecily and
her boyfriend must be trying to avoid being found in a
compromising position by the tabloid reporters.

Neville shrugged and continued walking. Whatever
their reason for discretion, it had nothing to do with
him.

He reached his motel and began packing. He made
a habit of moving every day or so. After he'd packed,

Neville looked in the Yellow Pages for a motel within striking distance of his goal. He ran his finger down the listing, stopping at the River Oaks Inn.

It was time to pay a visit to Chez Culpepper.

Fourteen

"No one here," said Mack, looking into the last bedroom. Cecily still held on to the waist of his jeans. She bumped into him every time he moved.

She peered over his shoulder. "Darn. I wish we'd gotten here faster. We almost caught him." Her breath tickled the side of his neck.

"You can let go now." Cecily was too close. He reached behind and unhooked her fingers from his jeans. He turned to face her. "You really wanted to catch him, didn't you?"

"Of course." She puffed out her cheeks and blew a stray strand of hair from her eyes. "As long as he's free, I'm trapped in this silly excuse for a marriage."

"No, you're not. You could get a divorce."

"I know I can get a divorce—as a matter of fact, I have an appointment with a divorce lawyer on Monday. That's not what I meant. But I need to get *him*. He hurt me. He hurt Cyrus. And all those people he stole from. I want to hurt him back." She bared her teeth.

"Revenge." Mack grinned. Cecily looked more like a

tigress than a spoiled socialite. Who would have thought that a madcap heiress had fangs? "You want to get even."

"I do." Her snarl morphed into an embarrassed smile. "I guess that makes me a bad person."

"That make you a good person, as far as I'm concerned. Bad guys should be punished. If I didn't think that, I wouldn't . . ." Mack stopped abruptly. He'd almost said he wouldn't be a policeman.

"You wouldn't be a bodyguard?" asked Cecily.

"Yeah. Something like that."

"I'm going to clean up the mess in the kitchen."

Mack surveyed the bedroom one more time, then followed her to the kitchen. A large, aromatic pool of liquid was spreading across the kitchen floor.

"No sign that anyone was here except for that." Cecily pointed to the shards of heavy glass on the floor. "That decanter should not have been sitting on the island. It should have been in the liquor cabinet in the living room."

Mack sniffed. "What was in it? Brandy?"

"Delamain cognac. Neville's favorite—because it's the most expensive, I expect." Cecily opened a cabinet and took out a roll of paper towels. Squatting, she reached for the decanter stopper, which had rolled under the island.

"Wait! Don't touch that," Mack ordered, kneeling beside her. "There may be fingerprints. Get me a bag— paper or plastic—to put it in."

"You're awfully bossy—sometimes I think you forget who is in charge. If there are prints on this, they'll be Neville's."

"Or a burglar's." Mack stood. "Where are the grocery bags? I'll get them."

"There are plastic Baggies in the pantry." Cecily pointed to a door next to the refrigerator.

Mack found the Baggies, took one, and carefully placed the crystal stopper in it.

"Neville was here, Mack. No burglar did this. What is it that cops on TV always say? Oh, I remember—no signs of forced entry. Whoever drank the cognac had a key and knew the codes. It had to have been Neville." She continued picking up pieces of broken glass.

"We don't know that anyone drank the cognac. Someone could have left the decanter out the last time they were here."

"The only people who know the codes—besides Neville—are me, Cyrus, and Iris. None of us are brandy drinkers. Well, in a pinch, Cyrus might drink cognac. But not with an unopened bottle of Jack Daniel's in the next room. Neville was here. I'm sure of it."

"Why would Neville have come here?"

"Maybe he intended to stay here until . . . he's done whatever he's come to do. We don't use the beach house much anymore, especially in the winter. He knew that."

"Could he have left something here? Something valuable?"

Cecily dropped the last large piece of the decanter into the baggie Mack held open. "Like money? Or jewels? Or a rare and valuable stamp collection?" She tore several towels off the roll and began sopping up the puddle of cognac.

"Yeah. Like that."

She rocked back on her heels. "I don't know. I hadn't thought about that possibility—that Neville might have come back here for something he left behind." Her face fell. "Darn. What if he did retrieve something? He could be on his way back to Brazil."

"His leaving something valuable behind was only a theory—one of several."

"Another one being that I would empty my bank account for him?"

Mack knew better than to answer that one. "You didn't think he'd come back just for you?"

She laughed out loud. "Not hardly. I did assume he wanted to see me again—to talk me into giving him money. I admit that particular theory has some basis in fact." Cecily gave Mack a wry grin. "Neville is arrogant enough to think that he could persuade me to do that."

"With some reason—he did talk a lot of people out of a lot of money," Mack pointed out.

"Yes, he did. And he talked me into marrying him."

"Were you in love with him?"

She shrugged. "I was in love with the pretty facade he presented to me. As it turned out, there was nothing real about the man I fell in love with. He was smoke and mirrors. A fake, a fraud, and a scoundrel." Cecily giggled. "I am not a good judge of men."

Mack grabbed a handful of paper towels and knelt to help Cecily mop up the brandy. "Whew! This stuff is potent. You could get drunk on the fumes."

Cecily raised her head. "I do feel strange. Maybe it is the fumes." She held out her hand. "Look. I'm shaking."

"Brandy fumes, or the aftermath of an adrenaline rush." Or the rush of sexual attraction. That was what was making him sweat. Mack tossed the wet bundle of paper towels into the waste basket. "Come on. Let's get some fresh air." He could only hope that cold night air would have the same effect as a cold shower.

His hand on her back, Mack steered Cecily to the sliding glass door in the living room. He opened it—the door stuck briefly. Then, with a slight thump, it slid open. "Is that the noise you heard?"

Cecily nodded. She walked onto the wooden deck and took a deep breath. "It's a balmy night. For December."

She looked up at the night sky. "And there are stars, after all."

"And a moon." The moonlight on the water made a silver swath to the horizon.

"When I was a little girl, I used to think you could walk on the moon highway all the way to . . ."

"Italy?" Mack guessed, his heart clenching.

"Yes. Silly, wasn't it?"

Mack put his arm around Cecily's waist and pulled her to his side. He wanted to comfort her.

"Mack . . . ?"

"If you could go for a walk on moonlight, where would you go?" he asked.

"Nowhere. I'm happy where I am." She looked at him. "And I'm very happy you're with me." She gave him a luminous smile.

The smile did funny things to Mack's pulse. He couldn't decide if his heart rate had speeded up or slowed down, or both. Maybe that was what a heart attack felt like.

Or love.

Joe had been right. Not the first look, maybe, but one special look—the way he was seeing her now—and he knew. Cecily Culpepper Barton was the only woman for him.

But he was not the man for her.

She had told Olivia exactly what she wanted from him—she wanted a temporary lover, a transition man.

Mack felt a pinch in the neighborhood of his heart. He ignored it. He wasn't having a heart attack. That was what the first crack in a heartbreak felt like. He would get used to it.

In the meantime, he was going to make a few good memories. "Let's go back inside."

She shook her head. "Not yet."

"It's cold out here. You're shivering." He was shaking, too, but not from the temperature. He was hot, and getting hotter. He took a step back, toward the open door.

"I'm not cold. Come here, Mack." She leaned her back against the deck railing and opened her arms.

"What for?" he asked.

"Golly. I bet you could guess if you put your mind to it. Come here."

"Who's bossy now?" He walked into her arms.

"Me. I'm in charge, remember? You are in my power." She wrapped her arms around his waist and rested her cheek on his chest. "I can hear your heartbeat."

"Does it sound erratic to you?"

"No. A little fast, but steady. Thump-thump-thump. Like that."

"That's the surf." Cecily's body pressed against his was affecting more than his heart rate.

"No. It's your heart." She took his hand and placed it under her left breast. "My heart is beating faster, too. Mack . . . kiss me." She closed her eyes and lifted her face.

Mack felt sweat break out on his brow. "Is that an order?"

"Uh-huh." Cecily slitted her eyes open. Mack was staring at her, his expression . . . pained. She opened her eyes wider. "Don't you want to kiss me?" Her lower lip trembled.

With a groan, he caught her lower lip between his teeth and gently ended the tremors. He soothed her lips with his tongue, seeking entrance into the moist warmth of her mouth.

A dreamy sigh escaped her lips as she parted them, allowing Mack access. Meeting his tongue with hers, she gloried in the taste of him. She wiggled closer, wrapping her arms around his neck.

Mack's mouth left hers, but he didn't stop kissing

MAKING MERRY   199

her. His lips trailed a path along her jawline, down her neck. She shivered when his hot mouth found the sensitive spot where her neck met her shoulder.

Mack must have felt the small shudder. He held her closer and asked, "Are you cold?"

"Are you kidding? I'm so hot you could fry an egg on my—on me."

"You shivered."

"You tickled my neck."

"I'm sorry. I should stop—"

"No! Says who? You? Not your decision, Mr. Armstrong. I'm in charge, remember?"

"Cecily—"

She put her hand on his mouth. "Hush. I order you to kiss me again. On the mouth."

Mack slid his arm around her and pulled her close. "And if I refuse? What will you do?"

"Uh, I'll . . . think of something." She lifted her face for his kiss.

"Think fast," he said, his mouth touching hers. "If we're going to stop, we have to do it . . ."

"Now?"

". . . soon." He kissed her again. When the kiss ended, Mack said, "Cecily, I have to tell you something."

"Not now. Later." Cecily slid her hands under the hem of Mack's sweatshirt. "You don't have buttons. I was looking forward to undressing you slowly, button by button."

"You don't have buttons, either," said Mack. "Listen to—"

She took her hands away. Without her hands on his bare skin, Mack could almost think clearly.

Then she pulled her sweater over her head and tossed it onto a deck chair. He learned that Cecily liked sexy lingerie. The bra she wore was nothing but a scrap of lace. Almost before that fact had registered, she'd reached behind her back and unhooked it. She tossed the bra aside. He didn't see where it landed. "Touch me, Mack. Now."

Mack shoved his hands in his pockets to keep himself from grabbing. He knew what he wanted—her. He knew what she'd told Olivia she wanted. But he wanted her to be sure. "Cecily . . . have you thought this through? It may not be a good idea."

"It's the best idea I've had in years. What's wrong? Don't you like being at my mercy? I confess. I was teasing about being in charge. I won't tell Cyrus anything that will get you fired."

"You couldn't," said Mack. "Cyrus isn't my boss."

"Of course he is. He hired you to protect me from myself."

"No, he didn't. I'm not a bodyguard."

"Of course you are. Those clippings—"

"Came from a dossier the Media Relations Department prepared for me."

"Media—you're a reporter?" Cecily felt a chill that had nothing to do with the cool breeze blowing over the water. She crossed her arms over her bare breasts.

"No. The H.P.D. Media Relations Department. I'm a cop, Cecily."

"Why would the Houston Police Department send a cop to be my chauffeur? Does Cyrus know who you are? Oh. Silly me. Of course he does. That's why he fired Jenkins so abruptly. But why now?"

"When Captain Morris—my boss—learned that Neville was broke and on the move, we thought he might be coming after you."

"Why didn't you tell me? Oh. Why do I keep asking stupid questions? You thought I would help him. How could you? After what he did to all those people? To Cyrus? I know everyone thinks I'm an idiot. But I'm not that stupid, and I do know right from wrong."

"We didn't know what you would do, Cecily. You were still married to him, and you wouldn't tell anyone why—"

"That's not true. Olivia knows why. I tell her everything."

"Yeah," Mack mumbled. "Why are you still married to him?"

"Because I didn't want to make another mistake. I thought as long as I was married, I wouldn't fall in love with another lying, cheating son of a gun."

"I'm sorry I lied to you."

"I know. At least you had a reason. Of sorts." Cecily shivered. "You were right. It is cold out here. I'm going back inside." She picked up her sweater and held it in front of her.

Mack followed her into the living room. "Cecily, I couldn't tell you who I was, not until I knew how you felt about Neville."

"I said you had a reason." She turned her back to him and pulled her sweater on. "So, all that kissing was just to find out whether or not I was going to be faithful to Neville?"

"No. Cecily, I kissed you because I wanted to, not for any other reason."

"You had another reason the first time—you wanted to keep me from seeing that folder."

"I could have done that some other way. I didn't have to kiss you. I *wanted* to."

"Uh-huh."

"I want you, Cecily. But, face it, I am not your . . ."

"My what? My type? Just because you lied about who you were? I'm sure Cyrus had something to do with that."

"He had his reasons, too. He wanted to protect you. Cyrus thinks Neville is going to try to kidnap you—hold you for ransom. Of all the theories, that one is now the most likely."

"Kidnap? He could have told me that."

"Yeah. He probably would have, if he'd known how you feel about Neville. But you didn't share that with him. And you didn't tell him you thought Neville was at the beach house tonight. Why not?"

Cecily's lower lip came out. "I didn't want to upset him," she said defensively. It was getting harder to hold on to her anger. Mack looked so worried.

"That's the same reason he gave me when he told me to keep quiet about being a policeman—he said he didn't want to upset you."

"He was afraid I'd do something to help Neville, too. Neither one of you had any faith in me. That's why you pretended to be a chauffeur and then a bodyguard."

"I had to be close to you, Cecily. Close enough to protect you from Neville."

The thought of Mack protecting her dissolved the last shred of anger. "Oh, well, close is good. Why are you all the way over there? Here we are, alone together." She switched off the lamp. "Moonlight and surf. Don't you want me?"

"Oh, yeah. I want."

"Why?"

"Why? What kind of question is that?" He wasn't going to tell her he loved her. She'd run like hell—if she believed him. "Why do you want to make love with me?"

Wanting wasn't loving. But if that was all she could get, she'd settle. She couldn't tell Mack she thought she might be falling in love with him. He'd never believe it. Not when all she'd blathered about was sex without strings. "Because you're here. And I'm here. And it's been three years."

"Same here. We're attracted; we're consenting adults, so why not?"

"No reason. Except . . . I almost wish you'd waited to

tell me the truth about who you are. I liked being in control."

"You're still in charge, Cecily. I won't do anything you don't want me to do. As long as all you're after is fun, I'm game."

Fun and games? That was what Mack wanted? Cecily opened her mouth, ready to object. This was serious business. She closed her mouth, swallowing her objections. Mack had told her he had commitment issues.

She was probably overreacting anyway. She wasn't falling in love. An affair was probably all she could handle right now. She would need time to put her marriage to Neville behind her. She couldn't really expect to jump from one marriage into another.

It had been three years.

But she hadn't taken even a baby step toward a new relationship in those three years. Now she was about to take a giant step. "Fun and games. Right."

"Are you mad?"

"No. Why would I be mad? My bedroom is this way." She took his hand and led him down the hall.

When they reached the door, Mack asked, "Did you make love with Neville in there?"

"No. He preferred the master bedroom. Ugh. You sure know how to destroy the mood. Why would you bring that up?"

"I don't know. Forget I said anything. Lead on, Cecily." As they entered her bedroom, Mack asked, "You're sure you want to do this?"

"Do what?" asked Cecily coming to a sudden stop right inside the door.

Mack bumped into her from behind. "I knew it. You don't."

"Don't what? What are you talking about?" Cecily took three steps toward the bed. Mack must be having second thoughts. Well, so was she. She hadn't done anything like this in . . . never. She'd never made love with a good man, a man like Mack. She looked over her shoulder. He was still in the doorway, one shoulder propped against the door frame.

Mack was eminently lovable.

Quickly Cecily turned away. She resumed staring at the bed.

What if she was right? What if she fell all the way in love with him after tonight? What if she was in love with him already? He didn't love her. He wouldn't love her—how could a man like Mack love a woman who had married a criminal?

"Cecily? Do you want to go home?"

"No. I want to go there." She pointed at the bed. "With you. Now." She had to get over thinking love entered into what was about to happen. Like Olivia—and Tina Turner—said, "What's love got to do with it?"

"You're sure?"

Out of the corner of her eye, Cecily saw Mack push away from the door and start toward her. She turned to face him. "Of course I'm sure. Why wouldn't I be sure? What's the big deal? Oh, I know. You're probably worried because I haven't done this in a while. I'm pretty sure I remember how to do it. If not, you can refresh my memory."

"I'm not worried about you. I'm having a serious case of performance anxiety." Why had he told her that? Nothing like lowering expectations, he thought, disgusted with himself. "Earlier, I thought I was having a heart attack. Now I'm about to panic."

"Really? You don't look panicky. How do you feel?"

"Hot. Cold. Shaky. I'm having trouble breathing. And my pulse is hopping." He was beginning to sweat again, too, but he kept that to himself.

"Weak?" she asked, smiling.

He grinned at her. "Definitely weak—especially my knees."

"Poor baby. I think you should lie down." She took him by the hand and led him to the bed.

She gave him a small push, and Mack let himself fall backward onto the bed. "What are you going to do?"

"I'm going to make you feel better," said Cecily, letting go of her doubts. Mack's weakness—even if he was only pretending—made her strong.

"You can do that?" asked Mack.

"Yes. I can." She knelt next to the bed. "First, we need to loosen your clothing." Cecily untied his shoes and slipped them off.

"I feel better already," said Mack, wiggling his toes.

"Good." She got up and sat on the bed, her hip next to his. She unbuttoned his jeans, then slowly slid the zipper open. Mack raised his hips, allowing her to tug his jeans off. "How's your breathing now?" she asked.

"Shallow. Fast. Like my heart rate."

"Oh, my. That calls for mouth-to-mouth resuscitation." Cecily crawled onto his body and gave him a long, luxurious kiss. "Better?"

"A little. I think I need another treatment."

Cecily kissed him again.

Mack arched his back.

"Am I too heavy?" Cecily murmured against his mouth.

"A few ounces, maybe. I think it's your sweater."

"Oh, well. I can fix that." Straddling him, she crossed her arms and pulled her sweater over her head. When she could see again, Mack was frowning. "What's wrong? Still too heavy?"

"No. We don't fit," he said. "I have bare legs. Your chest is bare." He closed his eyes. "The imbalance is making me dizzy."

"Well, take off your sweatshirt." Cecily got off the bed

and unbuttoned her slacks. She kicked off her shoes, then pushed her slacks and her panties down and off. "I'm naked."

Mack tossed his sweatshirt to the floor. "So am I."

"You're staring at me."

"Yeah, I am. I like what I see." He leaned back against the headboard of her bed. Patting the bed next to him, Mack said, "Come here."

"There you go, snapping orders again."

"Sorry. Please come here, Cecily." He grinned at her.

"I would, but I can't seem to move. I think I could, if you would close your eyes for one second."

Obediently Mack shut his eyes. But the grin remained in place. That dimple did strange things to her pulse, but she could move now that he wasn't looking at her. She climbed onto the bed. "You can open your eyes now," she said.

His eyes opened and his gaze met hers. Her mouth went dry. She'd never been the focus of such intense desire. Mack *wanted* her. She took a deep, shuddering breath.

"Cold?" Mack asked.

"Hot. I think I have a fever."

"It must be going around. I think I've got the same fever." He studied her intently. "We need protection."

"No, we don't. Neville is long gone."

"Not the kind of protection I was talking about," he said, grinning.

"Oh." She could feel her cheeks heat up. "There may be condoms in the master bedroom. Daddy and Iris were here last October."

Mack got up. "Bedside table?" he asked, walking away from her.

Admiring the view, Cecily sighed an affirmative sound. "Uh-huh."

When he returned, he had a box in his hand. "This should be enough," he said.

"How many are there?" she said, admiring his full-frontal nudity. She'd admired Mack's body clothed. Now, naked and aroused, he made her mouth water.

"Eight. I counted."

"Eight? *Eight.* That's not . . ."

". . . enough?" He showed his dimple again.

He was teasing her. She could do that. "Well, we can't use them all—we have to leave at least one in case Cyrus brings Iris here again anytime soon."

"If you insist," he said, winking. "Seven, then? We'd better get started." He took a condom out of the box. When he'd taken care of protection, Mack lay down next to her.

She rolled on top of him, fitting her body to his, rubbing her breasts against the hard muscles of his bare chest. "Don't forget who's in control here, Mister Armstrong."

"Never," said Mack as his hands stroked her back. "I have only one request—don't take too long. Not the first time, anyway. I'm ready to explode."

"I'll keep that in mind," Cecily said, rising on her knees. Straddling him, she took his erect penis in her hands. "Is this the site of the potential explosion?" she asked.

Mack groaned and reached for her breasts. His eyes were squeezed shut, and his brows were drawn together in a fierce frown. "Cecily—"

"I know," she gasped. "You want me to hurry." She guided his erection to the entrance to her vagina. He raised his hips, surging upward and burying his penis inside her. "Oh!"

Mack's eyes snapped open. "Did I hurt you?"

"O-o-o-oh, no-o-o-o. Nothing hurts. Everything feels

very, very good." She moved, sliding up the length of him, then settling down again. "Extremely good," she moaned.

"Glad to hear it," said Mack, matching his thrusts to the rhythm she set.

Sensations blossomed into an almost painful tension, before ending in pleasure so perfect Cecily wanted to weep with it. She screamed Mack's name, then fell on his chest in a boneless heap.

After minutes or hours, Cecily rolled off him. She cuddled up to Mack and said in her sultriest voice, "That was good for me."

"I aim to please," said Mack, grinning.

"Stop that. You know what that dimple does to me."

"Yeah." Mack's grin widened, and the dimple deepened.

Trailing her hand down his chest, Cecily used one finger to trace around his belly button.

Mack grabbed her hand. "The same thing that does to me." He sobered. "I hate to admit it, but I think I dimpled too soon."

"Is that so? Well, quality beats quantity every time. One outstanding time isn't shabby, especially for a man of your advanced years."

"Advanced years? Are you calling me old?"

"If the age fits . . ."

Mack rolled over and pinned Cecily beneath him. "I was wrong." He grinned again.

Cecily faked a swoon. With her eyes closed, she sighed, "Oh, goody."

Two condoms later, Cecily said regretfully, "We have to go. If we're not home before Cyrus and Iris get up, they'll be worried."

Mack stood and stretched. "You're right. It's time to get this show on the road. I need to take the broken glass to the crime lab first thing, and I've got to tell Cyrus to change the alarm codes."

"My, you're all business all of a sudden."

"I'm supposed to be doing a job here. I have to say, the fringe benefits are outstanding."

Later, on the way back to Houston, Cecily asked, "Mack, what happens next?"

"We wait for Neville to make his move."

"I wasn't talking about Neville. I was talking about us."

"That's up to you, Cecily. You're in charge."

"No, I'm not. I never was, was I? Darn. I liked being heartless and ruthless and having a sexy man at my beck and call."

"So? What's changed? I like it when you beck and call."

Cecily smiled. If the smile was a little watery, that was okay. Mack couldn't see in the dark. What had changed was that she'd gone and done it again.

She'd fallen in love.

But it wasn't the same. Not at all, not even if he had kept a few things from her. Mack had told her the truth about himself when it became important. She could just see Neville doing something like that: "Oh, my dear, before you say, 'I do,' there's something you should know. I'm a crook."

Neville had been an illusion, but Mack was not another fantasy man. He was real, solid—a good man to his core. Falling in love with a man like that was smart, not stupid.

She narrowed her eyes. If all that was keeping her from having Mack in her life forever was his fear of commitment, she could do something about that. She had proof that he was susceptible to her, even without having his job on the line.

She could work with that.

"What are you smiling about?" he asked.

"I'm smiling because I'm happy," she said.

"Did I have anything to do with that?" he asked, grinning.

"Oh, yeah. Lots." She leaned back and closed her eyes. Neville had been a dark cloud over her life for years, but now there was a silver lining, in the form of one very sexy police officer.

All she had to do to make them both happy was to make him fall in love with her.

Fifteen

Sunday morning, Mack arrived for breakfast before Cecily and Cyrus. "Where is everybody?"

"Cecily is sleeping in, I think. You two got home late last night. Another date?" asked Iris.

"Not exactly." Mack tugged on his collar, even though it was open and not constricting his breathing. Explicit memories of Cecily were responsible for that.

"And you left again early this morning—I saw you back your truck out of the garage."

"I had some things to take care of." After dropping Cecily off at home, he had taken the decanter remnants to the crime lab. Then he'd driven around for a while, trying to talk himself out of being in love with Cecily. "Is Cyrus around?"

"I heard the elevator a few minutes ago. He must be in his study."

"I've got to tell him something," said Mack, heading down the hall. He needed something to concentrate on—something familiar, something that he knew how to deal with.

"Mack, come on in," said Cyrus. "I'll be with you in a

minute." He hit a few keys on the computer and then turned to Mack. "What's going on?"

"Neville Barton is back in town." Mack quickly summarized the facts: Neville's call, Cecily's hunch, and the broken decanter.

"So that's where you and Cecily were last night. The beach house."

"Yes, sir." Mack felt heat in his cheeks—he hoped to hell Cyrus didn't notice he was blushing.

"Cecily figured out where he was from the background noises during Barton's second call?"

"That's right."

"Smart girl. And she took you along to help her catch him. That proves she doesn't care a rat's ass about the SOB." Cyrus twirled his mustache and grinned.

"Yes, sir. It does. She knows I'm a cop."

"She knows you're a policeman?" Cyrus stopped fooling with his mustache and gave Mack a speculative look.

"Yes. I told her. There was no reason to keep her in the dark about it, now that she's proved she wants to see Barton caught as much as we do. And she is in danger—Barton is still on the loose."

"You're right, of course." said Cyrus. "She needs to be on her guard. Does she know I know?"

"She figured that part out for herself."

"Son of a bitch," said Cyrus. "Does she know about the phone tap?"

"No. I didn't tell her about that. I said the police department got word that Barton was on his way to the States, and that's why you had asked for police protection—she guessed right away that you were the source of the tip."

"Like I said. Cecily is a smart girl—chip off the old block. But she doesn't know about the wiretap—let's keep that our little secret, shall we? If she knows we've been listening to her calls, she'll skin us alive. She has a thing about privacy—I blame all that unwanted publicity she gets from the *Scoop*. Is that all?"

"No. You need to have the security codes changed as soon as possible. You should probably have the locks rekeyed at some point. Barton got into the beach house with a key, and he knew the codes. Cecily said you hadn't changed them since he left town."

"No, we didn't. Good idea. I'll call the security company right away." Cyrus reached for the telephone.

There was a shriek from the foyer. "What?" said Cyrus, dropping the phone.

Cecily burst into the study.

Iris was right behind her, wiping her hands on a kitchen towel. "What's wrong? Why did you yell?"

Cecily had a stack of mail in one hand, a single letter in her other hand. She waved the letter under her father's nose. "Neville has a daughter! Why didn't your fancy spies know that?"

"What? That SOB got some other woman pregnant?"

"Twelve years ago. He was married before, Daddy. And he has an eleven-year-old daughter. Read this."

Cyrus scanned the letter she handed to him. "Well, we'll see about this. It may be some kind of scam."

He handed the letter to Mack before Cecily could take it back. "A scam?" she asked. "By the State of Texas?"

"By this Hannah Barton."

"Daddy," said Cecily, shaking her head, "she's eleven years old. I don't think Hannah is a con kid, even if her father is Neville Barton. Mack, I need the letter, please. I have to call and tell them I want to be—what did they call it?—her guardian?"

"Her managing conservator," Mack quoted.

"That sounds so . . . legalistic. But it means I would have custody of her, right? Be her guardian?"

"Yeah," said Mack, handing her the letter. Cecily seemed awfully excited about having a preteen stranger dropped in her lap.

"Let's make sure she is your stepdaughter first," said Cyrus. "I'll have someone run a check on the marriage between Barton and this girl's mother, and take a look at the kid's birth certificate. Shouldn't take long."

"The Department of Protective Services has already done that. All I have to do is sign a few papers, and they'll bring Hannah here. The letter says a home evaluation isn't needed for a stepparent."

"It won't hurt to double-check," Cyrus insisted.

"While you're double-checking, I'm calling the agency."

"Cecily, it's Sunday," said Iris. "There won't be anyone in the office. Where has this child been for eleven years? Does the letter say?"

"Yes. Her mother died when she was five. Hannah has been living with her grandmother—her maternal grandmother. She died earlier this year. Oh, poor thing. Hannah must be scared to death, thinking she's all alone in the world. Darn it! This letter came on Friday, and I let it sit there all day yesterday."

"I glanced at the mail—all I saw was catalogs and Christmas cards. This must have been stuck inside something." Cyrus reached for the telephone. "Bureaucrats may not work on weekends, but International Ops is available twenty-four-seven. They can check this out today—and they can explain why they didn't find out about a prior marriage when they checked on Neville for me."

"Daddy. You don't have to do that. This is not a scam. She is my stepdaughter. I knew I stayed married to Neville for a reason. This is it." Cecily got a funny look on her face. "Oh, golly. I'm going to be a mother."

"You're not going to faint, are you?" Mack asked, taking her by the arm. He steered her to a chair. "Sit down."

"I'm all right." Cecily sat. She looked at him, but Mack had the feeling it wasn't him she was seeing.

Dreamily Cecily said, "Hannah can have my old room. It has a canopy bed. Little girls love canopy beds . . . I think." She bent over and put her head on her knees. "I don't know how to be a mother. This is happening too fast. A woman is supposed to have time to get used to the idea—nine months, at least. Do you think my old room will do?" She raised her head and looked at Iris.

"What are you asking me for? I don't know any more about being a mother than you do."

"You do, too. You were the best mother I ever had."

Cyrus got a funny look on *his* face. "You think of Iris as your mother?"

"Closest thing to it I ever had," said Cecily.

Iris blinked rapidly. "Your old room will be fine for starters. She can always move to another room later if there's another one she likes better."

"Provided she stays," Cyrus cautioned.

Cecily paid no attention to her father. "Maybe even to the extra room on the third floor. Or I could move back to the second floor. She might get lonely all by herself."

"Hey," said Cyrus, his mustache quivering, "what am I, chopped liver? I'm on the second floor, right across the hall from the kid's room. And you're an elevator ride away. And we don't know she's going to stay."

"Yes, we do. Her name is Hannah, Daddy. She's a girl, not a baby goat." Cecily stared at her father, her eyes wide. "Golly. I just thought of something—you're going to be a grandfather."

Iris burst out laughing.

"Neville Barton has a lot to answer for," said Cyrus,

tugging on his beard. "I'm not going to be grandfather
to a crook's kid—girl—not unless . . ." Cyrus trailed off,
staring at Iris, who was glaring at him. "She might need
a grandmother, though, now that I think about it."

Mack watched as Iris blushed a deep red. He was beginning to feel like an intruder. The Culpeppers—and
he put Iris in that category—were dealing with a family
problem. He wasn't part of the family. He began edging
toward the study door.

"It's not Hannah's fault that her father is a criminal,"
said Cecily. "I don't think she's seen Neville in years. If
ever."

"Probably never," said Iris. "Neville never struck me
as the fatherly type."

"I'm going to call Mrs. Phillips first thing tomorrow
morning," said Cecily, getting up and wandering around
the room. She seemed to be in a daze.

Iris and Cyrus were staring at each other, identical
silly grins on their faces.

Mack cleared his throat. "I've got to call the crime
lab. See if they got any prints off that decanter. I'll use
the phone in my apartment."

"What are you talking about?" asked Iris. "What
crime lab? What decanter?"

"The Houston Police Department," said Cyrus.
"Mack isn't a chauffeur, Iris. He's a policeman."

"What?" Iris looked at Mack. "You're a cop? Why didn't
anyone tell me?"

"No one told me, either," said Cecily. "Daddy and
Mack thought I would give Neville money and help him
escape again."

"Well, they're both idiots, then," said Iris. She resumed glaring at Cyrus. "You wouldn't lift a finger to
help him."

"See?" Cecily blew a lock of hair away from her face

and gave Mack an accusing look. "Some people trust me."

"I know you wouldn't help him leave Brazil," said Iris.

"Oh, he's not in Brazil any longer. He's here, in Texas. Mack and I almost caught him last night. He was at the beach house."

"We think," said Mack. "So far, the evidence is circumstantial. I took some evidence to the crime lab this morning. We'll know for sure as soon as they check for fingerprints."

"I'm already sure," said Cecily. "No one but Neville could have gotten into the beach house without setting off the alarm."

"You went to the beach house last night to catch Neville? Cecily Jeanne! What were you thinking? That man is dangerous."

"I know that, Iris. That's why I decided to let Mack help me. But Mack broke a decanter, and Neville got away."

"Wait a minute." Mack said, indignant. "We don't know for sure that Neville was still around when we got there. He could have left right after he called you. And I ran into the counter because you forgot to tell me it was there."

"True. It was my fault—partly." She winked at him. He grinned back. Cecily's mouth dropped open. "Don't do that," she hissed. "Not now."

"Neville called you?" Iris asked. She looked from Cecily to Mack and back again. Her eyebrows rose.

Cecily nodded. "Saturday night. I heard background noises that made me think he was at the beach house, and I was right. He had been there."

"Good grief," said Iris. She turned to Cyrus. "Aha! So that's why you decided to fire Jenkins out of the blue.

You knew Neville was on his way here—that's why you contacted the police. Why didn't you tell me?"

Cyrus's mouth dropped open. "Uh . . . well, I . . ."

Mack took pity on him. "International Ops found out Barton had left Brazil; they told Cyrus. Cyrus reported it to us. We guessed Neville might try to contact Cecily. Cyrus agreed to let me act as Cecily's chauffeur. He couldn't tell you, not without blowing my cover."

"Nice try, Mack," said Cecily, patting him on the shoulder. "You wouldn't be here if Cyrus hadn't asked for police protection for me."

Cyrus jumped in. "I've had Neville under surveillance for years. I'm sorry I didn't tell you, C. J. You had a right to know."

Mack shook his head. Cyrus wasn't going to admit he'd overheard Neville's first call, not until he had absolutely no choice. Well, he could understand that. He hadn't told Cecily he'd been listening to *all* her calls for days.

"Well, I forgive you, Daddy. There were some things I didn't tell you—like, Saturday night was not the first time Neville called."

"Really?" said Cyrus, attempting an innocent look.

"Really. He called a couple of weeks ago and asked me to meet him."

"Imagine that," said Cyrus, stroking his beard. "Why didn't you tell me?"

"I didn't want to upset you. Why didn't you tell me you were keeping an eye on Neville?"

"I wasn't sure how you felt about him. And I didn't want to upset you."

"You two should talk more," said Iris. "As a matter of fact, we should all stop treating Cyrus as if he's made of glass. He's a tough old bird."

"Does that mean I can have steak for dinner?" asked Cyrus.

"A tough old bird on a heart-healthy diet," Iris corrected. "Cecily, don't you have an appointment with a divorce lawyer tomorrow?"

"Yes. I'll have to cancel. I can't get a divorce now."

"Why the hell not?" Mack blurted. Three sets of eyebrows rose at his outburst.

"Because I won't be Hannah's stepparent if I'm not married to Neville. The letter from the Department of Protective Services is clear on that point—the only reason they contacted me was because they can't find Neville. That makes me Hannah's next of kin." Cecily looked at Mack, who had a peculiar expression on his face.

Panicky—that's how he looked. As if he wanted to bolt from the room. It suddenly occurred to her that a man who found it hard to commit to one woman might find commitment even harder if that woman had a child.

Cyrus said, "Cecily, I think you need to slow down and think this over. You don't know anything about this child. Any way you look at it, she's not your responsibility."

Cecily shifted her gaze from Mack to her father. She couldn't think about Mack right now. "I think she is. I can be a good stepmother."

"I don't doubt that, but—"

A buzzer sounded faintly. "What was that?" asked Cyrus.

"The oven timer," said Iris. "I've got blueberry muffins in the oven. Does anyone want breakfast?"

"Sounds good to me," said Cyrus, getting up from his desk. "Come on, you two. You both look like you could use a bite to eat, and a nap. What time was it when you got home?"

"I don't know," said Cecily. "Late, but I'm too excited to sleep now." She started after them, but Mack put his hand on her arm, stopping her.

"We need to talk," he said.

"About last night?" she asked.

He recoiled, dropping his hand. "Lord, no. Why would you want to talk about that? I wanted to tell you what you need to do if Neville calls you again."

"Oh . . . Neville. I almost forgot about him." Cecily turned away with a shrug. She should have known better—any man with commitment issues would shake in his boots at the hint of the dreaded relationship talk.

Mack grabbed her by the shoulders and whirled her around. "You can't do that! You cannot let your guard down until he's in custody."

"All right. I won't. What should I do?"

"If he asks you to meet him, agree. You name the time and place. Then you tell me. Immediately. We'll set up a trap for him."

Cecily nodded. "Okay, I will. You're staying here, aren't you?"

"Yeah. I'm staying." He took her face in his hands. "Until this is over."

She opened her mouth to ask what "this" he was talking about. Before she could get the words out, Mack kissed her. The kiss was hot and hard and felt a little desperate. But that could have been her imagination.

"Why did you do that?" she gasped, once the kiss ended.

"You're under the mistletoe," he said.

She glanced up. "So I am. Imagine that." She'd forgotten she'd put mistletoe everywhere, including Cyrus's office.

"Meet me after breakfast." It was an order, not a request. "My place."

"To make our plans to capture Neville?" asked Cecily. It must have been very difficult for him to suppress his bossy tendencies for the few days he had pretended she was in charge.

"No," said Mack.

"No? We haven't decided on a place for me to meet him."

"No, that's not why I want you to come with me."

"Oh. What did you have in mind? Hannah? Do you want to talk about Neville's daughter?" She did. She wanted to know how he felt about children. And she wanted to talk about last night.

"Nothing to talk about until we know more about her. I want you to come with me so we can do it."

"Do it?" Cecily raised a brow.

Mack groaned. "Make love. After today, that's going to be more difficult."

Cecily felt her pulse speed up. Mack wanted her still. Even though she was a stepmother. That was a good sign, wasn't it? "More difficult because of Hannah? Or Neville?"

"Both. I'll be busy being a cop. You'll be busy with your new daughter."

"Right. But we'll find a way." She would make sure they found a way to be together. Her plan to make Mack fall in love with her depended on it. "We'll just have to be discreet. Which we would have had to be, anyway."

"Because of Cyrus and Iris? They're having their own fling, aren't they?" Mack asked.

"Yes. How did you know?"

"We used their condoms, remember? How long has it been going on?"

"Years. They think I don't know—well, Cyrus thinks I don't know. Iris knows I know, but she pretends I don't. Most of the time. She did tell me she's thinking about proposing."

"Marriage?" Mack paled.

"What else gets proposed?" Cecily asked, a little testily. Mack had commitment issues for other men, too? Convincing him that he needed a wife and an eleven-year-old daughter was not going to be easy.

"Why hasn't Cyrus asked her to marry him?"

"I'm not sure. I think he's afraid of making another mistake. Huh. Just like me—or the me I used to be. I guess I do take after my father." She put her arm through his. "Let's go get breakfast."

After coffee and muffins, Iris told Cyrus she wanted to do some Christmas shopping.

"Go with Cecily," said Cyrus. "Mack won't mind driving both of you."

"I don't need a bodyguard," said Iris. "I'll drive myself. As it happens, I want to look for a present for Cecily. I don't want her with me. She has a bad habit of peeking into other people's shopping bags."

"Oh, well, in that case, I'll drive you," said Cyrus, getting up from the table. "I need to look for a few things myself. Come on, let's go."

"Hold your horses. I've got to clean up the kitchen," said Iris.

"We'll take care of the kitchen," said Cecily. "You go on."

"Well, if you're sure." Iris took off her apron and handed it to Cecily. "What are you going to do today?"

Cecily gave a huge yawn. "I'm going to take a nap. How about you, Mack? What are your plans?"

He grinned at her. "I'll think of something."

Early Monday morning, hours before dawn, the security alarm screeched, waking Cecily from a sound sleep. As it turned out, she hadn't taken a nap on Sunday, after all. Mack and she had found a better way to spend the time.

She grabbed a robe and headed for the stairs. On

the second floor, she met Cyrus coming out of his room. "Are you all right?"

"Fine. Lucky Mack told me to get the security codes changed. That son of a bitch must have tried to get in here. He's coming for you, Cecily. Kidnapping is what he's got in mind, just as I thought. That's why I arranged to have a policeman on the premises."

"I know, Daddy. Mack explained all that to me." The alarm shut off. "Iris must have gotten to the keypad."

When Cecily and Cyrus got downstairs, Iris and Mack were in the kitchen. "Did you see who it was?" asked Cyrus.

"No. By the time I got here from the garage, whoever it was had gotten away. I did hear a car start up, from somewhere down the block."

"It must have been Neville," said Cecily. "Who else would try to break in?"

Sirens sounded in the distance.

"That's the police," said Cyrus. "The security company would have called them once the alarm was tripped."

"I called them, too," said Mack.

The police examined the doors and confirmed what the security company had reported—that someone had attempted entry by way of the front door. Lab technicians arrived to look for fingerprints and other evidence. Mack stayed with them while Cyrus ushered Cecily and Iris to the kitchen.

"It must have been Neville," said Cecily. "He would know that we were less likely to hear the front door open than the kitchen door."

"Right. Iris has ears like a bat," said Cyrus. "Alarm or no alarm, anyone sneaking in the back door wouldn't get past her."

Cecily shot a startled look at Iris. She'd been sneaking out through the kitchen. Iris gave her a knowing smile.

When the police had completed their work, Mack walked them out the front door, then returned to the study.

"I'm glad that happened before Hannah got here," said Cecily. "Neville won't try to break in again now that he knows we've changed the codes and the locks. Oh, Lord. What if he tried to kidnap her instead of me?"

"The man is desperate, Cecily," said Cyrus. "No telling what he'll try next. I don't want you going anywhere without Mack. And maybe we should wait a few days before letting Neville's daughter move in."

"Why?"

"She might help Neville get to you—she is his daughter, after all. We don't know what kind of relationship they have."

"I don't think they have any kind of relationship. Neville never said one word about a daughter. As a matter of fact, he told me he had no family at all."

"He didn't tell you he'd been married before, either," Cyrus pointed out. "He really is a piece of—"

The doorbell rang.

Cecily started. "Who could that be? The police again?"

"Maybe they found Barton," said Mack, heading for the front door.

Cecily led the way to the foyer, but Mack opened the door.

"Good morning, all."

"Jade Jones," said Cecily, rolling her eyes. "What do you want?"

"Good God," said Cyrus. "I'm not talking to the press."

"I'll deal with Ms. Jones," said Cecily. "You all go back to bed."

"Good idea," said Cyrus, yawning. "Good night, all. Come on Iris. I'll walk you to your room."

"I know where my room is, you old goat. I'll walk you to the elevator."

"Fine. Come on, then."

Mack stayed put.

Cecily asked Jade, "Now, what was it that you wanted?"

"A story, of course. What were the police doing here? And who is this?" Her gaze fastened on Mack.

"No story here. The alarm went off," said Mack. "It turned out to be a false alarm."

"I know you," said Jade. "You're a cop—and Cecily's mystery man. I thought I recognized you the other night at the Millennia. What's going on?"

"He's not a cop. He's my chauffeur. Good-bye, Jade," said Cecily, attempting to close the door.

"Chauffeur? Ha!" said Jade. "A policeman on the premises—must have something to do with your fugitive husband."

"Wait," said Mack. "You can't print that story. You'll be interfering with a police investigation."

"Oh, yes I can. Freedom of the press, and all that. So, I was right about Neville. Is he back in town?"

"We don't know that for sure. Not yet. How about a trade?" asked Cecily. "I've got a better story for you."

"Yeah? I'm listening."

"I'm going to be a mother."

Jade's mouth dropped open. "No kidding? Who's the father?" She slanted a speculative look at Mack. "You?"

"No way," said Mack, a little too firmly as far as Cecily was concerned.

She took Jade into Cyrus's study and, under Mack's watchful eye, told her about Hannah Barton. "She'll be here tomorrow. Give us a few days to get acquainted, and I'll give you an interview. How about next week some time?"

"Exclusive? With pictures?"

"Yes. Provided you hold off on any mention of Mack's presence."

"Mack *is* here because of your husband, isn't he? That's the only thing that makes sense."

"Ms. Jones," said Mack, "I'm sure the department will issue a press release when my assignment is ended. You don't work the crime beat, do you?"

"No. Society and human interest—that's my beat. But I have ambitions. The inside story of the capture of Neville Barton would be a coup for me."

"Hold off on mentioning me until Barton is in custody, and I'll give you an interview about his capture."

"So will I," said Cecily.

"A second interview? About your part in bringing your husband to justice?"

Cecily nodded. "We just don't want you to print anything now that will scare Neville off."

"It's a deal," said Jade, sticking out her hand. Cecily shook it.

"Glad you see it that way, " said Mack. "Let me show you out."

"I'll see you next week, Ms. Culpepper," said Jade.

"Fine," said Cecily. Once she and Mack were alone again, she said, "Do you think she'll keep her word?"

"I hope so. But she may decide one scoop now is worth more than two scoops later." He started down the hall toward the kitchen.

"Where are you going?"

"Back to my apartment."

"I think you should check my room. Someone may be hiding under my bed."

Mack gave her a heated look. "I'm pretty sure the uniforms checked out the entire house."

"I'm almost positive they didn't make it to the third floor. I'm sure they didn't look under the bed. Or under the covers, for that matter. What if a very thin burglar is hiding under the comforter?" She batted her eyelashes at him.

"Lead the way, Ms. Culpepper. Never let it be said that the Houston Police Department failed to do its job."

As they tiptoed up the stairs, Cecily whispered, "I told you we could be discreet."

Sixteen

Cecily called the Department of Protective Services the first thing Monday morning. Her plans to welcome Neville's daughter home were immediately thwarted by the mountain of paperwork needed to transfer custody from the State of Texas to her. She ended up keeping the appointment with the lawyer after another call verified that Ann Roberts handled adoption matters as well as divorce cases.

The attorney's advice had been to file the petition for stepparent adoption first—the adoption would be finalized in six months. Then she could file for divorce. Ms. Roberts had also assured Cecily that Neville would not have grounds to object to the adoption. According to her, Neville had forfeited his parental rights in about six different ways, including abandonment and failure to provide support.

Cyrus had received verification of Hannah's parentage on Tuesday, the documents transferring custody had been signed and filed the next day, and Hannah's arrival had been scheduled for Thursday at one o'clock.

That was today. Cecily glanced at the clock on Mack's

bedside table. Today, in a little more than seven hours, she would meet her daughter.

Cecily stretched, smiling at the ceiling.

Life would be perfect as soon as she met Hannah, and as soon as she figured out how her campaign to conquer Mack's fear of commitment was going. She turned on her side and looked at him. He was pretending to be asleep, but she knew better. His breathing had changed minutes ago—he was awake and waiting for her to attack him again.

Cecily would have gone nuts if she hadn't had Mack to keep her grounded—he was the only one around willing to listen to her obsess about Hannah. Of course, that could be because of the outstanding sex they'd been sharing. And because of his need to protect her— after the crime lab confirmed that the partial print they'd found on the broken decanter belonged to Neville, Mack had stayed close to her. Very close.

She flopped on her back again. He could make the first move this time—being in charge was fun, but exhausting. "It's been days since Neville tried to break in. What do think he's up to?" she asked.

Mack faked a yawn, then answered, "He's probably trying to figure out a way to get to you."

"That won't be easy. Maybe he'll give up and go away."

"I don't think so. He had to be pretty desperate to risk arrest again. He'll make another attempt. This time, we'll be ready for him."

"I wish he would call again—I hate waiting."

"I know. You barely give a man time to recover before you're on him to perform again."

Cecily snorted. "You've been asleep for hours. And you wake up ready. You're just waiting for me to take advantage of your morning erection."

"Yeah, I am."

"You're grinning, aren't you? I can almost see the dimple."

Mack reached over her and switched on the lamp. He was grinning.

Cecily fell back on the pillow and put her hands over her eyes. "Don't do that. I want to talk about Neville. Do you think he'll call again?"

"I don't know if he'll call, but I think he'll make another attempt to get to you." Mack tugged the covers down to her waist.

Cecily crossed her arms over her bare breasts. "Yes, but when? Soon?"

"Soon." Mack lowered his head and kissed her left breast. "He's probably stayed in the country longer than he intended. He's got to be anxious to get this over with."

Cecily squirmed, but only a little. She was getting better at resisting Mack's advances. The first few days, she'd gone weak every time he touched her—not the way to maintain control of the situation. "I know how he feels. I'm anxious, too. In a few hours, I'm going to meet my daughter."

"In a few hours, we'll have to stop meeting like this." He used his forefinger to trace around her stiff little nipple, then cupped her breast with his palm.

"You think?" Cecily said, trying not to wiggle in delight.

"Don't you?" He looked surprised.

"We've been sneaking around pretty successfully so far. Cyrus and Iris don't suspect a thing."

"That's different." He removed his hand from her breast.

Cecily felt a sudden chill. She had managed to distract him, but she couldn't remember why she'd thought that was what she wanted to do. Mack was too willing to give up their secret meetings. He was talking about ending their affair. She couldn't let that happen. Sex was all she had going for her in her campaign to entice him into a permanent relationship. "Different how? Because they're adults?"

"Yeah. And because they're sneaking around, too."

"There is that. But I think we'll find a way to be together, even after Hannah is here."

"What are you going to tell her about her father?"

"I don't know. I hate to be the one to tell her what a rotten human being he is."

"She may have figured that out for herself."

"I hope so. Maybe her mother or her grandmother told her. Mrs. Phillips did say that Hannah read the stories in the *Snoop* about him. And me. Oh, Lord, she probably thinks I'm an idiot. *You* did."

"Only until I saw you in person. One look, and I knew you couldn't be an idiot."

"Really? One look, and you knew I was smart?"

"Smart enough to be drooling over me."

Cecily sucked in a breath. "I was *not* drooling."

"Your mouth was hanging open, and you almost tripped over your own feet. Then you told me that whopper about getting carsick if you rode in the backseat."

"That wasn't a whopper."

"No? What was it?"

"A teensy-weensy little white lie."

"You lied to get close to me," Mack said smugly. He turned onto his side and grinned at her.

"So did you—telling me you were a chauffeur, and then a bodyguard."

"I was only doing my job."

"You do good work," said Cecily. Maybe she would make the first move, after all. She slipped her hand under the cover.

"I'm glad you approve," said Mack, rolling on top of her.

Thursday afternoon, Mack stood at the foot of the staircase, leaning against the newel post. He watched as Cecily paced the foyer, stopping every few steps to look out the window next to the front door. Lately, he found himself looking at Cecily every chance he got—time was running out for them, whether Cecily was ready to admit it or not.

He wouldn't be around much longer. Captain Morris was talking about ending the assignment. Once he moved out of the garage apartment, he wouldn't be able to see Cecily every day. Who was he kidding? He wouldn't see her at all. No matter what had happened between them, Armstrongs still did not move in the same circles as Culpeppers.

Today, she was waiting for Barton's daughter to be dropped off. Cyrus and Iris were waiting with her. Iris and Cyrus sat side by side on the bench, watching Cecily pace back and forth.

"They're late," Cecily said, as the grandfather clock chimed the hour. "They said she would be here at one o'clock. It's one o'clock."

"Just," said Iris. "Look. A car is turning into the driveway now."

A gray sedan stopped in the driveway. The door opened. A woman got out, leaned over, and said something to the passenger.

"Why isn't she getting out of the car? Oh, golly. She must be scared to death. I'm going to go—"

Iris put a hand on Cecily's arm. "Wait. Let the social worker handle it."

"Okay. It's all right. Here she comes. Oh, look. She's a blonde. And tall. Isn't she tall for eleven?"

"Scrawny is what she is," said Iris. "We'll have to put some meat on her bones."

"All knees and elbows," said Cyrus. "Just like Cecily was at her age."

Cecily opened the front door before the social worker rang the bell. "Hello, I'm Cecily Cul—Cecily Barton."

"Hello, Mrs. Barton. I'm Nancy Phillips. And, as you've guessed, this is Hannah Barton. Say hello, Hannah."

Mrs. Phillips was carrying a small suitcase.

"Hello," said Hannah, not moving from Mrs. Phillips's side.

"Let me take that," said Iris, reaching for the suitcase.

Mrs. Phillips gave Iris the suitcase, then turned to Hannah. "I'll be leaving now, Hannah. If I don't see you again, have a merry Christmas." She gave the little girl a hug. "You have my number if you need any help with anything."

"Yes, thank you," said Hannah.

"I'll walk you to your car," said Cyrus, taking Mrs. Phillips's arm.

Cecily stared at Hannah. She looked like she wanted to hug her, too, but she hesitated.

Mack was pretty sure the sight of Neville's daughter had frozen Cecily immobile. He pushed away from the newel post.

"Are you hungry," asked Iris. "Have you had lunch?"

"Yes, ma'am. Thank you. We ate before we came here." Hannah's gaze darted from Iris to Mack, then settled on the huge Christmas tree in the foyer. She tilted her head back, staring at the gilt angel on the top of the tree. "At McDonald's."

"Oh . . . good. If you get hungry later, come on back to the kitchen. I've got Christmas cookies baking. I'm the cook, Hannah. My name is Iris."

"Pleased to meet you," said Hannah, with a nod of her head.

"Yeah, Hannah." Mack knelt in front of Hannah. Eye to eye with her, he said, "Iris is the cook—and a very good one, too. I'm Mack, the chauffeur. The guy who looks like Santa Claus is Cecily's father. You can call him Mr. Culpepper."

"Does he do that on purpose?" asked Hannah, her eyes wide. "Look like Santa, I mean."

"Yeah. Cyrus is eccentric. Do you know what that means?" Mack stood up and took Hannah's hand.

"Crazy? Like her?" Hannah tilted her head in Cecily's direction.

"You think I'm crazy?" blurted Cecily. Hannah had succeeded in jolting her out of her frozen state. "Why?"

"I read it in the newspaper. You're a madcap heiress. Madcap means crazy. I looked it up in the dictionary," Hannah said solemnly.

"Really? I thought it meant impulsive. But I never looked it up. I'm not crazy, Hannah. And neither is Cyrus. Don't be afraid of us."

"I'm not scared." Hannah moved closer to Mack. "Do you know where my dad is?"

"No, Hannah. I haven't seen him in a long time."

"Neither have I."

There was an awkward silence. Hannah clung to Mack's hand and looked at the Christmas tree again. "Big place, isn't it?" said Mack. Hannah looked overwhelmed to him. So did Cecily, for that matter. "Cecily will take you on a tour, I'll bet. You need to be able to find your way around. No one wants you to get lost."

Cecily nodded her head vigorously. "Oh, yes. That's right. You need to be able to find your way around the house—it's your home now." She flashed Mack a grateful smile. "Good idea. Would you like to see your room, Hannah?"

"I have a room here?" Hannah's eyes widened.

"You certainly do. You're going to live here, you know. Your room used to be my room. It's on the second floor. We can take the elevator if you want." Cecily picked up Hannah's suitcase.

"An elevator? Is this a palace?"

"No. Just a big house. Too big for only three people. We're glad you came, Hannah. Now there will be four of us."

"Four? What about Mack?" asked Hannah, leaning into his side. "I thought he lived here, too."

"Not in the house, but close by. Mack has an apartment over the garage. Come on, Hannah." Cecily held out her hand, breathing a sigh of relief when Hannah took it.

Cyrus returned from escorting Mrs. Phillips to her car, and Mack walked out the open front door as he walked in. "Mack? Where are you going?" Cyrus asked.

"I need to gas up the cars. I'll see you at dinner, Hannah. Like I said, Iris is a great cook. See ya."

"Bye, Mack," said Hannah.

"I've got some work to do. Welcome, Hannah," said Cyrus.

As they followed Cyrus down the center hall, Cecily pointed out the rooms. "That's Cyrus's study. You can go in there when the door is open. If it's closed, he's working. Or sneaking a cigar."

"He smokes?" asked Hannah.

"He tries. He's not supposed to—smoking is bad for you, you know." At Hannah's nod, Cecily added, "It's all right to tell on him if you catch him with a cigar."

"Really?"

"I heard that," Cyrus growled.

Cecily winked at Hannah. "Really. It's for his own good." She opened the pocket doors to the family room. "This is where we spend most of our evenings—the television is in here."

"Another tree?" said Hannah, eyeing the gaily wrapped packages under the tree.

"This is the family tree. The one in the foyer is for show. A few of those packages have your name on them, by the way."

"Which ones?"

"I'll show you later. Let's finish the tour first." Back in the center hall, Cecily pointed to the doors in the opposite wall. "The living room and the dining room are across the hall, and the kitchen is at the end of the hall. We'll check those out later." Cecily led Hannah to the elevator between Cyrus's study and the family room.

"It's not a very big elevator," said Hannah once they were inside.

"No. Would you like to punch the button for the second floor?"

"Okay." Hannah pushed the button.

When the door opened, Cecily got off and led Hannah to her room. The door was open. Hannah stopped in the doorway. Behind her, Cecily tried looking at the room as if she were seeing it for the first time.

Her four-poster bed had a white eyelet canopy, which matched the dust ruffle. The yellow-and-white checked spread was piled with pillows covered with green and yellow checks and prints. The window seat had lemon yellow and grass green cushions.

"If you don't like the colors, we can change them. Maybe you would prefer pink? And I know there aren't any toys, but I didn't know what kind to get—are you a doll or a stuffed-animal person? I like both, myself. Mine are in the attic. I should have brought them down, but I didn't think about it until just this minute. Hannah?"

"It's beautiful," Hannah sighed, taking one step into the room. "The most beautiful room I've ever seen." She smiled.

Relieved, Cecily laughed. "I'm glad you like it. Your bathroom is through that door." She pointed to the door on the right. "The other door is the closet. Shall we unpack your bag?"

"Yes, please."

Cecily picked up the suitcase and put it on the bed. "I'm very glad you're here, Hannah. I'm sorry I didn't know about you sooner."

"I guess my dad didn't tell you about me."

"No. No, he didn't. I don't know why."

"Maybe he thought you wouldn't want me," said Hannah.

"If he thought that, he was wrong. I've always wanted a daughter." Cecily giggled. "And having one who can walk and talk and dress herself makes things much easier for me."

Another grin curved Hannah's lips. "Because I'm not a baby."

"Right. Not that I have anything against babies, you understand. But I've always thought eleven-year-olds were special—eleven was my favorite age."

"It was? Why?"

"Because when you're eleven, you're old enough to understand almost all the things grown-ups talk about, but young enough for kid stuff."

"Is getting old bad?"

"Not bad so much as inevitable. Except for the lost boys."

"*Peter and Wendy*. I read that book."

"Did you? Do you like to read?"

"Yes. Gran said I always had my nose in a book."

"There used to be a bookcase in this room—it must be in the attic. And my books—the ones I had when I was your age—are around here somewhere. We'll look for them later." Cecily hung the last pair of jeans in the closet. "There. All unpacked. What would you like to do now? Shall I show you my room?"

"Okay. But . . ." Hannah frowned.

"What, Hannah? Ask me anything. I want you to be happy here."

"When is my dad coming home?"

"Oh . . . dear." Cecily mirrored Hannah's frown. Nothing like getting hit with one of the hard questions before she was ready. She took a breath, then said, "Well, maybe we had better talk about your father. This may take a while, Hannah. Let's sit down. You take the window seat, and I'll sit on the bed."

When they were seated, Cecily said, "Hannah, I've never been a . . . a parent before. So I may not always get things right. But I think it's important for us to be honest with each other." She used up her first breath and paused to take another one. "The fact is, I don't think Neville—your dad—is ever coming back. Not for us, anyway."

"He left you behind, too, didn't he?" Hannah gave her a solemn look. "I read about it in the *Scoop.*"

"Yes. Yes, he did."

"Did he tell you he was coming back?"

"No, he didn't. He didn't even tell me he was leaving."

"He told my mother he would come back for us once he made his fortune. That's what she told me."

"Oh . . . well . . ." Cecily didn't know what to say.

"He lied," Hannah said matter-of-factly.

"Yes. I'm afraid he did. How did you know?"

"Gran told me he wasn't coming back. And I read about him in the paper, too. He did have a fortune, but he didn't come after me. I was pretty sure he wasn't going to even before that." She looked out the window.

"But I kinda hoped he would," Hannah said, her voice soft.

Cecily got up and walked to the window seat. "I know about that kind of hoping, Hannah. My mother left me."

Hannah met her gaze. "Your mother died?"

"No. She left. About that fortune, Hannah, the truth is, your father stole it. If he does return, he's going to jail. That's how I know he isn't coming back to get us."

Hannah nodded. "Why do you think he left us?"

"I don't know. What I do know for certain is that it isn't because there's anything wrong with us." Cecily knelt down so that she was eye to eye with Hannah. "I promise you this, Hannah. I will never leave you."

Hannah's eyes widened. "Truly?" she whispered.

"Truly. Cross my heart and hope to die." Cecily made an X over her heart.

A giggle came out of Hannah, a happy little-girl giggle. "Stick a needle in my eye."

"If I ever tell a lie," finished Cecily. "How about a hug?"

Hannah launched herself off the window seat into Cecily's open arms. Cecily hugged her fiercely, blinking away tears. "Now, tell me what you want for Christmas. We have some shopping to do."

Hannah looked around the room. "I think Christmas has already come."

"Well, if you think of anything special, just let me know. I'm famous for my gifts, you know. I try to get people exactly what they want."

"What if they don't tell you what they want?"

"I figure it out, anyway."

"How?" asked Hannah.

"I watch them. I see what they like and what they don't like. I already know you like books. So I could get you books for Christmas."

"But you don't know which ones I've already read—except for *Peter and Wendy*. Or which one I really, really want."

"Not yet. I'll find out."

"Even if I don't tell you?"

"Even if. Is that a challenge?"

"Maybe. I'll have to think about it. Can I see your room now?"

"Sure. Do you want to take the elevator or the stairs?"

"Elevator, please." In the doorway, Hannah stopped and looked back at the room. "This isn't really my room, is it? Not forever."

"It's yours for as long as we both live here. But we might move to another house someday." Cecily hoped it would be to the house Mack was looking for, but she wasn't ready to tell Hannah about her and Mack. She didn't know if there would be a Cecily and Mack much longer.

"Move? Both of us?"

"Yes. We're family, Hannah. Families stick together."

"Not all of them. Your mother didn't. My dad didn't stick."

"No. But Neville isn't . . ."

". . . a nice man?"

"Exactly. But there are nice men in the world. One of us might get married someday. That would involve a move."

Hannah giggled. "I'm too young to get married."

"And I'm still married to your father. So we'll probably be living here for a while."

They walked across the hall to the elevator.

"You have mistletoe everywhere," said Hannah, pointing to the bunch hanging from the light fixture in the hall. "Third floor?"

Cecily nodded, and Hannah pushed the button.

The elevator door opened, and Cecily let Hannah exit into her sitting room. Hannah headed for the small Christmas tree in the corner by her worktable. "Another tree!"

"Just a small one, for decoration." Cecily pointed to her worktable. "I use that table to wrap packages, and I needed a Christmas tree for inspiration."

"Can I help wrap presents?"

"Yes, you may. I'd like that. But first we have to go buy a few more." Cecily sat on the sofa and patted the cushion next to her. When Hannah was sitting next to her, she said, "I just had a thought, Hannah. Have you heard the saying 'Two wrongs don't make a right'?"

"Sure," said Hannah.

"Well, I think in our case, they do. Neville left you, and he left me. That's two wrongs. But if he hadn't left both of us, we never would have met. And this feels right to me."

"To me, too." Hannah gave her another one of her sunny smiles. "Getting left is something we have in common. Having things in common is good, isn't it?"

"Yes. Yes, it is."

"Where did your mother go? Does she visit you?"

"She lives in Italy now. She never visits."

"Oh. Italy is the country that looks like a boot. I got an A in geography."

"I knew you were smart. I could tell. That's one more thing we have in common. How do you feel about Christmas?"

"I love Christmas. I think your house is so pretty, with all the decorations. And you've got three trees—I never knew people could have more than one at a time. I wish . . ."

"What, honey? What do you wish?"

"That I could have gotten here in time to help decorate the trees."

Cecily grinned at her. "You know what? Mack doesn't have a tree. We'll get another one and help him decorate it. How about that?"

"Cool." Hannah drew her brows together in a frown. "But I thought you didn't like Christmas. I read about 'Cecily's Christmas Curse' in the *Scoop*."

"You read the *Snoop*—I mean, the *Scoop*—a lot."

"I wasn't supposed to, but whenever Gran started cussing, I knew there was something about my dad in the paper, so I would. I won't read it if you don't want me to."

"I think you're old enough to read the newspaper, as long as you know not everything you read is true. Cyrus always says, believe nothing you read and only half of what you see. But then, Cyrus is a cynic."

"What's a cynic?"

"A grumpy old man. But he has a good heart."

Hannah giggled. "Does he know he looks like Santa Claus?"

"Oh, yes. He knows."

"He must like Christmas a lot."

"Well, I'm not so sure about that. But I do. I think my Christmas curse is over, Hannah. I just got the best Christmas present ever. You." Cecily gave Hannah another hug. "If you would rather be on this floor with me, there is an extra room up here. It's empty now, but we could turn it into a bedroom in nothing flat."

"Oh, no. I love my room. I don't want to move."

"Okay. Cyrus's room is right across the hall from yours. In case you get scared in the night."

A small frown wrinkled Hannah's brow. "There aren't any pets here, are there?"

"Not at the moment. Why?"

"I wouldn't be afraid if I had a kitten."

"Oh. A kitten. Well. Isn't that interesting?" Cecily smiled, recalling all the kittens waiting to be adopted at the animal shelter. A kitten with a bow around its neck would make a perfect Christmas present. "Is there anything else you need to make you feel at home?"

"Friends. I made friends at Little Lambs. I've been there for almost a month, you know."

"I know. You'll make more friends when you start school," Cecily assured her. "I talked to the principal at the middle school, by the way. She said you can wait and start after the Christmas holidays. I thought you would like an extra week to get used to being in a new place. But if you want to make friends sooner . . . ?"

"I can wait." Hannah tilted her head to one side. "Can I ask a question?"

"Ask anything," Cecily said bravely. Surely she wasn't going to ask about the birds and the bees—not this soon.

"Am I going to have an allowance?"

"Why, yes. You are."

"How much? I want to know because I would like to buy presents for my friends at Little Lambs Children's Home. There are twenty-six of them. Twenty-six presents would cost a lot."

"Not that much. Besides, we don't have to worry about money." Cecily grinned at Hannah. "Cyrus is loaded."

"So I can buy the presents?"

"You can. And that won't count as part of your allowance. I'm not sure what the going rate for an eleven-year-old's allowance is—I don't remember what I got. Did your grandmother give you an allowance?"

"Uh-huh. I got two dollars a week, plus lunch money."

"We'll start with that. Oh! You might be interested in this—Iris pays for chores."

"She does? What kind of chores?"

"Clearing the table after meals, taking out the garbage.

That kind of thing. You can ask her. She may have to adjust her pay scale for inflation—it's been a long time since she paid me for those chores."

"When can I ask her?"

"How about right now? I think it's time to try those Christmas cookies she's been baking all week. Cookies and milk?"

"Yes, please. I like this place," said Hannah. "I like you."

"Oh, Hannah, I like you, too. I think this is going to work out just fine."

Seventeen

By the following Thursday, the day of the promised interview with Jade Jones, Cecily was exhausted. She hadn't realized how hard parenting was—even for a child old enough to walk and talk and dress herself. As she patted concealer onto the dark circles under her eyes, she couldn't keep grinning at her reflection. She was exhausted, but feeling very, very useful.

And happy.

For the most part. There were a few clouds on the horizon—a stormy one that resembled Neville's too-perfect features, and the one with the silver lining, which she hoped was not about to tarnish.

If Neville and Mack were clouds, then Hannah was the sun, shining her smile on everyone in the house. Cecily credited Hannah's Gran with giving her grand-daughter a solid foundation built on love. That strong beginning had to be the reason Hannah had adjusted to her new home and family so quickly. There had been only a few problems, and most of those had revolved around Neville.

Hannah said she knew her father was not going to

come for her, but Cecily got the definite impression that Hannah's heart still held a tiny seed of hope that Neville might show up someday. She had read Cecily a story she'd written about a Robin Hood–like character who'd left his wife and child, a son, to make his fortune so he could give it to all the poor people in the kingdom. Once everyone had everything they needed, the hero returned home to his family.

Of course, they all lived happily ever after.

Cecily didn't know what to do about Hannah's longing for a father, but it was early days yet, and she was figuring out how to be a mother day by day. That had to be what was so exhausting—weighing every act, every word, for its possible effect on Hannah.

Cyrus complained that the kid had taken over. Cecily discounted his grumbles—she noticed that he didn't kick Hannah out of his study whenever she dared breach his fortress. That was several times a day now. The first time, Hannah had gained entry by telling Cyrus she needed to use his unabridged dictionary. The first word she'd looked up had been *inflation*. That had prompted Cyrus to give her an impromptu lecture on economics and the advantages of the capitalist system.

Since Hannah had apparently stayed awake during his monologue, Cyrus was convinced she was a born entrepreneur. If she was, she must have inherited her business bent from Neville. Cecily didn't mention that to Cyrus. She knew he would teach Hannah ethical behavior along with any other life lessons he imparted.

Hannah spent time with Iris, too. Her grandmother had taught her a few recipes, which she showed Iris, and Iris, slipping into the role of honorary granny, reciprocated by teaching Hannah a few new ones. She and Hannah baked more Christmas cookies, then moved on to candy. A few more samples of their concoctions, and she was going to have trouble fitting into her clothes.

Mack also had a new admirer—apparently his dimple worked on preteens as well as adult women. It didn't take a psychiatrist to figure out that Hannah's puppy worship of Mack had a lot to do with her need for a father. On their shopping trips, while she had suggested gifts for Mack's family and for the girls at the Little Lambs home, Hannah had turned to Mack for advice on appropriate gifts for the boys.

When Hannah had said she wished she could see her friends open their presents, Mack had come up with the idea for a Christmas party.

She should have thought of that—she had planned many a holiday party, acting as Cyrus's social secretary and hostess.

Cecily dipped a brush in the powder pot, then brushed the powder on her face. If he ever got over his commitment issues, Mack would be a good father. And a wonderful husband. Cecily frowned. Too bad she didn't have a clue how he felt about taking on one or both of those jobs. So much for being in control; Mack had set the tone of their relationship—light—from the beginning. The few times she'd gotten up the nerve to ask a relationship question, he'd deflected her with a grin or a teasing remark.

She had to come to grips with the fact that Mack might not be around much longer. There had been no sign of Neville Barton for almost two weeks. The H.P.D. had begun making noises about having one of their detectives on the scene indefinitely. So far, Cyrus had managed to convince George Deeds to put pressure on the chief of police to leave Mack in place. But if something didn't happen soon, Mack would leave.

Not that she couldn't still see him. But Cecily feared

that once he moved away, she would lose whatever attraction she did have for him. She couldn't blame him because he didn't want to talk about their future—hadn't she set out to show him that she was the perfect woman for a brief, no-strings affair? She was convenient, willing, and eager to be with him as much as possible.

She yawned. That might explain her exhaustion. What with making love with Mack every chance she got, spending hours a day in on-the-job motherhood training, planning a Christmas party for twenty-six children, and preparing to be interviewed by the *Snoop*, she didn't have much time to spend sleeping.

She missed Olivia. If she'd ever needed her best friend more, she couldn't remember when. Olivia didn't have any more experience with children than she did, but she knew a lot about men. She could have used a few of Olly's cheeky comments to keep her grounded. But after the Texans failed to make the playoffs, Olly had taken Rory to the Bahamas. They weren't coming back until after New Year's.

She and Mack were still keeping their affair to themselves, so she couldn't talk about him with Iris or Cyrus. Hannah was too young and impressionable to take Olivia's place as confidante. So, in the continuing melodrama of Cecily and Mack, she was on her own.

There was a knock on her dressing room door. "Come in," said Cecily.

Hannah pushed the door open. "Do I look all right?" She twirled around, showing off one of her new outfits, a red-and-green plaid skirt and a red sweater.

"You look adorable. And very Christmasy. I thought you were going to save that skirt and sweater for the party."

"I was. But I decided jeans and my red sweatshirt with the Christmas tree on it would be better 'cause most of the other kids won't be dressed up. The invitation did say casual dress."

"Right. Good point. Jeans **prob**ably would be better, considering the games we have planned."

"You look pretty, too," said Hannah, giving her an admiring glance. "How long will the interview last?"

Cecily pulled a brush through her hair, then gave her head a shake to settle her hair into place. "I'm not sure. If I had to guess, I would say not more than an hour. Why? Do you have something else to do?"

Hannah nodded. "I asked Mack if he would take me shopping. He said he would, as soon as we're done."

"Shopping? I thought we'd finished. Well, I can always look for a few more stocking stuffers."

"You can't come with us," said Hannah, her tone decisive. "I'm shopping for a present for you. Iris told me that if you came along, you'd peek."

"Iris ratted on me, did she? Well, you don't have to stay for the whole interview, just for a picture. I'll ask Ms. Jones to take the picture first, then you can go with Mack."

"Okay." Hannah jumped up and twirled around again. "I can't wait until Saturday. I've never given a Christmas party before—only birthday. And Gran was the hostess for those—I was the guest of honor. Right?"

"That's right." Once Cecily had explained to Hannah that she would be the hostess of the party, Hannah had taken her role very seriously. She had consulted with Iris about the menu, and with Cyrus about the location. She had decided on hamburgers and hot dogs grilled on the indoor grill. They'd decided to open the pocket doors between the living room and dining room and have most of the party there, except for the gift-opening ceremony. That would take place around the large tree in the foyer and would be the last event before the party ended.

"I think I heard the doorbell ring. That's probably the reporter and the photographer from the *Scoop*."

When the photo session was over, Cecily remained with Jade in Cyrus's study. Iris called Mack and told him Hannah was ready to go shopping. Mack found Hannah in the family room, staring at the pile of presents under the tree. "What's up, squirt?"

"There sure are a lot of presents under this tree," said Hannah. "Almost as many as are under the tree in the foyer."

"I counted ten with your name on them," said Mack. "I think that on Christmas morning, you'll find everything you wanted under that tree."

Hannah gave him a solemn look. She shook her head. "I don't think so."

"Why not? Cecily is very good at figuring out what people want."

"I know." Hannah's expression turned mischievous. "She got you exactly the right thing."

"Yeah? Care to give me a hint?"

"Nope." Hannah pressed her lips together and made a turning motion with her thumb and forefinger.

"Your lips are sealed?"

"Tick-tock, my lips are locked." She took one last look at the tree, then got her coat off the chair. "I'm ready to go now. What are you going to get Cecily for Christmas?"

Mack took her coat from her and held it while she got her arms in the sleeves. "I don't know." Contrary to his usual habit, he'd actually spent time trying to come up with an idea for a present for Cecily. He'd drawn a blank—what could he possibly give a woman who had everything? "You got any good ideas?" He held out his hand.

"Yes. I know what I'm going to get her." Hannah took his hand, and they walked out the front door.

Mack had parked his truck in the driveway. He got Hannah settled in the truck, seat belt fastened, then started the engine. "Where to?"

"We have to go to an art supply place. Cecily is an artist, you know."

"No, I didn't know that. I knew she used to work at an art gallery—that's a place that sells paintings."

"I know. She explained it to me. And she showed me some of the pictures she drew when she was in college. She's very good. Cecily draws kittens and puppies really well."

"Huh. Imagine that. She told me she didn't know how to do anything useful."

Hannah frowned. "She told me she didn't have any talent—she said she was a greeting card artist, not a real artist. Do you think Cecily has self-esteem problems?"

Mack shot her a surprised look. "Where did you hear about self-esteem problems?"

"From the shrinks at the orphans' home. They called them counselors, but they were shrinks."

"Oh. Well, I think Cecily doesn't know what a great girl she is. Maybe we should tell her."

"Yeah. And show her. She said she wasn't a real artist because a lot of pictures of kittens and puppies end up on birthday cards, you know? But I think she likes drawing them, so I'm going to get her sketch pads and charcoal. Then I'll tell her how good her pictures are. Every one."

"That's a very good plan, Hannah. I think you may be as good at this gift thing as Cecily is. And I know of an art supply store. Maybe I'll find something there I can give her. If you don't mind me stealing your idea."

"I don't mind. You could get her some water colors. Or pastels—those are kinda like chalk. I looked artist stuff up on the Internet. Stealing ideas isn't the same as stealing money, is it?"

"Not this kind of idea."

"I didn't think so." Hannah was quiet for a minute, then asked, "Did my dad steal money from you?"

"What?" Her question surprised him. "No. I never met your father."

"But you don't like him," said Hannah.

"What makes you say that?"

"Well, you don't, do you?"

"No. I don't like Neville Barton." Mack winced. He could have said something less definite—Hannah was just a kid. He looked at her. His blunt answer hadn't bothered her, as far as he could tell.

"Cyrus doesn't like my dad, either. He says my dad hurt his girls—he meant Cecily and me—and he doesn't like people who hurt people he loves. He said love is important for families. More important than money." Hannah giggled. " 'Course, he's loaded, so that's easy for him to say."

Mack barked a laugh. "Loaded, huh? Well, then, are you ready to spend some more of his money?"

"Yes. He gave me a hundred dollars. I'm supposed to get two presents for Cecily—one from me and one from him. Cyrus doesn't shop well. Iris told me he usually gives people money for Christmas."

"Does he? I guess Cecily doesn't approve of that."

"Nope. She says giving money and gift certificates is lazy. And Iris said it showed a lack of imagination."

"Right. I've heard them say that. Are you going to get Cyrus's present for Cecily at the art supply store, or is there somewhere else we need to go after that?"

"I thought maybe we could go to that art gallery where she used to work—she needs a painting for her bedroom. I was going to look for one with dogs and cats—just so she'd know that they don't all end up on greeting cards. I want her to know she's talented."

"That's a good idea, Hannah, but I don't think

you've got enough money for that. Paintings at that gallery cost a lot more than one hundred dollars."

"Cyrus said I could charge it to him. It is his gift, after all."

"Oh, well. In that case, we'll hit Objet d'Art before we go home." Mack thought about the ugly painting over his fireplace. "I'm not sure we'll find any cat and dog pictures there, though. We might have to try a few places before we find what you want."

"That's okay. Shopping is fun. Especially with you," Hannah said. "You never said why you don't like my dad."

"For the same reason Cyrus said—I think dads should take care of their families, not run away and leave them."

"Not even if they have to seek their fortune?"

"Not even then. It doesn't take a fortune to take care of a wife and a couple of children."

Hannah nodded. "I figured that out when I was nine. Gran didn't have a lot of money, but she took good care of me. All you need is enough for a home and food and clothes." She slanted a look at him. "Do you have that much money?"

"Yes." Mack gave her a wary look out of the corner of his eye. Was the kid matchmaking? That seemed unlikely. He'd heard Cecily explain the adoption-and-divorce scenario to Hannah. She knew that Cecily and her father were still man and wife.

And she didn't know that he and Cecily were having an affair. Mack shifted his position on the bench seat. He really hated sneaking around. But he would have hated not having Cecily in his bed even more.

"So why don't you have a wife and children?" Hannah asked.

"I have commitment issues—that means I'm not ready to settle down," said Mack.

"Will you be ready soon?"

"I don't know, Hannah." Mack spotted the art supply store and turned into the parking lot. "Here we are," he said, grateful that he could end Hannah's speculation about his ability to support a family. He could never support a family that included not one but two heiresses—Cyrus had confided that he'd had his attorney draft a codicil including Hannah in his will.

There was no point in even dreaming a thing like that was possible. He and Cecily were having an intense, exciting, and brief affair, emphasis on the brief. As long as he kept that firmly in mind, he could enjoy the time they spent together. He would save feeling guilty about deceiving Hannah, Iris, and Cyrus—three people he'd come to care about—for later.

After a successful shopping trip—they had found a oil painting of a Persian cat at Kmart—Mack drove home. "Let's take these packages to my place. We can wrap them there. I'm not very good at wrapping packages, though."

"I am. I'll go get the wrapping paper from Cecily—she has tons of it." Hannah got out of the truck. "Thank you for taking me shopping, Mack."

"No problem, Squirt. Thank you for helping me find the right present for Cecily." He had ended up getting her an easel. Pretty lame, now that he thought about it. She probably had an easel.

At breakfast the next day, Cyrus said, "I noticed a few new presents under the tree in the family room."

"Those are the ones Mack and I got," said Hannah. "I really love shopping," she said with a satisfied sigh.

Iris and Cecily exchanged a high five. "Yes!" said Cecily. It was amazing how many ways Hannah reminded her of herself—she could almost believe that they were related by blood. Hannah was smarter, of course. And she had a serious side—no one would ever call her a madcap.

Hannah looked up from her pancakes. "What did I say?"

"Iris and I love shopping, too. Cyrus and Mack don't get it."

"Is it a girl thing?" asked Hannah.

"Must be," said Cyrus. "Makes sense. When there were cavemen—and women—the men were hunters and the women were gatherers."

"That's not right," said Iris. "Women had to hunt for food before they could gather it."

"Yeah," said Cecily. "Shopping requires both skills, too—hunting for bargains and gathering them in."

"So what you're saying is that men are completely useless?" asked Mack, pouring syrup on his pancakes.

"No!" came a chorus of three female voices.

"You have your uses," said Cecily, winking at him.

He grinned, making her blush. "Yeah? Like what, for instance?"

"You drive us to the stores," said Hannah. She looked at Cyrus. "And you pay for the things we buy."

"Smart kid," said Cyrus. "Already knows what males are good for." He got a stunned look on his face. "Oh, good God. How long will it be before we have hordes of young men coming around to see Hannah?" Bringing his brows together, he gave Hannah a suspicious look. "You don't have a boyfriend, do you?"

Hannah looked him in the eye. "Cyrus, I'm eleven. Eleven-year-olds don't have boyfriends."

"How old do you have to be these days?" asked Iris, bringing another stack of pancakes to the table. "Before you have a boyfriend, that is."

"Thirty," said Cyrus, reaching for the newspapers next to his place mat. "At least."

"Ah. That explains why Cecily doesn't—" Iris stopped.

Hannah giggled. "Cecily is married. She can't have a boyfriend."

Cecily's gaze went to Mack. He was frowning. Did he think of himself as her boyfriend? Or not? She really did have to get up the nerve to talk to him. Soon.

"Right. No boyfriends for either one of you. Ever. That will make my life a lot easier," said Cyrus. He handed the folded *Houston Scoop* to Hannah. "Here. Look for your picture."

Hannah opened the newspaper. "Oh! Look, Cecily. Our picture is right on the first page."

Cecily leaned over and looked at the paper. The headline read, *Cecily's Christmas Blessing.* "Oh, good. They gave up the alliteration. And the picture turned out well, too. I think I'll call Jade and ask her for a copy. We can have it framed."

"You and that reporter have gotten awfully chummy," said Cyrus. "Considering all the grief she's put you through over the years."

Cecily quickly scanned the rest of the story. "Nothing grief-inducing in this story. Maybe I should have gotten chummy with her sooner." She knew Jade was on her best behavior because she wanted the story of Neville's capture, but Cecily kept that to herself.

She hadn't told Hannah that she and Cyrus intended to help the police recapture Neville. What would Hannah think once she found that out? She wanted to believe that Hannah would forgive her—better yet, that she would think there was nothing to forgive. But that might be wishful thinking on her part.

"Is everyone sure we have everything we need for the party tomorrow?" asked Iris. "I've got the food front under control, except I think we might need a few more gallons of ice cream."

"Is there room in the freezer?" asked Cecily.

"I think so."

"We have dozens and dozens of cookies to go with the ice cream," said Hannah. "But I have to fill the favor bags today." She planned to give each of her guests a bag of Christmas cookies and candy to take back with them.

"Maybe we'd better go over the checklist after breakfast," said Cecily. "Just to make sure everything is under control."

"I'll be in my study," said Cyrus.

"Do you want me to hang around? In case you need to go for more supplies?" asked Mack, rising from the table. "If not, I'm going downtown. I need to check in," Mack said.

Cecily gave him a startled look. Did that mean his boss had called him? Her heart stuttered. He couldn't be leaving this week. She'd counted on his being around at least until after Christmas.

If he left before then, no matter what the headline in the *Scoop* said, her Christmas curse was still in force.

That Friday morning, in a motel room a few miles from River Oaks, Neville Barton saw the photograph and read the story about Cecily and his daughter in the *Houston Scoop*. Cecily had taken in Hannah—she'd had a tendency to fret over strays, he remembered. He'd had to claim he had a serious allergy to pet dander to keep her from taking in every cat and dog they came across.

Hannah. Silly name. Old-fashioned, just like Alice, his first wife. He'd almost forgotten about them. He had taken to reading the *Scoop* as well as the *Chronicle* because he'd been looking for an announcement about the next party at the Culpepper mansion—Cyrus always had some kind of fancy gathering during the holiday season. He hadn't expected a children's party—he would have preferred a nighttime event—but he'd take what he could get. He had already been in Houston longer than he'd anticipated.

Neville read the story again.

According to the newspaper, there would be a Christmas party at the Culpepper mansion for the twenty-six children currently resident at the Little Lambs Children's Home on the twentieth of December—tomorrow, in other words. He scanned the party plans—games, food, cake and ice cream—until he came to the item he wanted. Yes, there it was—there would be a Santa Claus to pass out gifts to all the guests. The reporter had noted that even though Cyrus Culpepper looked the part, he would not be donning a Santa Claus costume for the occasion.

Neville didn't understand that remark. Cyrus had never looked like old Saint Nick to him, but he hadn't seen the man in three years. Neville tossed the paper aside and reached for the Yellow Pages. Now, what was the name of that agency the Culpeppers used for temporary help? Ah, yes: Heaven Helpers. Neville looked the number up and dialed.

When a woman answered, Neville used another of his many talents. In a perfect imitation of Cyrus's voice, he said, "Hello. Cyrus Culpepper here. I believe my daughter hired a Santa for a children's party tomorrow."

"Let me check. That's right, Mr. Culpepper, we have that booked for Saturday from two until six."

"Well, we won't be needing a Santa, after all. At my daughter's insistence, I'm taking over the role." Neville imitated Cyrus's chuckle. "But please, send me a bill anyway. I don't want to ruin some other Santa's Christmas."

"Why, thank you. And if I may say so, Mr. Culpepper, you'll make a very good Santa Claus. Your beard is the real thing."

Another chuckle, and Neville hung up the telephone. He went back to the telephone book. Now all he had to do was find a costume shop.

He had a way into the Culpepper mansion.

Eighteen

Saturday evening after the party was over and the
guests had gone, everyone headed for the kitchen.
Cecily followed the others, stopping along the way to
check each of the downstairs rooms. When she got to
the kitchen, Cyrus, Iris, and Mack were at the table.
Hannah was standing in front of the open refrigerator
door.

"Did any of you see the Santa Claus leave?" asked
Cecily.

"I didn't," said Iris, getting up and walking to the refrigerator. "What are you looking for, Hannah?"

"Something to eat. I'm starving."

"That's not possible," said Cyrus. "You had a ham-
burger and two hot dogs. Plus a handful of cookies and
two dishes of ice cream."

"Hours ago," said Hannah, staring into the depths of
the refrigerator.

"How about some scrambled eggs?" asked Iris, taking the egg carton out of the refrigerator. "You must
have the contents memorized by now. Close the door,
Hannah."

"Breakfast food?" asked Hannah, closing the refrigerator door. "For dinner?"

"I hadn't planned on cooking dinner tonight. I thought we'd all be full from the party food. If you don't want scrambled eggs, how about an omelet? Omelets are suitable for breakfast or supper."

"An omelet sounds good to me. I'm feeling a little peckish myself. I cooked more than I ate," said Cyrus. "I want sweet pepper and onion in mine."

"Omelets all around, then?" asked Iris. "Egg white for Cyrus, of course." She began cracking eggs, separating the yolks from the whites for some of them.

"I want mushrooms in mine," said Cecily, joining Iris at the counter. She opened a cabinet and took out a cutting board. "I'll chop the peppers and onions. I wish I knew where that Santa got off to."

"He must have gone out with the last batch of kids," said Iris. "What kind of omelet do you want, Mack?"

"Is there any cheese?"

"Cheddar or Swiss?" asked Iris.

"Cheddar, please," he said. "And mushrooms, onions, and pepper. If it's not too much trouble."

"I want cheese in my omelet, too," said Cyrus. "Something to make the egg whites look yellow."

Iris exchanged a look with Cecily. "All right," she said. "I don't think a little cheese will kill you."

"Can I grate the cheese?" asked Hannah, opening the refrigerator again. She found the block of cheddar and put it on the counter.

"Sure," said Iris. "Do you know where the grater is?"

"Yep. Why were you looking for the Santa Claus?" Hannah asked, getting the grater from the cabinet.

"Santa Claus isn't going to have a very good Christmas, I'm afraid. He left without his check," said Cecily.

"Send it to the agency," Cyrus said. "They'll get it to him."

"I will, but I had a cash tip for him, too. Oh, well, I'll just write another check and send it along to the agency, too." She got the onions and peppers and began chopping.

"That was the best party, ever," Hannah said, grating away. "Everyone said so. And Miss Wilson said if we hadn't given the party, there wouldn't have been one this year. Donations are down because of the economy." She shot an accusing look at Cyrus. "You said it was going to get better."

"It will. I explained about business cycles, remember? And I didn't say when it would get better—probably next year some time. By the way, thank you for inviting me to your party—I had a real good time."

"You're welcome," Hannah said, using her formal hostess tone. "Thank you for coming."

"The economy and the party will both be better next year," said Cecily. "The party, for sure."

Hannah's eyes widened. "Next year? We're going to have another party next year?

"Don't you want to?" asked Cecily. "Of course, next year there may be different children, some you don't know, but we can ask Miss Perkins to help with finding the right gifts for them."

"I would like to have another party," said Hannah. "But I wasn't sure we would be here next year."

Cecily stopped chopping onion. "Of course we'll be here next year. Where else would we be?"

Hannah shrugged. "I don't know. I thought maybe we'd move to another house."

"Why would you do that?" asked Cyrus. "There's plenty of room here."

"Too much room, if you ask me," said Iris. "But it is a good house for parties, I have to admit. I imagine you could talk Cyrus into having the party here, even if you and Cecily do decide to get your own place. Speaking of that—have you found a house yet, Mack?"

"No."

Iris nodded. "That's understandable. You haven't had much time to look, what with carting Cecily all over town."

"That's not why—my real estate agent hasn't called with any new listings."

"Most people don't want to move during the holidays. Wait until next year; there will be plenty of new listings, you'll see," said Cyrus. "But I don't see why Cecily and Hannah need another house."

"I didn't know you were looking for a house," said Hannah. She had stopped grating and was staring at Mack. "Why?"

"I'll be moving soon," said Mack.

"Why? Don't you have to drive Cecily until she gets her license back?"

Cecily had explained her loss of license to Hannah, using herself as an example of the unpleasant consequences that followed doing the wrong thing. Now she tensed, waiting for Mack to explain what he meant by "soon."

"Uh, well . . . it's this way, Hannah," said Mack, obviously searching for the right words. "I've got another job. This one was just temporary."

"That's not fair! Nobody told me that. You can't go, Mack! You're going to ruin everything!" Hannah dropped the grater and ran from the room.

Cecily went after her. She found Hannah in her room, sitting in the window seat and staring out at the night.

"Hannah, you're not crying, are you?"

"No." She didn't look around, but her voice sounded weepy to Cecily.

"Why are you so upset? We'll see Mack even if he doesn't live here."

"But we won't see him every day."

"That's true. But we will see him." Cecily felt a surge of protectiveness. Mack could dump her, but she'd be damned if she'd let him dump Hannah, too.

"When? Where? Will we see him every week?"

"I don't know, honey. He may be busy. You will be busy, too. New school, new friends." As soon as she said that, the thought struck her: With Mack gone and Hannah in school, she would have a lot less to do.

"I thought Mack was part of the family. You said families stick together," Hannah said accusingly.

"They do. But Mack isn't really a part of our family. He's a friend. A very good friend. He explained that he has another job."

"Why does he need another job? Isn't Cyrus paying him enough money?"

"I'm sure money isn't the issue, Hannah. Mack is a very smart man—he needs a job more challenging than driving me around town."

Hannah turned around and looked at Cecily. She had tear stains on her cheeks. "Did you know he was looking for another job?"

"I knew this was a temporary job for him," Cecily said. She wanted to tell Hannah that Mack was a policeman, but then she'd have to explain that Mack's job was to catch Neville. She wasn't sure how Hannah would feel about that. And Mack had asked her to keep his secret.

"Oh. I hadn't thought about that. Driving is a pretty easy job. I guess it isn't the right job for Mack." Hannah scrubbed her cheeks with the heels of her palms, then gave her a suspicious look. "Are you sure we'll see him after he moves?"

"Positive." She knew Mack wouldn't do anything to

hurt Hannah. She only wished she could be as certain that he would want to see her, too.

"I'm ready to back downstairs," said Hannah.

"Good." Cecily held out her hand. "Let's go."

At the elevator, Hannah asked, "When do you think Mack will leave?"

"I think he'll be here for the rest of this month. But I don't know that for sure. I don't think he knows, either. When we get back to the kitchen, I think you should tell him you're sorry you yelled at him."

"Okay. I shouldn't have yelled." Hannah stuck out her round chin. "But he shouldn't go away."

Cecily felt the same way, but she didn't say that out loud.

In one of the second-floor guest rooms, Neville listened to the murmur of female voices coming from what had been Cecily's room when he'd last been in the Culpepper mansion. Hannah had identified it as her room on the tour she had given him and her guests. He had raised a few brows when he'd asked—in a voice none of the Culpeppers had heard him use before—if he could go along on the tour. But no one had objected, and he'd been able to check every room in the house.

The painting was nowhere in sight. Too bad. He might have spent the time since the party ended retrieving it. Then, once the house was quiet, he could have walked out the front door with the painting under his arm. Cecily must have banished his wedding present to one of the many closets—too many for him to search when there were people around—or to what remained of the attic. He had surreptitiously checked the new entrance to the attic during the tour of Cecily's apartment. It had been locked, with a dead bolt.

Ah, well, he had a backup plan—one with a trifle more risk, but one he was confident would succeed. During the course of the party, he had observed that Cecily and Hannah had become very close in a short period of time—happily for him.

Neville had just finished shedding the Santa suit when he'd heard their footsteps on the stairs. He'd worn a black sweater and black pants underneath the costume. He walked to the door, which he'd left open a tiny crack, and strained to make out what Hannah and Cecily were talking about. He heard Cecily tell Hannah they needed to return to the kitchen, then the hum of the elevator—another change to the mansion. He assumed Cecily's new quarters on the third floor had precipitated the need for an elevator.

Once the hum of the elevator ceased, Neville left his listening post at the door. He stretched out on the bed and settled down to wait.

Cecily had taken Hannah back to the kitchen. He sneered. Cyrus and his good-ol'-boy affectations—buy American, eat in the kitchen—just like plain, everyday folks. What a crock! Not that he thought wealth should be flaunted—that smacked of vulgarity. But wealth should be enjoyed to its fullest. The best of everything—that was what he wanted. And what he'd had.

In a few hours he would have it again. This time he would invest more prudently, and he wouldn't make the mistake of dipping into his principal. That was one bit of Cyrus's advice that he should have heeded.

He had not completely stripped himself of valuable assets, however. His mistake had been in underestimating the Houston Police Department. Their actions had prompted his hasty departure and forced him to leave a good portion of his wealth behind.

At nine o'clock he heard footsteps in the hall. He re-

turned to the door and put his eye to the slit. Cecily and
Hannah went into Hannah's room again. Half an hour
later, he heard footsteps climbing the stairs to the third
floor. He surmised that Cecily had tucked Hannah in—
how parental of her—and was going to her own room.

Around ten, Cyrus went to his room.

Shortly after Cyrus retired for the night, Neville
heard footsteps on the stairs from the third floor. Using
his peephole, he saw Cecily going downstairs again.

Where was she going? Not to the kitchen for a snack—
she had a kitchen upstairs. He supposed she might be
going after something she didn't stock in her third-
floor kitchenette.

Neville waited a few more moments, then carefully
slipped out of the bedroom and followed Cecily downstairs. The soft-soled slippers he wore made not a whisper of sound on the stairs. She did go to the kitchen,
but Cecily didn't stop there. She went out the back
door. Neville went to the window and watched as she
disappeared into the garage.

She was going to the chauffeur's apartment. Neville's
lip curled. A chauffeur. He had thought Cecily had
higher standards than that.

Quietly he made his way back to his hiding place. An
hour later, he heard footsteps on the stairs. Cecily was
returning to her room on the third floor.

When the house had been silent for another hour,
Neville took the plastic bag with the chloroform-soaked
cotton pad in it and walked down the hall to Hannah's
room.

Cecily was drifting off to sleep when the telephone
rang. "Who would be calling at this time of night?" she
muttered, fumbling for the receiver. "Hello?"

"Cecily, my dear. Did you enjoy making merry tonight? I saw you leave for your rendezvous with your chauffeur."

"Neville?" Cecily came wide awake. "What do you want? How could you have seen me?"

"Ho, ho, ho. Did you think changing the security codes would keep me out?"

"You were the Santa? How did you—"

"Never mind that," Neville interrupted. "I've got my daughter."

"Hannah?" Her heart stopped, then began beating again, sluggishly. Cecily croaked, "Why? Where are you?"

"Never mind where I am. Pay attention to me, Cecily. I want Alejandro's painting, and I want it tonight. Bring it to the beach house."

"The beach house?" she repeated stupidly. Everything seemed to be moving in slow motion, including her brain. "Is that where you are?"

"Of course not. I'll call you there in two hours and tell you where to bring the painting. If you call the police, or bring anyone with you, I'll know. I'll take Hannah away, and you'll never see her again."

The threat broke through her strange lassitude. Galvanized, she jumped from the bed. "No! I'll do exactly as you said. I'll get the painting and I'll be at the beach house as soon as I can. Let me talk to—"

There was a dial tone.

Cecily dressed quickly and ran to the garage apartment.

Mack opened the door before she knocked. He was dressed—he hadn't been when she'd left him. That thought had barely registered when something else caught her attention. The painting was no longer hanging above the mantel. It was on the coffee table.

"What are you doing with the painting? I need it. Now. Neville's got Hannah."

"I know," said Mack.

"How do you know? He just called."

"I heard."

"What do you mean you heard?"

"Your phone is tapped."

That slowed her down again. "You've been listening to my phone calls?" Cecily felt a spurt of anger. "Oh, I don't have time for this. Give me the painting. I have to go."

"I'm going with you," said Mack.

"No. Neville said he'd know if I brought someone with me."

"I'm not letting you go alone. You can't drive without a license. Don't worry, Cecily. We'll get Hannah back. Together."

Cecily let him take her in his arms. "I'm going alone, just like Neville ordered. I'm taking that silly painting and I'm getting my daughter back." She remembered what he'd confessed, and punched his shoulder. "You listened to my calls!"

"I had to do it. I stopped as soon as I was sure you weren't going to help Neville. I wouldn't have picked up tonight, but I had a hunch it was Neville."

Cecily pushed herself out of the comforting circle of Mack's arms. "Did you call the police?"

"No. Not yet."

"You can't do that, Mack."

"All right. I won't. Provided you let me go along."

"But if Neville sees you—"

"He won't. Think about it, Cecily. He's alone, except for Hannah. No one is helping him. He must have taken her to the beach house. He won't have time to send you running all over the island. If we call the police, they can send a SWAT team, and—"

"SWAT? With guns? No! Oh, Mack, I'm afraid he'll hurt her. You can come, if you promise to stay out of sight. But no one else. Please! We've got to hurry."

Mack picked up the painting. "All right. We'll do it your way. Why does he want this thing? I thought it wasn't valuable."

"It isn't. Neville paid a few thousand dollars for it. I doubt he could sell it for as much as he paid."

"Then he's hidden something valuable in the frame, or behind it. A safety deposit box key, maybe."

"We don't have time to look for it."

"You're right. Let's get going." Mack, painting in hand, walked out the open door and down the stairs.

Cecily followed.

Mack put the painting in the backseat of the Camaro, then turned to her. "Listen, Cecily, if Neville isn't at the beach house when we get there, he'll have to be close by. Otherwise, he wouldn't be able to tell if you were alone or not when you arrive. Think. Where could he be that would give him that kind of view?"

"I don't know. The boathouse, maybe."

"What kind of boat?"

"A motor cruiser. Twin-engine."

"Full tank?"

"Probably. Cyrus has someone take it out once a month or so, to make sure it's in good shape."

"Neville arrived by boat. He may be planning to leave the same way. He could have arranged for another boat to meet him off the coast."

"Mack, even if Neville is hiding in the boathouse, he may not have Hannah with him. He might have left her somewhere."

"I don't think so. He must know you wouldn't give him the painting until you have her back."

"He might try to take it away from me."

"He might, but he'll be in a hurry. He won't have time to fight with you. Here's what we'll do. I'll drive to Galveston. Right before we reach the island, we'll switch.

You can let me out of the car before we get to the beach house."

"What will you do?"

"Watch and wait until I see what's going on. If I see Neville go into the house without Hannah, I'll look for her in the boathouse. If he's got her with him, you keep him talking. I'll get to him one way or another."

"What does that mean?"

"I'll take him, if I can. If not, and if I'm sure Hannah is with you, I'll let him go. The Coast Guard can have the pleasure of chasing him down."

"All right."

They were halfway to Galveston before Cecily thought to ask, "How long has my phone been tapped?"

"Since I moved in." Mack stiffened, bracing for an explosion.

"Since before that. Cyrus heard the first call from Neville, didn't he?"

"I don't—yeah. That was what prompted his call to the police." He didn't feel like keeping Cyrus's secrets any longer.

As they speeded toward Galveston, Mack thought about what would happen once they arrived. He should have called for backup, but he was pretty sure Cyrus would be taking care of that.

One way or another, his assignment as Cecily's chauffeur would be over in a few hours. Then what?

He had been in the study when Cyrus had called and chewed out the International Ops agent for failing to report that Neville had been married before. After a while, Cyrus had had to admit that all he'd asked for was confirmation of Neville's net worth, not for a complete background check. When the call had ended, Cyrus had explained that he always had Cecily's suitors' financial status checked out.

Mack scowled at the taillights ahead of them. He could imagine how his bank account would stack up to the likes of Lance Ebersol and the guy with the yacht. He had saved enough for a healthy down payment on a modest house, but aside from that, his assets consisted of his truck, a few sticks of furniture, and the wage he earned as a detective.

He had to stop deluding himself. When the assignment ended, Cecily would disappear from his life faster than eyewitnesses to a bar brawl.

"Go faster," said Cecily, ending his reverie. "Hannah must be scared to death."

"She's going to be okay, Cecily."

"I know. I just want this to be over."

A mile from the turnoff to the beach house, Cecily stopped the car and watched Mack slip out into the night. It wouldn't be night much longer—it was after five o'clock.

She continued to the house, stopped the car, and got out. Cecily opened the passenger door and retrieved the painting. She leaned it against the house as she unlocked the side door. Upon entering, she disarmed the security system using the new codes. She brought the painting inside. Taking it with her, Cecily went to the living room and sat down on the edge of the sofa.

And waited.

The phone rang. She answered it. "Neville? Where is she?"

"Have you got the painting?"

"Yes."

"Good. Bring it to the patio door."

"I want to see Hannah first," said Cecily.

He didn't answer immediately. Finally, with a disgusted sigh, he said, "All right. I'll bring her to you."

A few minutes later, Neville entered the sliding glass door, carrying Hannah slung over his shoulder.

"What have you done to her?"

"Nothing she won't get over." Neville continued through the living room to the kitchen. He dumped Hannah's limp body in a kitchen chair, then ordered, "Find something to tie her with. Now."

"Why?"

"Do it. And hurry. It will be dawn in another hour or so."

Cecily opened the pantry and took out a roll of twine. "Will this do?"

"Yeah. You first. Sit down." He motioned Cecily into another of the kitchen chairs. When she was seated, he said, "Put your hands behind your back."

She did, and he used a double strand of the kitchen twine to tie her hands together. Then he did the same with her feet.

"Cecily?" said Hannah. Her eyes fluttered open. Her voice sounded weak.

"I'm here, sweetie. Don't be scared."

"I'm not scared. I feel sick. I think I'm going to throw up." Her eyes closed again.

"What did you give her?" asked Cecily.

"A harmless anesthetic, that's all. She'll be fine."

"Who are you?" asked Hannah, opening her eyes and staring at Neville. "I don't like you."

"Is that anyway to talk to your dear old dad?"

Hannah eyed him sleepily. "You're not my dad."

"Yes, I am. I said I would come back for you, and I did." Neville laughed harshly. "Never say I didn't keep my word." He quickly bound Hannah, then picked up the painting and left.

"Is he really my dad?" asked Hannah, once they were alone.

"I'm afraid so," said Cecily.

"He really is a bad man, isn't he?"

"Yes. But not as bad as he could be. He didn't hurt us. He only wanted that painting."

"Why? It's ugly."

"I don't know why. Mack thinks he might have hidden something in it."

"Is Mack here?"

Cecily nodded. She didn't understand why Mack hadn't confronted Neville before he tied them both up. What if Neville had gotten the jump on Mack? What if Mack was lying on the beach? "Hannah, Mack may be in trouble. We'd better try to get loose."

She scooted her chair across the tile floor until she was back to back with Hannah. "I'm going to try to untie your hands."

After breaking several fingernails, Cecily managed to get the knots undone. As soon as she was free, Hannah untied her own feet, then started to untie Cecily.

"There's a pair of scissors in that middle drawer. That might be faster."

Hannah got the scissors and cut the twine binding Cecily's hands and feet.

Cecily reached for the telephone, but before she had a chance to dial 911, Cyrus burst through the door, followed by Iris and several policemen.

"Are you all right?"

"I'm fine," said Cecily. "I think Hannah is, too, but Neville gave her some kind of drug. Where's Mack? Have you seen him? How did you get here so fast?"

One of the policemen asked, "Ma'am, where is Detective Armstrong?"

"I don't know—"

"Here," said Mack, standing outside the sliding glass doors on the deck. He had the painting with him.

Cyrus asked, "Where is Neville? You didn't let that son of a gun get away, did you?"

"No. He's on your boat, handcuffed to the railing. He's not going anywhere." Mack fished in his pocket

for a key, which he handed to one of the uniformed policemen. "Here, take him into custody—there's an outstanding warrant for his arrest. I already gave him the
necessary warnings. I'll be with you in a minute."

The policemen left.

Mack knelt in front of Hannah. "Are you all right,
squirt?"

"I am now." She threw her arms around Mack and
gave him a hug. "I want to go home."

"Cyrus and Iris will take you both home. I've got to
stay here. I'm a policeman, Hannah. That's my other
job."

"Oh. You were after my father."

"That's right."

"Why didn't you come after him before he tied us
up?" asked Cecily.

"I didn't know if he was armed or not. I waited until
I was sure he wasn't going to hurt you; then I followed
him back to the boathouse."

Cecily turned to Cyrus. "Daddy, how did you know
where we were—oh! I forgot. You had my phone tapped,
too."

"What does that mean?" asked Hannah. "Why would
Gramps want to listen to your phone calls?"

"What did you call me, young lady?" asked Cyrus,
doing his best to scowl.

"Gramps. Cecily said we're family, so that makes you
my grampa."

"Daddy, you didn't answer my question—have you
been listening to my phone calls?"

"Only the middle-of-the-night ones. This one almost
gave me another heart attack. I didn't know if I should
come after you or not. Iris thought we should. I called
the police on the way here." Cyrus gave Hannah a hug.
"Are you sure you're all right, kid?"

"Yeah. I don't feel like throwing up anymore."

"Neville said he gave her a mild anesthetic," said Cecily.

Iris leaned down and sniffed the collar of Hannah's pajamas. "Smells sweetish—chloroform? That stuff's dangerous."

"We'd better get you to a doctor, Hannah."

"Doctor? Do I have to, Mom?"

"Mom? You called me Mom." Cecily's eyes filled up with tears. She blinked them away.

"Don't get all mushy, you two. Save that for later." Cyrus grabbed Mack's hand and shook it. "Mack, thank you. We'll see you at home once you're finished with Barton. Get the painting, Iris. We'll stop at an ER on the way home."

There was a patrolman in a car parked behind Cyrus's Escalade. Cyrus told him they were leaving, then got Iris, Cecily, and Hannah, and the painting, in the SUV. He backed out of the driveway.

Cecily looked out the rear window for a glimpse of Mack. She didn't see him.

Nineteen

The emergency room doctor checked Hannah and found no ill effects from the chloroform, except a little residual grogginess. He prescribed fresh air and rest. They took her home, and Cecily put her to bed. Before leaving her room, she opened the bedroom window a crack, then joined Iris and Cyrus in the study.

Alejandro's painting was leaning against Cyrus's desk.

"What is it about this work of art?" asked Cyrus, staring at it. "There's nothing taped to the back, or to the frame. The only thing left is to check out the painting itself. There must be a false back or something. Should we take it to an expert and have it dismantled?"

"I can do it," said Cecily. "I've framed enough paintings, I know how to get the canvas out of the frame without damaging it." She carefully removed the painting from the ornate wooden frame. "Aha!"

"What is it?" asked Iris.

"There are two paintings attached to the stretcher bars." She looked around. "I need something to get the staples out."

Cyrus opened his desk drawer and took out a letter opener. "Here. This should do it. It has a steel blade."

Cecily used the letter opener to remove the staples. "Now, let's see what we have here." Turning the paintings faceup, she lifted the ugly painting away. "Golly," she whispered, awestruck.

"What? What is it?" Iris hurried to her side and looked. "Oh. It looks like a van Gogh."

Cyrus stared at the painting. "Maybe it's a forgery—something Barton thought he could sell for a lot of money."

"He could have sold it for a lot of money, all right. It's real," said Cecily.

"Are you sure?"

"Well, I'm not an expert. But I know this particular painting was sold at auction four or five years ago—at a time when Neville would have had the funds to buy it."

"You'll have to turn it over to the police," said Iris. "If he bought it with stolen money . . ."

"I'm sure he did. Either that, or he stole it from whoever bought it at auction. I remember the buyer wanted to remain anonymous."

"But anyone who bought something like this would surely have reported its theft," said Cyrus, stroking his beard.

Cecily nodded. "True. Neville must have bought it. He fancied himself a connoisseur of all things expensive."

"How much did this item go for, do you remember?" asked Cyrus.

"Not exactly. Ten or fifteen million—somewhere in that neighborhood."

Cyrus whistled. "Nice neighborhood. If he spent that much money on this painting, that goes a long way toward explaining how he managed to run out of money so soon."

"It also explains why he chose Diego's painting—it's

the right size," said Cecily. "I always wondered about that—there were much nicer paintings at the gallery at the time Neville bought my wedding gift."

Iris stared at the painting. "Ten million dollars? No wonder he risked coming back to get it. But why didn't he take it with him in the first place?"

"He must not have had enough time. And he wouldn't have been welcome in my bedroom, which is where he thought it was hanging. Neville never would have thought to look for it in the garage apartment," said Cecily.

"Did he even know there is a garage apartment?" asked Iris.

"I don't know. The first time he called, he asked about the painting—he wanted to know if I still had it. He must have had at least a few bad moments over the years thinking about what I might have done with it." She grinned. "I certainly hope so."

"I'll bet he was looking for the painting at the beach house," said Cyrus.

Iris nodded in agreement. "And he tried to get in here to look for it the night the alarm went off. I'm glad Mack had you change the security codes. Where is he, by the way?"

"I don't know," said Cecily. She'd been wondering the same thing. He would come back. She was sure of that. What she wasn't at all sure of was what she would say to him. She couldn't just throw herself at him and beg him to love her. She'd gotten braver over the past few weeks, but she wasn't *that* brave. What she really wanted was for him to declare his love for her first. That would make things so much easier.

"When did you put the painting in the garage apartment?" asked Cyrus.

"The day I found out he'd left Houston for parts unknown. I almost threw it away, but I couldn't do that to Diego."

"And luckily, not to van Gogh, either. What are you going to do with it, Cecily?" asked Cyrus.

She shot him a startled look. "Me? It's not mine."

"Yes, it is. Neville gave it to you as a wedding present—he may have thought he was only giving you the Alejandro, but a gift is a gift."

She looked at the painting again. "Well, then . . . I know exactly what I'll do with it. I'll sell it and use the proceeds to repay all his victims. That won't be enough to repay everyone one hundred percent of their losses. Still, it will help."

Cyrus scowled. "I don't know if that's such a good idea. If you pay off the victims, Neville may be able to negotiate a more favorable plea bargain. After what he did to you and Hannah, I want him to stay in jail for a long, long time."

"Oh, I don't think that's going to be a problem," said Iris. "That nice young patrolman told me that kidnapping for ransom is a very serious felony."

"Ahhh," said Cyrus, satisfied. "I hadn't thought of that. Kidnapping *is* a much more serious crime than theft—even theft on the scale Neville practiced. Well, then, what are we going to do with this until we can sell it?"

"I'll call my old boss at Objet d'Art. He'll take good care of it, if I tell him he can handle its sale. He has a climate-controlled vault."

"Sounds good to me," said Cyrus. "Now, I don't know about you two, but I'm going to take a nap. I'm too old for this kind of excitement—chasing down fugitives and discovering priceless works of art. It's been quite a night." He looked at the sunlight streaming in the study window. "Night and morning."

After checking on Hannah, Cecily went to her room. She took off her clothes and put on a robe; then she lay down on top of the covers. She closed her eyes, but she couldn't sleep. She couldn't stop thinking about all that had happened since Neville's late-night call.

The call. Her eyes popped open.

Mack had heard it. So had Cyrus.

Mack had heard all her calls, since the day he'd moved into the garage apartment. Oh, good grief. What had she said to Olivia about him?

What hadn't she said? He'd known she planned to seduce him. He'd known what his dimple did to her. And he'd heard her say all she wanted from him was sex. Cecily's heart sank. What if he took her at her word?

At least Olivia had left town before she and Mack had made love. Wouldn't he have loved hearing her critique of that?

Cecily picked up a pillow and put it over her hot face.

She couldn't face him.

Tossing the pillow aside, she sat up. Oh, yes, she could. And she'd tell him exactly what she thought about sneaky, underhanded eavesdroppers.

Mack arrived at the Culpepper mansion Sunday at dinnertime. He declined Iris's offer to fix him a plate. Now that he didn't have his undercover identity to hide behind, he felt awkward, exposed. He wanted to do what had to be done quickly, so he could leave and go back to his normal life.

When Iris protested, he told her, "I've got to get back to the station tonight." He turned to Cecily. "Captain Morris wants you to come downtown tomorrow to sign a complaint against Barton for kidnapping. The assistant DA assigned to the case will want to talk to you, too, in a day or two, about testifying before the grand jury."

"Don't I have to go?" asked Hannah.

"No, not if you don't want to." Mack had talked about Hannah with his boss. After consulting with the district attorney, they had decided Hannah's testimony against her father, while potentially very powerful, would not be needed. Cecily and Mack had both witnessed enough to be able to make a kidnapping charge stick. "Don't worry, Hannah. You won't have to testify against your father."

Hannah puffed out her cheeks. "He's not my father. He's a sperm donor."

"Hannah!" Cecily gasped. "What do you know about sperm?"

Hannah gave her a puzzled look. "I'll explain it later, Mom." She looked at Mack. "I want to complain, and I want to testify, too. I'm the one he kidnapped. And he knocked me out, too, with chloroform. Isn't that a crime?"

Mack ruffled her hair with his hand. "It sure is, squirt. Assault and battery. You're a very brave girl to want to do that."

"Can I go, Mom?" asked Hannah.

"We'll see," said Cecily, obviously still off balance from Hannah's sperm-donor remark.

Mack grinned. "You sound just like my mother—she always said, 'We'll see,' when she didn't want to come right out and say no."

"Will you be there?" Cecily asked him.

He couldn't tell if she wanted him to be there or not. "No. I've got a new assignment; I need to get up to speed with my partner."

"I see," said Cecily, nodding.

"Where's the painting?" asked Mack. "I need to take it to the crime lab. They should be able to figure out why Barton wanted it so badly."

"We know why," said Cyrus. "We already took it to

Objet d'Art. It's safely stowed in a climate-controlled vault."

"Are we talking about Alejandro's painting? What did you find in it?"

"A priceless masterpiece," said Hannah. "I saw it. It was much nicer than that other painting."

"Neville hid a van Gogh behind Alejandro's canvas," Cecily explained.

"Cecily is going to sell it and use the money she gets for it to repay Neville's victims. They should get about fifty cents on the dollar," said Cyrus.

"What does that mean?" asked Hannah. "Fifty cents on the dollar?"

While Cyrus explained, Cecily turned to Mack. "When will you be moving out of the apartment?" Her tone was neutral, as if she didn't care one way or another.

"Tonight. It won't take long to pack up the clothes I've got there. Someone will be by in a day or two to uninstall the wiretap."

"Where will you go?" she asked.

"I'm staying with my parents until I find a house." He started moving toward the door. "I'll be going now. Thanks for all your help—and for all the good food."

"You're welcome in my kitchen anytime, Mack," said Iris, giving him a hug and a smacking kiss on the cheek.

"You're going?" said Hannah, following him to the door. "Will you come back to see me?"

"Sure thing, squirt. Just give me a call and I'll be here."

"Okay. What's your phone number?"

Mack took a card out of his wallet. He jotted a number on the back and handed it to her. "My number at work is on the front. My parents' number is on the back. I'll be there when I'm not working, at least for a few weeks."

"Okay." Hannah hugged him around the waist. "Thank you for saving me."

"You did a pretty good job of saving yourself," said Mack.

"Well, I'll miss you," said Iris, sniffling.

"Me, too," said Hannah. Her lower lip was trembling, but she managed a grin for him.

"So will I," said Cyrus, taking his hand and giving it a vigorous shake.

They all looked expectantly at Cecily.

"Good-bye, Mack." That was all she could get out before her throat clogged,

Mack nodded, then walked out the door.

Cecily couldn't believe it. He'd walked away from her so easily, making no attempt to see her alone. He could have asked her to help him pack. He might have insisted on taking her to sign the complaint against Neville right away. He could have . . . Cecily stopped.

She could come up with hundreds of ways for him to have gotten her alone. The fact remained, he hadn't come up with even one.

Because he didn't want to be alone with her. His hasty departure made it clear—the case that had brought him here was closed. Their affair was over.

She could go after him. Maybe she had it all wrong. Maybe he was waiting for her to ask him to stay. Cecily took a step toward the kitchen door, then stopped. She couldn't do it.

She remembered thinking that if she could manage to help capture Neville, she would feel good about herself. Brave.

Well, she'd been wrong about that. She was still a coward, too afraid of being rejected to chase after a man who found it so easy to walk away from her. Tears welled in her eyes. She blinked them away. Hannah was looking at her curiously. "Are you all right, Mom?"

That made her grin. "Yes. Better than all right." And she was. She had Hannah. Neville was on his way out of her life and into prison. She and Cyrus had begun to talk to each other. She might not have Mack, but she'd get over his loss. Someday.

In the meantime, she had a lot to keep her busy.

On Monday she met with the police and the district attorney. On Tuesday she met with Neville, at his request.

Cyrus drove her to the jail.

"Do you want me to go with you to see him?" he asked.

"No. I'll be all right, Daddy. I just want to make sure he doesn't have some kind of plot involving Hannah."

Neville entered the visitors' room, dressed in an orange jumpsuit. He did not look his best with bleached blond hair—and dark roots were beginning to show. "Cecily, my dear. Thank you for seeing me. I know you must be a little peeved with me."

"Peeved? That's not how I would put it. I came because I wanted to tell you to your face that I'm filing for divorce."

"You really know how to kick a man when he's down, don't you, princess."

"I am not a princess, I never was. What do you want, Neville?"

"Since you brought it up, let's talk about the divorce first—I don't think you've thought this through."

"Oh, yes, I have. I don't want to be married to you any longer."

"If you're not married to me, you won't be Hannah's stepmother."

"I know that."

"She's in your custody because of our marriage. Marriage ends, custody ends."

"I've filed a petition to adopt Hannah, Neville."

"Your petition will be denied if I object. I am her bio-
logical father. If I don't waive my parental rights, you
can't adopt Hannah. Not to worry, though. I will waive
my rights . . . if."

"If what?"

"I understand from my lawyer that you intend to reimburse my so-called victims. He tells me that will allow
him to negotiate a favorable plea bargain for the theft
charges, since the funds for restitution come—indi-
rectly, to be sure—from me."

"If you take that argument to its logical conclusion,
Neville, the funds come from the people you stole from."

Neville shrugged. "My attorney is not so sanguine
about the kidnapping charges, however. So, if you agree
to drop those charges, I'll give my blessing to your adopting Hannah."

"I intend to adopt Hannah. I do not need your blessing."

"You won't succeed. Not unless I waive my parental
rights."

He seemed awfully sure of himself. But Cecily was
positive he was wrong. "Is that what your lawyer said?"

"No. He is a criminal lawyer. But we have a law li-
brary here in the jail. I looked it up."

"You didn't look in the right place, Neville. You don't
have any parental rights. You lost them when you abandoned Hannah. My lawyer explained it to me when she
filed the adoption petition." Cecily stood up and sig-
naled the guard that she was ready to leave. "Good-bye,
Neville."

She met Cyrus on the first floor. He hustled her out
of the building and into the Escalade. Once they were
in the car, Cyrus slanted a glance at her.

"You look a little flushed. Are you all right?"

"I'm mad."

"What did he want?" Cyrus asked.

"He wanted me to drop the kidnapping charges, in exchange for not objecting to my adopting Hannah."

"Slimeball. I never should have let him near you."

"Daddy, we need to get something straight. Neville was my mistake, not yours."

"Not entirely. If I had gotten a complete background check on him when you first met him, we would have known about his marriage, and Hannah, a lot sooner."

"And he would have explained it all away. I can hear him now—explaining with tears in his voice that he was widowed, with a child, a child who preferred her grandmother to him. You know he would have, Daddy. Neville could talk his way out of anything."

"I don't know . . ."

"I do. I was the one who fell for his good looks and smooth talking. Neville Barton was my mistake."

"You want full credit, do you?"

"I wouldn't call it credit, exactly. Credit for what?"

"Your mistake brought Hannah into our lives, Cecily. Mack, too, for that matter. And it made me do some hard thinking."

"About what?"

"Family. Love. Christmas. This is the season to make merry, you know."

"I know," Cecily said warily.

"You're not going to do anything foolish this year, are you?"

"I hadn't planned on it," said Cecily.

"Good. I knew this Christmas was going to be different."

"Not that different. There will still be a story about me in the *Houston Scoop* tomorrow. When I gave Jade the interview about Neville's arrest yesterday, she said they would run it in the Christmas Eve edition."

"Did she give you an advance look?"

"Yes. The words *madcap heiress* do not appear anywhere in the story. And the headline is going to read, *Cecily Culpepper Captures Crook*. Which isn't exactly true, since Mack did the actual capture. But the *Scoop* dotes on alliteration."

"I'm proud of you, C. J.," said Cyrus.

"Oh, Daddy," said Cecily. "I'm so l-lucky." And she was. She had a daughter. Her father was proud of her. She had gotten everything she'd wanted.

Except for the what she wanted most—Mack.

"Have you heard from Mack?" asked Cyrus, making her jump.

"No. Hannah has. He called her yesterday."

"That's good. She misses him."

"He's only been gone a couple of days," said Cecily, anxious to change the subject before she spoiled her newly declared independence by weeping all over Cyrus's neck. "That reminds me: What are we going to do about a driver?"

"Taken care of. I called Jenkins yesterday. He's back on the payroll as of the second of January." Cyrus cleared his throat. "Cecily, I'm sorry."

"What for?"

"For ever doubting you. I should have known you wouldn't have helped Neville."

"You would have, if I'd ever talked to you about him. I'm sorry I didn't."

"That's not your fault, either. If I'd been around more when you were a child, we might have gotten into the habit of talking to each other. As it was, Iris was your confidante, not me."

"Speaking of Iris—"

"I'm going to ask her to marry me."

"You are? When?"

"Tomorrow evening. I need to buy an engagement ring. Care to help?"

"Daddy, you know shopping is my life."

Twenty

On Christmas Eve morning, Cyrus called Iris, Cecily, and Hannah together in his study. "I think we should take a little drive."

"A drive? Where to?" asked Hannah, staring out the window that faced the courtyard.

Cecily knew she was looking at the garage—she'd spent more hours than she should have mooning over the garage apartment.

"You'll know when we get there. Come on, get your coats and let's go."

"Okay," said Hannah. She didn't sound overly excited by the prospect of a drive.

Once they were all in the Escalade, Iris in the front seat next to Cyrus, and Hannah and Cecily in the backseat, Iris looked over her shoulder at Hannah. "It's Christmas Eve, Hannah. Aren't you excited?"

"Yeah, I guess." Hannah sighed, staring out the window.

"What's wrong with you?" asked Cyrus, looking at her in the rearview mirror. "I've never seen such a long face." Cyrus's gaze shifted to Cecily's face. "Except for yours. I've never seen two such mopey faces. Are you two still stewing about Neville?"

"No, Daddy." The lack of Mack was what had her in a funk. She had a feeling that was what was bothering Hannah, too.

Iris snorted, "That man! He's got a lot of nerve, asking you to drop the kidnapping charges. Threatening to object to your adopting Hannah."

"He's a cad," said Hannah. "I'm going to divorce him, too."

"Are you, sweetie?" said Cecily. "That's good."

"And I don't want to be Hannah Barton," she said, crossing her arms over her chest and sticking out her round chin. "I want to be Hannah Culpepper."

"That can be arranged," said Cyrus, pulling into the parking lot of the animal shelter. "Here we are."

"This is a Culpepper Christmas tradition, Hannah," Cecily explained as they got out of the car. "We each get one present on Christmas Eve. You should get to pick which present you want to open, but I didn't know how to wrap a kitten, so—"

"A kitten? I'm going to get a kitten?" Hannah started dancing around the parking lot.

"That's right. You said you wouldn't be afraid if you had a kitten."

"Oh, I'm not afraid anymore," said Hannah, returning to Cecily's side. She quickly added, "But I want a kitten anyway."

There were only two kittens at the shelter: one tiger-striped yellow male and a tortoiseshell female. "A lot of people adopt at Christmas time," the shelter aide explained.

"I should have remembered that. Which one do you want, Hannah?" asked Cecily. "Or would you rather go to the pet store and see what they have?"

"Oh, no." Hannah stuck her fingers into cage. The tiger kitten attacked. "May I have them both?"

"Two kittens?"

"They could have fun playing with each other," said Hannah. "I'll be going to school soon, and one kitten would get extremely lonely." She gave Cecily her serious look. "Just like an only child."

"I think she's right, Cecily," said Iris. "We wouldn't want an extremely lonely little kitten moping around the house, would we?"

"Absolutely not. All right, we'll take them both."

"We need litter boxes and food and toys," said Hannah.

"I already got those—Iris hid them in the pantry. But I only got two dishes—one for food and one for water. We will need another food dish."

"Yes," said Hannah. "Cisco wants his own dish. So does Honey."

"Cisco and Honey? Those are their names?" asked Cyrus.

"Yes. I do get to name them, don't I?"

"Of course. Good names," said Cecily.

"We have plenty of dishes," said Iris. "I'll loan you one or two until we can get back to the pet store."

The kittens were duly adopted and placed in cardboard carriers for the trip home.

"They're going to climb the Christmas trees," said Iris.

"Yes," said Hannah. "That's what kittens do."

"Well, I don't think they'll hurt anything. Most of the ornaments are unbreakable. Misty broke all the glass ones years ago. Misty was my cat when I was your age," said Cecily. "She was a white Persian."

Hannah gave her a funny look. Before she could ask what that was about, Hannah ducked her head and began poking her fingers through the air holes in the pet carriers.

When they got back home, Cecily carried the litter box and bag of litter upstairs to Hannah's room. Hannah took the kittens. Cecily put the litter box in Hannah's bathroom, smiling at the sound of Hannah's giggling at the kittens' antics. When she returned to the bedroom, Hannah was sitting on the floor, and the kittens were climbing up the curtains.

"I think they like it here," said Hannah.

"I do believe you're right. You'd better show them where the litter box is. Don't forget to close the door when you come downstairs. Imagine having to look for two little kittens all over this house."

"Okay. Iris is right. This house is too big. Don't you think so?"

"Too big for just the four—six—of us? I suppose. But size has its advantages. We can each have our own space."

"I like cozy better. Like Mack's apartment."

"The apartment only has one bedroom. That would be a little too cozy, don't you think?"

"I guess. I bet he finds a nice, cozy house. With more than one bedroom."

Cecily decided a change of subject was in order. "Did Cyrus tell you what he's going to give Iris for Christmas?"

"Yep. He showed me the ring. She will say yes, won' she?"

"Oh, I don't think there's any doubt about that," Cecily laughed. "Except Cyrus's."

"I know. He's scared."

"Oh, my, Hannah. Look at the time. Cyrus wanted u in the family room at six o'clock."

Iris and Cyrus were waiting in the family room when Cecily and Hannah got there.

"Which present are you going to open tonight? asked Hannah.

"I don't know." Cecily eyed the oddly shaped package that Mack had put under the tree for her.

"I'm going to open this one," said Cyrus. "It looks like someone gave me cigars."

Hannah giggled. "That one's from me."

Cyrus tore off the paper. "Aha! I was right. Chocolate cigars—my favorite. Thank you, Hannah."

"You go next, Cecily," said Iris. "I can't make up my mind."

Cecily retrieved the gift with Mack's card. She couldn't wait until morning to see what he had given her, and it obviously was not what she wanted from him—the size and shape were all wrong for an engagement ring. She removed the bow and carefully slid a fingernail under the tape.

"Good God, Cecily," said Cyrus. "Tear the paper, why don't you? You never reuse it."

"Doing it this way makes the unwrapping last longer." She got the paper off. "Oh! An easel."

"Why would he get you something like that?" asked Iris. "I didn't know you planned to start painting again."

"Neither did I. But maybe I will."

"Here. You open this one," said Cyrus. He handed Iris an envelope.

"A Christmas card? What's in it? Money? My Christmas bonus?" Iris opened the envelope and took out a card. "Oh. A gift certificate—dinner for two at Maverick's Steak and Whiskey." She looked closer. "Oh, and it's good for today only. Cyrus—"

"Will you please take me to dinner tonight?" Cyrus asked, uncharacteristically humble.

"Tonight is Christmas Eve, Cyrus. Pizza-and-Scrooge night. It's a tradition."

"It's a rut. I thought we could do something different this year."

"But this is Hannah's first Christmas Eve with—"

"It's okay, Iris," said Hannah. "Cyrus discussed it with me. I think you should ask him."

"Do you? Well, then, yes, I will take you to dinner this evening, Mr. Culpepper." Iris's voice had a catch in it, and her eyes were suspiciously bright. "If we're going out, I have to change clothes."

"Get moving, woman," said Cyrus. "I'm starving."

"I hope you don't think you're going to get steak tonight."

"You'd be surprised what I think I'm going to get tonight," Cyrus said as he followed Iris out of the room. Hannah left, too.

Alone in the family room, Cecily picked up the discarded wrapping paper and then went to find Hannah. She was in her room, playing with the kittens. "Do you like your Christmas gift, Hannah?"

"Oh, yes. I love Cisco and Honey." She dangled the catnip mouse by its tail and giggled at the kittens' clumsy attempts to grab it. Tossing the mouse between the two felines, Hannah gave Cecily a solemn look. "But they weren't what I really, really wanted."

"No? Now you tell me. Let's go tell Iris and Cyrus goodbye. We'll probably be asleep when they come home."

Cyrus was helping Iris into her coat when Cecily and Hannah reached the bottom of the stairs.

"Hannah told me the kittens aren't what she wanted most for Christmas."

"That's all right," said Iris. "You aren't supposed to open the most important present on Christmas Eve."

"What I want most isn't under the tree, either," said Hannah.

"Then you're a day late and a dollar short, honey. The stores close early on Christmas Eve." Cyrus patted Hannah on the shoulder. "Whatever it is will have to wait until after Christmas."

"When it will probably be on sale," said Iris. "So you could have two for the price of one."

Hannah giggled. "I only want one."

"You girls gonna be all right by yourselves?" asked Cyrus, opening the door and ushering Iris out.

"Yes, Daddy. We'll be fine. The video is ready to go, and I'll order the pizza right away."

Once Iris and Cyrus were gone, Cecily and Hannah retreated to the family room.

Hannah said, "He's going to ask her to marry him, isn't he? She will say yes, won't she? Then she'll be my grandmother for real."

"I think that may be what will tip the scale in Cyrus's favor—she'll get us, too. Now. Let's call the pizza place. What do you like on your pizza?"

"Everything, but first . . . I know it's Christmas Eve, but you could get me what I want tonight."

"I could? What is it, Hannah?"

Hannah stuck out her round chin. "I want you to get me Mack for my father."

"Oh. I don't think—"

"You love him, don't you?"

"Does it show?"

"Uh-huh. You've been very sad ever since he left."

"Not that sad—you make me happy. I do love Mack, Hannah. But I don't know if he loves me."

"Did you tell him you love him?" asked Hannah.

"No, but . . ." Cecily almost said, *but he should have known*. He had heard everything she had ever said about him.

But she had never told Olivia she was in love with Mack. She had let Olly keep on referring to him as her transition man. She had never admitted she loved Mack out loud to anyone until this minute, when Hannah asked her how she felt. Her heart began to pound, and she felt light-headed. Could she do it? Could she tell Mack how she felt and what she wanted?

"What's wrong," asked Hannah. "You've got a funny look on your face."

"I think we'd better forget about the pizza. Let's get our coats. We're going to see Mack." If she couldn't be brave for herself, she could be for Hannah. She could try to get Hannah what she wanted for Christmas.

Hannah grinned. "Do you know where he lives?"

"Oh . . . no. He's staying with his parents, but I don't know their address. Maybe it's in the phone book."

"That's okay. I know. Mack gave me the phone number, and I called and asked for the address," said Hannah, following Cecily to the coat closet in the hall.

Cecily handed Hannah's coat to her, then put on her own coat. Hannah opened the front door.

"Wait. I forgot. The car keys are in the kitchen."

"Aren't we going to call a taxi? You can't drive."

"Yes, I can. I just don't have a license. I don't want to wait for a taxi." She might lose her nerve.

Once they were in the car, Hannah asked, "Do you think he'll say yes?"

"I don't know. I hope so." She took a deep breath. "But there is a chance he won't."

"I think he will," said Hannah. "Won't that be great? I'll have a mother and a father and a grandmother and grandfather."

"Two sets of those—Mack's parents would be your grandparents, too. Plus an uncle and an aunt—Mack's brother and his wife."

"Wow. That's not bad for an almost orphan."

"Nope, not bad at all, but let's not count our relatives before we get them."

Cecily drove cautiously, as if she'd had too much to drink. She still felt a little light-headed, and her heart kept beating faster and faster. When they got to the right street, she told Hannah, "Look for the house number—it's two-eleven."

"Two-nineteen, two-seventeen—there it is. Oh! Look at all the cars. They must be having a party."

"I forgot. Mack said his family has an open house on Christmas Eve. Hannah, maybe we should wait. This isn't the right time for—"

"Yes, it is. I see Mack's truck. He's here."

"Oh." Cecily's mouth went dry. "Good," she croaked.

"Are you scared?" asked Hannah.

"Terrified."

"Too scared to go in?"

Cecily took a deep breath. "No. Nothing ventured, nothing gained. Faint heart never won . . . anything. Love conquers all."

"What are you doing?" asked Hannah.

"Giving myself a pep talk. Okay. I'm ready now. I want Mack for Christmas, too."

Cecily found a place to park halfway down the block. She and Hannah walked back to the house. Through the windows, she could see what looked like dozens of people standing, sitting, talking.

Clutching Hannah's hand, she rang the doorbell. A man opened the door. "Merry Christmas," he said. "Come on in. Buffet's in the dining room. Help yourself. Christmas carols in the living room. Make yourself at home." He wandered away.

"I see Mack," said Hannah, standing on tiptoe and craning her neck.

"Where?"

"Over there in that corner."

"I see him." Mack was sitting in an overstuffed chair. A leggy brunette—a gorgeous, leggy brunette—was sitting on the arm of his chair. Cecily's heart stopped. "Oh, Hannah, he's here with a date. Let's go." She took Hannah's hand.

"Mack!" yelled Hannah, pushing through the crowd and dragging Cecily with her."

Mack looked up. And grinned.

His dimple made Cecily's knees go weak. "Hannah, I don't think I can do this."

"Mom! You promised," said Hannah. "Hi, Mack. Merry Christmas."

"Merry Christmas, squirt." Mack got out of the chair.

The brunette smiled at Cecily. "You must be Cecily, and you're Hannah. I've heard a lot about you both. I'm Sarah, Joe's fiancée."

"Oh," said Hannah. "You're going to be my—"

Cecily put her hand over Hannah's mouth.

"Your what, sweetie?" asked Sarah.

"Could we have a word with Mack?" asked Cecily. She could barely breathe.

"Sure. It's time I found Joe, anyway. I was just trying to cheer Mack up. I think you two can do that better than I was."

She walked to the piano bench and sat down next to a man who looked a lot like Mack.

"How did you get here?" asked Mack. "Taxi?"

"Uh, we drove."

"You drove? Without a license." His brows snapped together. "Cecily—"

Hannah tugged on his shirt. "It was an emergency. And she drove very carefully," said Hannah. "Don't be mad, Mack. She had to do it to get me what I want for Christmas."

"You're Christmas shopping on Christmas Eve?"

"In a manner of speaking. Mack, I know you think I do, but I don't tell Olivia everything."

"No? What did you leave out?"

"The most important thing of all. Olivia is the one who called you my fun—my transition man, not me. That's not how I think of you. I never did."

Hannah squeezed Cecily's hand. "You're taking too much time," she hissed.

"I'm almost there. Don't interrupt, Hannah. It isn't polite."

"What are you trying to say, Cecily?" asked Mack.

"I love you. I never told Olivia that I love you. I never told you, either, but that's because you left and—"

"Cecily!" said Hannah. "Hurry up!"

Cecily glared at Hannah. "All right! Have a little patience, Hannah. Mack, I love you. Hannah loves you, too. So, what Hannah wants for Christmas—what I want, what we both want more than anything, is—"

"We want you to marry us!" yelled Hannah.

The singing stopped.

"Is that right?" asked Mack, grinning.

"Yes. We do. We want you to marry us."

"I told her that's what I want for Christmas," said Hannah. "You for my dad."

Mack's grin faded.

"Well? Aren't you going to say anything?"

"As soon as I can swallow the lump in my throat." Mack swallowed. "There. Now. I love you, too. Both of you. And I will marry you. Both of you."

There was a cheer from the crowd.

Then a lot of people were hugging and kissing Mack and Cecily and Hannah.

"This is the best Christmas ever," said Hannah.

"Just wait until next year," said Mack, hugging both his girls. "Next Christmas will be even better."

And it was.

EPILOGUE

Christmas day, one year later

Olivia adjusted Cecily's veil. "I can't believe you're going to do it again."

"Get married?" asked Cecily.

"Get married on Christmas day. Aren't you afraid this date is jinxed for you?"

"Nope. Last Christmas turned out just fine—I proposed and Mack accepted."

"No, you didn't," said Hannah, looking at herself in the mirror. "*I* proposed. You were too scared."

"Right. I'm not scared now, though. I can't wait to be Mrs. Mack Armstrong." No knots in her stomach, not even a butterfly flutter.

There was a knock on the door. Iris stuck her head in. "Are you girls ready? Mack is going to faint if you don't come down those stairs pretty soon."

"Boys don't faint," said Hannah. "They pass out."

"Who told you that?" asked Cecily.

"Gramps. After he almost passed out at his wedding—it must be a guy thing." She grinned at Olivia.

"I explained that. Overcoming commitment aversion causes blood to drain from their heads. Naturally, they get dizzy on their wedding days." She gave Cecily one last look. "Okay, Iris. We're ready. Come on, Hannah, we go first. Cyrus will take Cecily down the stairs. Where is he?"

"Right here. I never saw a more beautiful bride. Well, not since the last time you wore white. This is going to be a beautiful wedding." Cyrus held out his arm, and Cecily took it. "Almost as beautiful as mine."

Cecily smiled. "I'm so glad we're having it here, at home, with just family."

"Maybe not just family," said Cyrus, holding out his arm for Cecily to take. "There's quite a crowd downstairs—I think a few of Mack's colleagues snuck in."

"No. They were invited—they're family, too. So are the Penns. And Mack has a big family."

"Nice bunch of people. You did good, C. J. Of course, you had my example to guide you."

"I know. This is a much better wedding than the last one—I didn't have a mother of the bride last time. Or my very own daughter to act as junior bridesmaid. And I didn't have Mack waiting for me at the bottom of the stairs."

Cyrus waited until Olivia had reached the bottom step; then he guided Cecily down the staircase.

Mack looked up and grinned, shamelessly showing his dimple.

Cecily grinned back and reached for the handrail, catching herself before her knees buckled. That dimple—she'd tried to convince Mack that she was immune. But he knew she'd be falling at his feet every time he grinned for fifty or sixty more years.

She could live with that.

Discover the Thrill of
Romance With

Kat Martin